Widow Wilkes

Shalene Marie

This book is a work of fiction. Although some historical events and persons have been referenced, many details have been adjusted for the benefit of the story and are in no way intended to be construed as facts.

First Edition, 2023

Contributors:

Editing: Krista Venero @ mountainswanted.com
Cover design: Marta and David DaSilva
        @ artbook_illustration@hotmail.com
Author: Shalene Marie @ shalenemarie.space

Shalene Marie

For Angie~

The friend I've had the longest in my life. The one where we can't even figure out when we met because we were so young. You are my rock, my devil's advocate, my sister, my teacher, my friend.

I know we have the kind of friendship that will stand the test of time because we've been through it ALL.

Thank you for your unfailing support. Thank you for always being there for me.

I hope you know that I will ALWAYS be there for you.

!Caution!
See author's website for full list of trigger warning's associated with this novel: https://www.shalenemarie.space/trigger-warnings

Chapter 1

England, 1362

Miranda Wilkes awoke with a start, roused from a restless sleep by an unshakable feeling that something was terribly wrong. A pair of stormy gray eyes made a sweep of her chamber, not finding a single detail out of place. The fire in the hearth was a mound of glowing embers, but a candle remained burning on the bedside table, casting a faint glow upon familiar surroundings.

Reacting on instinct alone, she threw her thin coverlet aside and bounded out of the massive canopy structure as if the feather mattress had caught flame. A slim hand clutched the brass candle holder on the bedside table, and she rushed from the chamber. She didn't waste a moment to collect her white bed robe for modesty, uncaring that her feet were bare.

It was midsummer in northern England, the point in the year when the temperature and humidity soared, even at night; nevertheless, the stone flooring in the keep always retained a threatening chill. Miranda's heart thumped in her chest. Fear coursed through her veins, causing her breath to labor. The wispy stark-white material of her cotte fanned out behind a petite figure, and unbound coal-black curls were a tangled mass flowing down her back.

But the lady noticed none of it as she held the candle high and padded down the darkened corridor with purpose.

Her only thoughts were of Edwin. He was her love, her life, her blood. He was her only child, and perhaps she was overly protective of him, but as a mother, she knew no other course. Every decision, every action was attributed to his happiness. She thought of him first, herself last. He became the light of her life the moment he was born, and in the six years since that day, nothing had changed that truth, and nothing ever would.

In appearance, he was the mirror image of his father, but in spite of her mixed emotions toward the man who had sired him, she attached none of that resentment to Edwin.

Gerald Wilkes was Edwin's father; at least, he had been. Nearly three years prior, during his return from a battle for their king, Gerald was accosted, robbed of his coin, and left for dead. As a knight, it was assumed that he fought valiantly for his life. Nevertheless, he succumbed to his stab wounds right there on the road.

Miranda had shed her tears for Gerald. He'd been her husband and the father of her son. His life had mercilessly been cut short, and, sadly, he'd died alone. But it was possible the Lord would frown down upon her because she felt no shame in admitting she didn't miss him. There was no love lost between them. Theirs had been a marriage of titles and lands, not love.

Miranda was a girl of only ten and five, and Gerald was more than a decade older when they vowed to remain together until death parted them. At such a young age, marrying a man of twenty and seven gave her cause to believe he was larger than life. But she was quick to amend such thoughts. In spite of being attractive, well titled, and wealthy beyond any man's dreams, Gerald was far from perfect.

"Attractive" was an understatement in reference to Gerald Wilkes. The man had been beautiful. He stood tall, no less than six feet, with a solid, sturdy frame. With a head full of blinding white-blond curls, and eyes the color of the earth and the sky combined, he was a striking figure in any room. But his looks were an eye-catching shroud, concealing the ugly being within.

He gave nothing of himself to their marriage, with the exception of Edwin. He was selfish, inconsiderate, faithless, and even slightly sadistic upon occasion. Miranda saw the first of that on their wedding night. In spite of her innocence, Gerald's consummation had been quick and painful. Knowing it was her duty, Miranda forced herself to be willing, but the man had simply taken his pleasure without a care for her inexperience, then left her.

At first, he sought her body whenever and wherever he pleased. She found her skirts being lifted while she tended to chores, at her bath, and even roused from slumber in the dead of the night. His visits were rough and uncomfortable and swift. Miranda allowed his attentions, but she remained cold and unmoved in his arms.

When the novelty of his bride wore off, he turned his focus elsewhere, and even though Miranda was grateful for it, it was a stunning blow to her pride. She felt used and betrayed. And Gerald made no attempts to hide his trysts from the public eye, which only added to her humiliation.

She confronted him with the concept of keeping his affairs private, but he merely laughed in her face and turned his back on her. The man had no respect for her, or their marriage. He ordered her about as he ordered their servants, ridiculed her lifeless bedroom behavior in front of their guests, and refused to hear any opinion, as if she was of no consequence to anyone. He may have never struck her in anger, at least not in that fashion, but she had been abused just the same.

Then she received the disconcerting news that her parents, delighted with their prize of wealth through the sale of her marriage, had decided they were going to see the world and all it had to offer. That decision left her younger sister, Rowena, on the Wilkeses' doorstep in need of a home.

Miranda gladly took her in, welcoming the only person she shared any real affection with during the entire course of her life. Her parents had been dutiful and diligent in the raising of their daughters, but the love of a mother and a father for either of them was never forthcoming. Always forgotten and overlooked, Miranda was overflowing with love to give when, at her own age of six, Rowena was born.

Without anyone else to share their affections, the sisters quickly became inseparable. In spite of their age difference, they trusted only each other, relied on only each other, confided only in each other. Initially, Miranda had welcomed her marriage. She had had high hopes she would find love, perhaps even the happiness she had been denied all of her life, and her only regret had been in leaving her younger sister behind.

With her hopes abruptly dashed like a wave breaking upon a rocky shore, Miranda found only the slightest lift in her strength of will when Rowena crossed the threshold of Wilkes Castle. Miranda possessed a strong constitution, but in her nightmare of a marriage, with Rowena standing at her side, she found herself at the lowest point she had ever been in all of her years.

Then she learned she was with child, and suddenly her world had a purpose. The meager candlelight in her life exploded into sunshine. She was able to withstand every act of emotional abuse Gerald bestowed upon her because she had a reason to look to the future.

Edwin's birth saved her from Gerald; in fact, he saved her from herself. Gerald was no less selfish, inconsiderate, faithless, and sadistic when their son was born. Edwin's presence merely changed her reaction to his unkind ways. She was able to find an indifference to her husband, a deaf ear to his abusive words, a blind eye to his sneering expressions, and numbness to his physical needs on those rare occasions when he sought her out.

As a father, Gerald was nonexistent; therefore, it was no loss to his son when he was murdered three years after his birth.

In the three years since her husband's death, a nearly blissful contentment had settled on their small family. Miranda, Rowena, Edwin, the servants, and the Wilkes army were the only occupants of the castle. Gerald's parents had passed on after their marriage, and her own had scattered into the wind, leaving all of the Wilkes wealth and lands in Miranda's capable hands.

Now, at twenty and two years of age, running the household was second nature to her. It allowed her maximum free time to spend with her sister and her son. Without the dictation of an overbearing husband, Miranda felt a freedom unlike any she had ever known, and she basked in it.

There was only one blemish in her state of natural contentment.

Frederic Bishop.

Bishop, a close neighbor, had made it known on several occasions that he desired the Wilkes lands, and he was willing to go to any lengths to get them. His threats were always veiled but clear, nevertheless. He visited often, and rather than bar his entrance and ignite his anger, Miranda indulged her guest with the hope that he would let go of his greedy intentions.

On the surface, they conversed civilly, but beneath their words, there was a palpable tension. And on Miranda's side, apprehension. But it was not for herself—it lay with Edwin, the heir to the Wilkes fortune. The lands may have been in her capable hands, but once her son became of age, everything would pass to him: the keep, the lands, and their armies.

At age six, Edwin was already wealthier than most of the earth's population. And not only that—he was also a member of the nobility, belonging to the House of the Lords. It was a foregone conclusion that he would be a knight. In fact, it would not be long before he began his training in preparation for the field of battle.

As a knight who possessed his father's white-blond curls and striking teal eyes, her son would certainly break many hearts on his path to becoming a man. And Miranda vowed to do everything within her power to ensure that man possessed his father's physical traits, and nothing else.

In the present moment, who he would become in the future wasn't forefront in her mind. The racing of her heart and her young son's safety was all that drove her toward his chamber in the late hours of the night.

As she raced down the long, dimly lit corridor of her late husband's home, a comment Bishop made during their last encounter replayed itself over and over in her mind. Rowena had taken Edwin out to watch the army go through their daily drills, and Bishop had inquired of his whereabouts. When she announced his absence, the neighbor replied, "I shall see him in time, 'tis certain."

Miranda had shrugged it off, believing it to be an honest response. Had she been mistaken? Had there been a warning in his tone? As an extra precaution, she had increased the number of guards posted around the keep at all times, but that did nothing to alleviate her fears that one day Bishop would act on his threats.

One merely had to look on him to feel suspicion well inside. Bishop was forty years of age, his height and frame comparable to Gerald's, but that was where the comparison ended. His long raven locks were always pulled back in a queue, adding menace to his square-cut jaw and piercing cobalt-blue eyes. He gave the superficial impression of being charming, but it was as transparent as glass.

Greed nearly oozed from the man's eyes, and his fingers clearly itched to hold more than his fair share of earnings. He was certainly not destitute, far from it. His own holdings were substantial, but it was never enough for him. Evidently his ambitions surpassed his means. And those ambitions included the Wilkes lands. It did not matter whoever stood between him and them.

"I shall see him in time, 'tis certain..."

Rowena's voice yanked her from her thoughts. "Something is amiss."

Miranda looked up to find her sister moving toward her as she crossed through a junction of perpendicular corridors. Her stomach dropped, hearing a like fear spoken aloud. "I feel it too," she admitted.

Rowena fell in step beside her. The girl's long black curls were as tangled as her own. Their hair and a meager height of five feet were common between them, but those were the only similarities they shared.

Miranda's eyes were the color of an approaching storm, yet held a contradictory calm no matter what emotion lay inside. Rowena possessed a beautiful pair of amber eyes, the color of a cat's, their father's eyes. They were expressive, revealing everything she felt at any given moment. The elder sister was petite in every sense of the word: delicate bones, modest curves, and a flawless ivory complexion. The girl of ten and six was considerably endowed, with shapely legs, full hips, an eye-catching bosom, and a lightly sun-kissed complexion.

"Beautiful" was applicable to both, yet in different forms of the word. Rowena was striking; there was no doubt about that. Her beauty shouted itself across the rooftops, whereas Miranda's beauty was demure, softly stated but ever present when one cared to look closely.

Wordlessly, the pair hurried to Edwin's quarters. Miranda crossed through his open door first, the light of her candle spilling into the darkened chamber. A wall sconce burned for him every eve, but it would have long since blinked out at such a late hour.

Fingers of candlelight slowly stretched the length of his bedchamber and finally reached across the foot of his little bed. But Miranda didn't see the covered mound of his feet. She rushed forward, causing the light to reveal everything.

In the back of her mind, she told herself he was curled up in the fetal position—that was why she hadn't seen his feet at the foot of the bed—but as her eyes darted to the empty mattress, the truth struck her like a physical blow.

"Edwin," she choked.

Rowena gasped at her back.

Frantically her eyes bounced around the space of his chamber, desperately hoping he would materialize, but in the deepest recesses of her soul, she already knew he was gone. Her son had been stolen from her. And Bishop had taken him.

The candle dropped from her hand. As it clanked upon the stone flooring, the flame doused and cast the room in inky blackness.

Rowena's mouth opened, and she screeched into the night, "Edwin!"

Chapter 2

Rowena's piercing cry roused the whole of the castle's occupants. Bleary-eyed knights, men-at-arms, and servants poured into the Great Hall, searching for the cause of the scream.

Unable to think coherently in Edwin's empty chamber, Miranda grabbed her sister's hand and dragged her down the long corridor and shadowed stairwell to greet the commotion in the hall.

The grim expression on Miranda's face and Rowena's panicked moans caused the crowd to hush in anticipation of what could only be bad news.

Tumultuous eyes scanned the crowd. When she spotted a tall, dark-haired gentleman with unruly curls, a full beard, and eyes black as night, she gave him a curt nod and headed for the dais.

Alfred Coombs was the captain of the Wilkes army, and her most trusted knight. He and a handful of knights followed her lead, trailing behind the sisters as they climbed a short staircase to the raised platform for family dining.

The captain took notice of her scandalous state of undress and immediately sent for a maid to collect a bed robe for her. Alfred pulled her chair, aiding Miranda's place at the head of the table, then seated himself at her elbow. The others followed suit, with the exception of Rowena. She paced at Miranda's back, unable to remain still.

Outwardly Miranda appeared calm, but her insides were trembling, her stomach twisted in fear. She laid her palms flat on the table and stared Coombs in the eye.

"Edwin's been taken."

His lips thinned, and a muscle ticked near his eye. "Bishop?"

She nodded. "I am certain 'tis none other. He desires my husband's lands. *Our home.*"

Acting swiftly, he gave a nod to an awaiting footman, wordlessly giving the order to send men in search of the boy. Then he glanced at Rowena. Once. Twice.

The maid returned and draped the bed robe over Miranda's shoulders. She thoughtlessly stretched her arms into the thin fabric. Her chest heaved, taking in a deep breath, forcing herself to remain logical. "How could he have possibly surpassed our walls? *How did he get to my son?*"

Coombs thought a moment, then the light of understanding glistened in his eyes. "Bishop's recent visit was a fortnight hence. A member of his entourage could have remained hidden within these walls."

Miranda's gaze fell. She felt the weight of guilt press on her shoulders. It had been a mistake to allow Bishop entrance. The blame was her own. She shook her head; it was not the time to be beaten down by self-defeat.

"Aye, your theory is certainly feasible. Now we must look forward," her words were steeped with a confidence she didn't feel.

"Bishop's a powerful man. He has strength in numbers, my lady. The mass of his army surpasses ours by more than a thousand men," he informed.

Miranda's jaw clenched. As her palms remained flat on the table, she rose from her seat, leaned toward Alfred and growled softly, "The man has my son. I will die without a second thought to ensure he is returned alive." With that, she calmly sat back down and wordlessly awaited a response.

"Every man within these walls is willing to sacrifice his life for your son. But we will need aid if we are to secure a victory against the vast size of Bishop's army." His expression was earnest.

"If we seek to use brute force, I do not have any assurance my son will not be harmed for our efforts." The thought caused an inward cringe.

"We do not know how to judge Bishop's capabilities," Rowena inserted as she continued to pace, wringing her hands in an agitated manner.

All eyes shifted to the girl as she spoke, but she didn't look up to see if anyone had acknowledged her remark.

"I am in agreement with my sister," Miranda added, causing their audience to shift focus once again. "We have known Bishop for many years, yet I cannot convince myself that he will not resort to violence during his criminal act."

Coombs's brow furrowed. "We cannot appeal to our Yorkshire overlord for aid. Bishop is his greatest ally. 'Tis certain Bishop's confidence in that allegiance spurred his hand in Edwin's abduction. Yorkshire is not an option. How do you dare to proceed, my lady?"

"I am at a loss, Alfred. I need the guidance of a higher power."

"You seek the Lord's wisdom," he assumed.

Gracefully, she rose to her feet and announced, "I need to see our King."

"The King?"

Chapter 3

The light of dawn streaked the horizon when Miranda and her entourage crossed under the portcullis and emerged beyond their castle walls.

Unable to bear witness to an ever-present fear in her sister's eyes, Miranda ordered Rowena to remain behind, temporarily passing off her duties as lady of the manor to the youth. Perhaps with her mind preoccupied with learning mundane details, the girl's panicked state would be relieved.

And with that accomplished, Miranda was forced to ask herself, *now how will I preoccupy my mind from fear*? At present, their king was sheltered at a neighboring estate, Colville Manor, which would shorten their travel time considerably. Nevertheless, it was more than half a day's ride, and in that time, she had nothing to do but torture herself with a vivid imagination.

Alfred's search party had returned before their departure and confirmed precisely what Miranda had already known deep in her heart. Edwin was well and truly gone—and in the hands of a man whose capabilities lay in the realm of the unknown.

Edwin must have been terrified. And it tore at a mother's heart to realize she could do nothing to ease his fears. A boy of six was defenseless against a seasoned man; fighting back would be useless for his meager size. The only reasoning that saved her from breaking into hysterics was the fact that killing Edwin would not serve the man any purpose. Bishop wanted the Wilkes lands, and her son was his only piece of leverage. He would not jeopardize that at any cost.

To use a child in such a fashion, for his own financial gain, was perverse, and it made Miranda's fingers itch to scratch the man's eyes from their sockets. It added fury to her emotionally precarious state.

She took a long breath to steady herself and looked to the dawn sky. There was not a cloud in sight. Already the heat was blistering, and as the day wore on, the temperature would only rise. She drew the back of her palm across the perspiration on her brow. In such humidity, they would have to rest their mounts often, and that would only delay their arrival.

It was possible their half a day's ride could drag into a day. The lady had donned lightweight attire for their travels: a form-fitting cotte, a single full-length lilac linen gown, and her silken locks had been drawn up into a net. But her luminous skirts were suffocating in spite of her forethought, and she could feel stray curls stick to her moistened nape.

Despite the less than comfortable conditions of a sweltering summer day, it would never occur to the lady to complain. In fact, she welcomed the misery. It was a refreshing distraction from her self-loathing over her son's abduction. She had been careless, reckless to allow Bishop's return to the castle on more than one occasion.

She had blindly hoped the man would develop a conscience and forget the unsavory intentions he possessed. Clearly, she had hoped in vain. And now her son had fallen victim to her foolish optimism. Forgiving herself would be an impossibility if anything happened to Edwin, if he was harmed in any way.

Miranda glanced at the man abreast of her. He rode his war horse, his posture rigid with self-discipline. He had not voiced a word since their departure, and she was grateful for it. He knew her well enough to realize it was the wrong time to press her for conversation and was respectful of that knowledge.

The hard-hearted man had been Gerald's most-trusted knight for as long as Miranda had known him. And her husband's death had done nothing to displace Alfred's loyalty to the Wilkes family or to her. Before Gerald's murder, the pair never had necessity to share words, and Miranda had never attempted to bridge that gap because she knew her husband would disapprove.

Following the loss of her husband, as lady of the manor, Miranda found herself consulting with him for a great number of reasons. And she soon learned she had an ally in an unlikely place. He always remained distant and professional, but there was mutual respect and an unspoken friendship between them.

Her gaze returned to the rutted road in front of them. "Speak to me, Alfred."

He stared at her out of the corner of his eye, a thick brunette brow raised inquisitively. "Unable to dispel thoughts of your son?"

"Horrible thoughts," she confirmed in a breath.

Coombs's jaw clenched. "Bishop's plan will not be served by harming your son. He may be ruthless, but he is not a fool."

"I want to believe that." Her voice was heavy with feeling. "I need to believe that."

"The King will not condone such behavior."

"Aye, Edward will understand, but he is distracted by politics. I fear he will not be able to attend to this matter."

"At this time, the good of our country may take precedence over your abducted son," Alfred admitted.

Miranda closed her eyes for a prolonged moment, then pinned her companion with a steady gaze. "If we're forced to abandon the keep to secure Edwin's welfare, 'twill be done."

"'Tis a matter of principle, my lady. If we abandon the keep, Bishop will seek to overtake the remainder of the Wilkes holdings. There will be no end to the man's ambitions."

"I will surrender the gown on my back to secure my son's safety. My husband's lands are not worth Edwin's life."

Coombs gazed at her, his expression pensive. "Do I perceive a deeply ingrained desire of vengeance upon your husband's name, my lady?"

Miranda drew in a sharp breath. Her mouth fell open to admonish the man's cutting tongue, but as her thoughts spun, she failed to put a voice to her words. Could it be true? In life, she had been helpless to retaliate against that letch of a man. Was it possible she sought to regain her pride through revenge upon his name in death?

For many prolonged minutes, she believed Alfred may be correct in his assessment. But then she thought of her son.

"That statement may hold truth if my son did not walk the earth, my son who shares the name of my deceased husband. Gerald may have besmirched his namesake with his every breath, but when Edwin steps into his role as heir, he will give the Wilkes name the respect it deserves," she concluded with a nod.

Alfred was quiet for a moment. "Gerald may have been lacking in his role as husband, but he excelled in his function as an ally and confidant," he defended.

"'Tis a shame he failed to see that a wife may be both," her voice was steeped in bitterness.

"Is there not any moment when you miss him?" Curiosity won out over propriety.

Miranda spoke softly, which forced Alfred to strain to hear over the clop clop of horse hooves. "I regret that Edwin has been robbed of a father, even a poor father." She evaded the question in a single statement. She turned her head away, dismissing the subject.

A relatively cool breeze whispered over the rolling green hills that surrounded the entourage and gave them a short reprieve from the heat. Miranda lifted her face toward the gentle gust. She welcomed the air as it lifted several damp locks from her nape.

The pair fell into a contented silence for the remainder of their journey to Appleta.

Chapter 4

Aware of their impending arrival from a messenger who had been sent on ahead, the lord and lady of Colville Manor greeted Alfred and Miranda as they crossed over the threshold into the Meeting Hall.

"To what do we owe this unexpected pleasure, Lady Wilkes?" Reissa Colville inquired. A warm smile of welcome lifted the corners of her mouth.

"I sincerely apologize for our abrupt arrival, my lady, but we must see the King with a matter of great importance." Miranda glanced at Viktor, Reissa's husband. He stood at his wife's side, his expression inscrutable.

Miranda and the Colvilles were distant acquaintances. Gerald and Viktor had never been friendly. Both possessed strong personalities, and, unfortunately, those personalities clashed. The Wilkeses had been invited to the Colvilles' wedding as a matter of propriety, and they had attended merely as a matter of propriety.

Gerald and Viktor hadn't exchanged a single word. And Reissa had still been a stranger to her surroundings, another victim of a marriage contract, so she was reclusive and unwilling to socialize with her guests.

Gerald's murder followed a short time thereafter. Released of the prison of marriage, Miranda sought to bridge the gap between herself and her neighbors with an invitation to the Wilkes holdings.

Reissa had returned a letter expressing her delight to visit, but, unfortunately, she was several months along with child and unable to travel at that time. Through correspondence, they agreed to set up a meeting in the future, but their lives carried on, and that agreement never fleshed out.

Now Miranda had returned to Colville Manor. She wished it was in regard to that long overdue social call, but, sadly, that was not the case.

Her eyes unwittingly assessed the couple in front of her. They had been strangers at their wedding; in fact, they met the same day they spoke their vows. From afar, Miranda had noticed their cold demeanor toward one another, and she wondered if they were doomed to the same fate as herself and her own husband. But as she studied them now, there wasn't a hint of that cold rapport between them.

Viktor stood close to his wife's side, as if he meant to be protective without consciously being aware of it. And Reissa leaned toward her husband, as if seeking his proximity, also without consciously being aware of it. Their body language spoke volumes, which made it clear to any observer that the couple had formed an unbreakable bond.

Many would be startled by that assessment because, at first glance, the pair seemed to be a complete mismatch. Viktor was a large, muscular man with black locks that curled at his nape, striking black eyes, and remarkable features. He was incredibly handsome, with a hard countenance and intimidating presence. He was a man who caused a woman to take stock of her own appearance, to strive for perfection simply to gain an interested glance.

And Reissa was a tiny woman, with straight strawberry blond tresses, ash-gray eyes, and fair skin. She was relatively plain, meek, and soft-spoken. Generally, men did not take a second glance; however, she had flourished in personality and appearance since her marriage. This husband and wife were not together *in spite* of their differences; they were together *because* of their differences.

Reissa's brow furrowed. "The King?" She glanced at Alfred, curious about the man's presence and status.

"Aye, we must speak to him immediately." Her hand lifted, gesturing to Coombs. "This is Alfred Coombs, the captain of my husband's army."

Reissa stared at the man, wide-eyed, startled by that knowledge. Viktor's response was less dramatic. A single black brow rose in silent inquiry. Both gave the man a courteous nod.

Reissa's eyes swung back to Miranda. "I hope all is well," she breathed, apprehension marking her feminine features.

Miranda glanced at Coombs, but she guarded her expression. "Is Edward available?"

Viktor spoke up, "Certainly. Follow me, my lady."

The group crossed the crowded hall and approached two men seated before a massive fireplace, a chess board separating them. Both men looked up to greet the arrivals.

Miranda recognized Edward immediately. While Gerald had been alive, the King had visited Wilkes Castle on numerous occasions. Miranda and Edward shared polite words during those short visits, but Gerald always monopolized the King's time while in residence.

Edward's long dark locks and beard had grown significantly grayer in the years since she had last seen him. But she would recognize those eyes, the hue of molasses, and that beak-like nose anywhere. A slash of straight brows gave him a deceiving appearance of menace, yet, for a man with such power, he was rather personable.

His eyes lit up in instant recognition, in spite of her limp, exhausted appearance. "My Lady Wilkes."

"The lady requests an audience with her king," Viktor announced. He gestured to the woman who stepped up to his side.

"Is that so?" His bushy brows rose.

"I apologize for interrupting your recreation, Your Majesty, but 'tis a matter of great importance. I must appeal to your kind nature for wisdom and aid," she implored, her voice filled with desperation.

His head tilted, clearly intrigued. "You have succeeded in gaining my attention, my lady. Let us take to the dais to discuss your matter of great importance." Despite the weight of his gold-spun finery, Edward rose with grace and guided the lady to the empty dais. They climbed the staircase, and a footman was quick to aid their seating.

The instant they were relatively alone, Miranda sat forward and came straight to the point. "Frederic Bishop has abducted my son."

For a moment, he simply stared at her, digesting the news she had imparted. Then finally he wondered, "Frederic Bishop?"

"Aye, Your Majesty."

"You are certain?"

"Aye."

"What are his intentions?"

Thoughtlessly, she tucked an errant raven curl behind her ear. "He desires the Wilkes Yorkshire holding."

"Your present home," he remarked. His features grew hard.

"We do not possess the army or the power to use reason, Your Majesty. Please help us."

Edward laid a palm flat on the table and took a weary breath. "As you are aware, Lady Wilkes, we have attained a tentative peace in this never-ending war. I must return to court. And Viktor and Reissa have kindly accepted my offer to join me there to offer their support. I cannot attend to this matter—"

Miranda felt the threat of tears burn at the back of her eyes. "I beg of you, Your Majesty; he is my only son—"

He held up a finger to ward off her pleading. "However, I will offer a surrogate." Coal-black brows furrowed thoughtfully as he scratched his beard.

"Your Majesty?"

"If Viktor had not agreed to attend court, I would retain his services in this matter, but I know of another. Return home, my lady; you shall have your aid."

Miranda bowed her head, feeling a modicum of relief. "I cannot express enough gratitude, Your Majesty."

"Now, go rest yourself, Miranda. You appear dead on your feet."

She gave her king a weak smile, curtsied, and began to exit the dais as he ordered.

Edward summoned Viktor to his side and immediately set his plan in motion. "Send for Crogan Adair."

Chapter 5

Crogan surfaced in sleep to hear an incessant pounding on his chamber door. An itch of irritation crawled up his spine as his eyes popped open to stare at the ceiling. He let out a heavy sigh and glanced down at the woman using his chest as a pillow. Her nose twitched, also affected by the noise, but she remained in slumber.

A callused hand lifted her arm from its resting place on his abdomen, then he gently but firmly pushed her onto her back, which freed his body from an unconscious embrace. With silent stealth, he rose from the feather mattress and stepped into a pair of navy braies while the banging of knuckles against the opposite side of the door continued.

He cursed under his breath, crossed the distance to the door and quickly opened it, putting an end to the noise that had yanked him from a satiated slumber. Crogan adored his cousin, but he was not pleased to see Brodie standing in the dim corridor, his fist held upright in mid-knock.

Brodie ignored the scowl on his cousin's handsome face and spoke quietly, "The King wishes to see ye posthaste."

The furrow in his brow deepened. "The King?"

"Of England," Brodie added with a hint of a smile.

"Edward?" Blunt nails scraped against the auburn stubble on his sculpted jaw. "When did he arrive?"

"Nae, cousin, a messenger carried the request. Edward resides at Colville Manor."

The last remnants of sleep fell away. A pair of sea green eyes widened as understanding dawned. "Colville Manor?! We must travel to England posthaste?"

Brodie's smile flourished. "Aye."

The lady's slumber was successfully disturbed by a trail of shouted epithets that echoed throughout the large chamber.

***

Crogan was far from happy. In response to the King's message, he found himself, his cousin Brodie, and a majority of his army marching the road to England under the light of a full moon.

An owl hooted in the distance. His hooded eyes located the animal on the branch of a nearby oak tree, but his head churned with such irritation that he failed to acknowledge any further presence. A sticky breeze combed through the deep auburn waves falling across his creased brow, causing moonlight to catch the golden highlights hidden there. The silky shoulder-length strands were pulled back in a haphazard queue, yet his hastily donned attire appeared immaculate.

With the exception of horse hooves thundering against the dirt road, the night was quiet and still, rather unlike the storm raging inside Crogan's head. Subconsciously, his chiseled jaw clenched against thought while he stared at the path that stretched out before him. But he did not see the path; he saw the vision of a woman. A woman he had loved. A woman he had lost.

If Crogan were a man to complain, he would have little to complain about in the course of his life. He was born into a wealthy, prominent family in Scotland. His parents were generous and loving people. As an only child, his mother doted on him to no end, while his father taught him the value of respect, honor, and loyalty. He was showered with love, education, and fine possessions. He wanted for nothing.

But the boy grew into a restless man. He longed for excitement; he longed to see the world. And so, he followed his desire across the oceans into the unknown. In those exotic foreign lands, he learned more about life than anything he could have read in a book. He saw the goodness in humanity, and the evil. He saw the atrocities done to one another, the outbreak of war at the drop of a hat, and the freedom to choose his own battles.

He could not be certain how or when he decided, but he found himself joining loyalty to England over France in their never-ending war. He entered into their bloodshed, fighting alongside the Black Prince in the Battle of Poitiers.

Impressed by his conduct during that battle, the Black Prince supervised a meeting between Adair and his father, King Edward III. Adair and the King became fast friends, and during the next four years, Crogan spent his time between his lands, lands passed from his father when he reached the proper age to oversee them, and time with his English comrades fighting for their cause.

In the year 1360, the Treaty of Bretigny was signed, initiating a tentative peace between England and France, but by then, Crogan had already seen the loss of the only woman he had ever truly cared for, with the exception of his mother.

In 1357, Brodie purchased a lovely young beauty from the auction block in Lanark and presented the woman to his cousin as a gift for the celebration of his thirtieth birthday. Adair appointed Dana Dillingham as a servant in his kitchen, but he knew from the moment he set eyes on her that he would have her.

She was a petite woman, small and delicate in bone structure, standing no more than five feet in height. With sparkling jade-green eyes and fire-red hair, she was truly a mesmerizing sight to behold.

Crogan had known countless women in his life, known them intimately, but he never possessed anything greater than lukewarm feelings for any of those women. But there was something different about Dana—something he could not label, could not name.

The lass of twenty years had been strong-willed, with a spirit to match. She swore he would never own her body. Nevertheless, he seduced her into his bed within days. Despite the vast chasm between their stations in life, the couple grew to love one another fiercely, and without regret.

Dana continued her duties in the kitchen while Crogan shared his time between home and battle. Prior to Dana's presence in his world, he welcomed the thrill of battle, welcomed that tangible feel of life that flowed through his veins while he looked out upon a vast army of men ready to sacrifice their lives for their country. But Dana changed everything. He dreaded leaving her. He counted the days until he could return home to be in her arms again.

Unfortunately, their bliss did not last. Tragedy befell his blazing beauty.

One morning when Dana arose early to tend to her duties in the kitchen, she stumbled in the stairwell. In her fall down the stone staircase, she struck her head with such force that her neck broke, and she died instantly.

Crogan found her limp figure lying on the mezzanine between floors. He had dropped to his knees, skinning them in the process, and pulled her into his arms. For several moments, he simply stared at her lifeless eyes, his brain registering the shocking truth of her loss, and finally a guttural cry emanated from his throat. His face was dry, too angry at fate for tears, so he raged at the world, sending his voice into the heavens, unable to understand why that had happened to her.

His shout brought the whole of the castle running to the source, but they all stopped in dead silence when they saw their master clutching the lifeless body of his lover in his arms.

Her death had followed the Treaty of Bretigny, leaving him two years to wallow in his grief without an outlet to channel his rage. It left him bitter and cold. He was quick to anger and foolishly impulsive.

It was because of that acquired impulsive nature that he invited the King's right to choose his wife. Knowing he would never find a woman he would deem fit to wed, but needing an heir to his domain, he requested that David II choose a spouse for him. And so David had agreed, albeit reluctantly.

Following greater than a year of consideration, David named Alice Farraday to be Crogan's future bride. As she was the daughter of another prominent family in Scotland, it was a smart match. The betrothal was instated, the contract signed, and upon the arrival of the new year, the couple would be joined as man and wife.

Crogan thought of the woman he had abandoned in his bed earlier that evening, his bride-to-be. Alice Farraday's only living relative was a grandmamma in failing health. With the marriage set for the new year, they traveled to Crogan's home six months early so the elder woman could be settled while she was still healthy enough for the journey.

They had arrived not seven nights ago. Admittedly, Crogan was not displeased with Alice; on the contrary, he was rather surprised by the striking young woman who had stepped into his Great Hall. She was average in height, falling halfway between five and six feet, with an alluringly voluptuous figure, shiny blonde curls, and watchful chestnut eyes. In terms of personality, she seemed intelligent, thoughtful, and charming.

Adair was further surprised when he found that she was candidly receptive to his advances. He had learned through experience that the lady was no innocent, but that made little difference to him. In truth, it absolved him of any guilt that he had bedded his bride prior to the ceremony. And it only seemed to be an added bonus that Alice was well versed in the ways of lovemaking.

She was not Dana—no one could ever replace her—but, aye, he was rather content with David's choice of lady to wife.

It had been his plan to bed her again upon waking, but those plans were forcefully discarded when Edward's urgent message interrupted his slumber. His scowl darkened at the thought.

"Do ye believe the Treaty has been broken?" Brodie questioned in reference to their abrupt journey.

"'Twould explain the King's urgency." Crogan glanced over at his cousin, who rode abreast of him. Brodie had his own lands to oversee, his own life to lead, but ever since Dana's death, he had remained close to Crogan's side.

At thirty and seven years of age, Brodie was two years older than his cousin, and, because of that seniority, the man felt a need to watch over and protect him. Although it was a certainty that Adair needed no man's protection.

Crogan was aware that Brodie remained because of his erratic behavior following Dana's tragedy, but rather than be insulted over the reason for his presence, he welcomed it without question. He enjoyed his cousin's company, and, selfishly, he would not tell him to go tend to his own affairs. The men shared the same blood, but beyond that, they shared a mutual love and unspoken respect for one another.

In many ways, they were very much alike. Both stood at six and a half feet tall and were broad-shouldered, with a bulk of muscle that gave fearless men pause. Both possessed green eyes, but Crogan's were a soft pale hue, and Brodie's shone with an emerald glow. Dark locks crowned their heads, Crogan with deep auburn waves and his cousin with brunette curls.

In terms of personality, confidence and arrogance were their most outstanding attributes, but those traits were well earned by way of skill and experience. When they set out to do something, no matter the act or subject matter, it was done without flaw. Both were charming and comedic; however, the light of humor and the spark of life that had once shone in Crogan's eyes blinked out the day Dana had her accident.

It was rare to see that warm side of his character break through the cold, bitter man he had become. It was as if an impenetrable stone cage had been built around his heart, and no one possessed the strength to surpass it.

"It seems ye have only just arrived home, cousin; a broken treaty is not welcome."

"A broken treaty is not welcome in England; *I* do not harbor any qualms in returning to battle for Edward's crown," Crogan divulged.

"Ties to the Lady Farraday will not dissuade ye from leaving Scotland if war ensues?"

Auburn brows drew together in a frown. He shook his head from side to side. "Nae."

The men had not discussed Alice at length since her arrival. It was obvious that Brodie sought answers to Crogan's inclination toward the chit.

"Was the news of your abrupt departure well received by the lass?" Brodie wondered.

Crogan hadn't told him outright, but his cousin could read him like an open book when it came to crossing that physical threshold with a woman. It was clear Brodie had discerned that Crogan and his betrothed had already explored the intimacies of the marriage bed prior to marriage.

A smooth brow furrowed once again. "Nae, the lass did not receive the news well a'tall. An' failure of explanation for such an abrupt departure succeeded in drawing a pout from that pretty mouth."

"Merely a pout? A lesser woman would scream an' rail an' bring the wrath of Hell down upon a man for departure without invitation to accompany her betrothed on his journey," Brodie pointed out.

"The lass will simply be my wife, not an added limb," Crogan's deep voice was decidedly firm.

"Ye are resigned to marry the lass, then?"

"My thoughts on the matter are irrelevant, cousin; the contract has been signed, an' I will honor it."

"*Lord help ye,*" Brodie uttered below his breath.

Chapter 6

All male occupants of Colville Manor were in the process of daily drills when the whole of Crogan's entourage arrived at their destination. Not above fighting alongside his men in battle, Edward led their regimen, and Viktor stood at his side. The bailey was filled with men in full armor, their arms poised with bows and arrows, ready to release the deadly weapons on command.

Edward's voice echoed off the stone walls of the keep as he shouted for action. Upon the words "fire all!" the arrows cut through the air, leaving a hum and whistles in their wake as they traveled through the air in rapid speed. The makeshift men of hay standing before the curtain walls were impaled with a skill their Scottish audience admired without question.

After taking stock of the army's successes, the king turned, preparing to meet his guests. Viktor dismissed the bailey of men, then joined the reunion.

Crogan dismounted and approached them with a smile on his face.

"'Tis always a pleasure to see you, Crogan, even in the direst of circumstances," the eldest man greeted with a grin.

After summoning a courteous bow, he admitted, "On this day, I hope these are not the direst of circumstances, Edward." They had dispensed with formalities long ago.

Viktor and Crogan shared a polite nod. The men were friendly acquaintances. They had only met briefly on several prior occasions due to their mutual relationship with the English crown.

The king's deep brown eyes looked to the sky, and upon observing an orange glow, he announced, "The sun sets, and I am famished. We shall discuss your urgent arrival over supper." With that, he spun on his heel and began toward the entrance to the keep.

"In anticipation of your timely arrival, my wife has prepared a feast for you and your men," Viktor informed, then lifted an arm and motioned for his guest to continue into the keep.

"We are most grateful for your wife's foresight and generosity. I look forward to meeting her at last." Crogan looked at Brodie and his men, signaling that they follow and partake of the meal.

After their squires had aided in the removal of the Englishmen's armor, the trio climbed the dais and seated themselves at the trestle table. While servants scurried about filling the table with an abundance of food, Crogan noticed a somewhat plain young lady rush up the dais staircase. Viktor stood while she looked to their guest.

As she smiled at him, Crogan amended his first thought. She was not plain at all; in fact, she was quite lovely, more so when a smile lifted her lips and sparkled in her ash-gray eyes. Shiny strawberry blond locks were artfully pulled back in a silver coiffe, which revealed a soft, creamy complexion.

"My Lord Adair, I must apologize for my tardiness; I was attending to my ward. 'Twould seem the most trivial challenge is a tragedy for a young girl," she explained and curtsied, her smile remaining. "I am Lady Reissa Colville."

As Crogan raised her delicate hand to his lips, he was struck with a hint of mild disappointment. The woman was his host's wife, which meant hands off, in spite of his piqued interest. "'Tis a pleasure to meet ye, my lady."

She motioned to the trestle table piled with a feast. "Let us dine." With that, she circled the wooden structure and seated herself in the chair Viktor pulled for her.

Crogan gazed at the couple seated across from him. It was obvious in every warm look, every bright smile, and every lingering touch that they were crazy about each other. Their actions were not overt, but a blind man could see their love for each other.

Once upon a time, he had known such happiness, but it had been shattered. He could not look at the Colvilles without his rage rising with a bitter taste in his mouth. His teeth tore a piece of chicken from the leg in his hand with gusto, so engrossed in his angered and distracted state that he failed to recall there was a reason for his visit.

In his mind, he could hear Dana's throaty laughter as she leaned closely over him while serving a tankard of ale during the supper hour. He could envision her lusty derriere as she lingered over a cauldron of stew hanging in the fireplace. He could feel the touch of her fingertips on his hand as they traveled the staircase to his chamber.

During confrontations, the lass was a spitfire, but during lovemaking, she was defenseless and gentle. In spite of her long absence, her soft whispers of passion still tingled in his ear while he could feel her palms smoothing over the mat of curls on his chest.

Crogan's jaw clenched, and he shook his head to remove the images and memories that continued to haunt him. He wanted none of it. She was gone—forever.

"I need your help," the King's admission jolted Crogan from his miserable reverie.

His gaze shifted to the right, taking in the regal figure seated at the head of the table. "Aye?" He offered his full attention.

As he spoke, the King subconsciously tugged on his long gray beard, a well-known sign that he was pensive. "One of my loyal subjects is in desperate need of aid, Crogan, and I have generously volunteered your services in the name of the crown."

"Generous indeed." Crogan gave a tight smile in the face of the King's audacity. However, he had to admit he was mildly intrigued. "'Tis nothing to do with a broken treaty, then?"

"Lord in heaven, nay," Edward assured, crossing himself. "The widow Wilkes has suffered the abduction of her only son. Without a husband to lean on, she sought my wisdom."

"Please help her, my lord. Edwin is merely a child," Reissa interjected, her stare imploring.

"The lady's husband?" Adair wondered as he scratched at the itchy stubble on his chin. He preferred to keep his jaw clean-shaven, but the urgency of the King's message had not allowed time for trivialities.

"Gerald Wilkes. Murdered by highwaymen several years past," Viktor joined in the conversation.

"Lady Wilkes is well aware of the man who has abducted her boy. She is certain he seeks to bargain the boy's life for her holding in Yorkshire. A ransom may already be awaiting your acknowledgment, my friend," the king added.

"An' the man who has taken her lad?"

"I know little of Lord Bishop," Edward confessed.

"Be warned, Adair, he has strong ties to Yorkshire's overlord. I do not wish to go to war with our neighboring territory. 'Twould be best to seek Bishop alone rather than appeal to Yorkshire. 'Tis certain the lady avoided her overlord for that precise reason." Viktor offered valuable guidance to his Scottish acquaintance, his dark eyes drilling intensely.

Crogan gave a curt nod, and a stray auburn lock fell onto his cheek. "Your aid is most welcome." *An' I am most grateful that ye are an ally rather than an enemy,* he thought silently as he gazed at the Englishman seated directly across from him. They were equal in terms of sheer body mass and height, but in terms of war, he feared he had much to learn from the younger man.

"An' what is the age of the lad?"

Reissa was quick to respond, "He has seen six summers, my lord."

Crogan's sculpted jaw clenched.

"Reissa and Viktor have kindly accepted my offer to attend court. We depart at dawn. Will you join in our departure to seek a destination differing from our own? A destination in great need of your services?" As King of England, he could not order a Scottish countryman to do his bidding.

"Nae," Adair returned. "My men and I will not depart at dawn. We will depart following the meal." A defenseless child needed his help. He would never consider denying such a request, whatever the circumstances may be.

The grin Reissa sent him gave him the impression that she could have circled the table to throw herself into his arms in gratitude.

"I will send a royal guard to officiate your arrival at the Wilkes Castle," Edward announced with a grin.

Chapter 7

Miranda stared out at a clear night sky, her petite form tucked in the window embrasure in her bed chamber. The moon descended toward the horizon. It would be dawn soon. The sunrise was not two hours away. She had not slept well that night, or any night since Edwin had been taken.

Her slumber was restless, plagued by dreams that she would never see her son again, dreams that brought about the end of his short life. In her mind's subconscious, she faced an unimaginable reality. She could see her son's limp, bloodied form lying amongst the rats in Bishop's dungeon. Her mouth opened to scream, but there was no sound as she thrashed on her feather mattress, helpless to save him, helpless to her own grief.

She woke, drenched in perspiration. The lady had been too exhausted to change into her bedclothes that evening, so she had fallen onto her mattress in full dress and allowed oblivion to claim her. Uncomfortable in her damp garments, she had risen and climbed into the cool window embrasure. She let the night air soothe the knots of tension in her body.

Curled up in the window seat for an indeterminate amount of time, she ignored the aches in her stiff figure and let her head fall to her raised knees. Her unbound raven curls tumbled forward, creating a curtain that shielded the forlorn look on her face.

Not only was Miranda worried about her son, but she was also concerned about her sister as well. Rowena fared no better than she. The girl barely slept, barely ate since Edwin's disappearance. Rowena addressed her minor duties in the manor like a zombie. The world did not seem to register in her thoughts.

In addition to her supervision of the household, Miranda found herself following her sister around, catering to her welfare like an overprotective mother hen. She forced her to eat, certain the girl would not touch a bite if left to her own devices. She read to her in the evenings, her voice sweet and melodic, soothing Rowe into much-needed rest.

All such responsibilities left the elder sibling utterly taxed by the time the sun set. During the day she held up, strong and invincible, wearing a brave face, allowing no one, especially her sister, to see that her insides quivered with apprehension.

Yet she could not stop herself from asking the questions, *what if she never saw her son again? What if he was lost to her forever?* The constant uncertainty was maddening. It drained her positive regard, not knowing if he would be returned safe and unharmed.

Unable to ignore her stiff limbs any longer, Miranda tossed her long locks over her shoulder and rose from a seated position. Suddenly restless, she began to pace. When the pacing did not calm her frayed nerves, she padded over to the washstand and splashed tepid water onto her face, washing away the salt of dried perspiration.

As she wiped the clear liquid from her skin with a dry cloth, a timid knock sounded on the door.

"Aye?"

A bleary-eyed serving girl entered. Miranda peered at her expectantly.

"Alfred ordered me to fetch you, milady. A royal messenger has brought word. The King's guest, a Scottish guest, is due to arrive momentarily."

A Scottish guest? Miranda was caught off guard by the news, but it mattered not. Any aid provided by her King was welcome. A thread wove through her being, drawing out her uncertainty, and, unexpectedly, a bud of hope grew in the recesses of her soul.

She took a deep breath, letting it wash over her like the water she had just used to douse her face. She gave the girl a ghost of a smile and a nod. "Rouse the others. I want a meal prepared, water heated for bathing, and chambers readied posthaste."

"Aye, milady." The girl curtsied and flounced out the door.

Unwilling to dally, Miranda quickly rubbed some mint paste on her teeth, braided her hair in a hasty plait down her back, and smoothed the wrinkles from her burgundy gown.

Without bothering to take stock of her appearance in a mirror, she rushed from her bedchamber and down to the Great Hall with the intention to greet her guests when they arrived; however, she was brought up short when she saw men-at-arms who bore colors of the Scottish crown filtering into the keep. The vast room was painted with tunics of navy blue and white braies. They must have discarded their armor in the bailey before entering, she thought distantly.

With a muttered oath, she hurried into the hall and found herself immersed in a crowd of strangers. Feeling far too short and a bit claustrophobic, she peered up into the nearest face. A man with kind blue eyes and a full blond beard smiled down at her.

"I am the lady of the manor, and I seek your lord, kind sir," she spoke.

"Ye seek Crogan Adair," he informed. With that, he clutched her elbow gently but firmly and guided her through the masses.

"Thank you," she muttered.

Seeing one of their own guiding a lady through the crowd, they quickly stepped aside, only to reveal more and more men. The mass seemed to be never-ending.

She soon realized he was accompanying her toward the entrance, and she began to wonder if his intentions were honorable after all. As he pulled her through the double doors and into the night, she dug in her heels. Alarm bells sounded in her head.

"The widow Wilkes, my lord," the soldier announced into the darkness.

Miranda looked up and saw a shadowy figure kneeling in the bailey, not several feet away. A young squire was in the process of raising a shiny hauberk over the man's head. Once the armor was lifted away, the blond soldier drew her forward, which gave her eyes time to adjust to the poor light of the moon.

At last, she was able to focus and clearly see as the figure stood to his full height. It forced her head to rise and tilt back to meet the face that looked down into her own. A tremor of trepidation shot through her body as she realized the man's size and took in his handsome face.

He was large; no one could argue that point. Her neck craned, and her own figure felt dwarfed by his height. He stood a full foot and a half taller than she. It was not only his height that instantly intimidated, but also the broad shoulders and the visible muscle straining against his tunic, across his arms, shoulders, and chest. It was the narrow waist, hardened thighs, and sturdy legs that made her feel like nothing but a child standing in the shadow of a god. She had to resist the urge to withdraw.

Deep shiny auburn locks were pulled back in a queue, but a stray lock fell across his cheek. It drew her gaze over the dark stubble on his stubborn jaw and gracefully rounded chin. His full lips parted as if to speak, but words did not follow, which caused her gaze to linger there. She noticed a glisten of moisture, giving her the impression that he licked his lips recently. He had a straight Roman nose; full, moderately arched brows; and a high, smooth forehead.

Finally, after taking stock of his remarkable appearance, she met his eyes. They were nearly black under the white light of the moon and the shadow of his bent head, and they were also centered directly on hers.

She felt her heart flip in alarm. It forced the lady to remind herself that he had arrived to give aid, not plunder the coffers.

She took a deep breath with the intention to speak, but words failed her. Her mind was blank. For a moment, her own name failed her memory.

"Ye are the widow Wilkes?"

Even as she acknowledged that the deep timbre of his voice raked across the pit of her stomach, she felt a scratch of irritation with the choice of his words. The word "widow" was a direct reminder of a husband best left forgotten.

She recalled her senses with a vengeance. "I am, but please do not address me as such. I expect to be honored as my lady, or Lady Wilkes." In direct result of her indignation, she overcompensated with a haughty arrogance that was not befitting of her kind nature.

Those assessing eyes narrowed. "My men and I have traveled through the night, *my lady. I expect* a meal and a soft bed."

Still rather shaken by the man's presence, she nodded contritely. "Of course. Follow me."

With that, she turned and realized the blond soldier had departed without notice. She marched into the Great Hall to find that his men were seated around the banquet tables, patiently waiting while the food was quickly being prepared. Bread, cheese, and ale had been dispensed to tide them over while venison roasted on spits over the fires.

As she crossed the distance, a pair of eyes bored into her back, causing her to feel rather self-conscious of the stature of her walk. She lifted her head a notch.

Alfred rose from his seat as he surveyed her approach to the dais. He bowed courteously as she climbed the staircase, then turned to the stranger on her heels.

"You must be Lord Crogan Adair," he assumed, his eyes also assessing.

"I am," their guest confirmed, his head held high. His gaze did not waver under such close scrutiny.

Alfred paused a moment and looked him over as a man would survey a piece of horseflesh. Finally, he gave a curt nod and offered his hand in welcome. "I am Alfred Coombs, captain of the lady's army."

Crogan looked at the extended hand and placed his own within it.

"We are grateful for your aid and prompt arrival, my lord," Alfred commended.

"As I will lead your men in addition to my own, indeed, *I* am grateful for *your aid*, Coombs," Crogan stated his place as leader of them all without batting an eye. With that, he moved toward the trestle table, leaving Alfred stunned and speechless in his wake.

Miranda had watched the display of authority in awe, but when her guest stepped toward her with the intent to seat himself at the table, she moved forward to address his comment.

She looked up and was startled to see that his eyes were not black at all. They were a soft sea-green hue that seemed rather contrary to his hard countenance. They were unsettling as they lingered on her face, awaiting her words. She swallowed over the tension in her throat and tested, "You seek to *lead* any effort against Frederic Bishop?"

"'Tis why Edward summoned my services," he validated. Casually, he hooked a thumb into the wide leather belt around his waist.

Alfred moved to face them. "With all due respect, my lord, I am captain of the Wilkes army. I obey the lady's orders, and none other."

Crogan spared the man a glance, then turned to Miranda, seeking her word on the matter. She looked from one to the other, her face an unreadable mask. She understood Alfred's pride in his people and his home; she understood his desire to command them as his station outlined, but Edwin's best interests were her only concern.

Alfred's pride and her own be damned. "The King trusts this man with Edwin's life, and I trust the King; therefore, we will trust in the man he has deemed worthy of my son's salvation."

She gave a final nod, stating her word as law, then moved to the head of the table, where a footman pulled her chair.

Alfred seated himself at her left, Crogan at her right. A chalice of wine had been dispensed to her place at the table.

Immediately, she reached for it and took a sip, looking for the crutch of spirits to calm her nerves. As she held it in her delicate hand, she felt a pair of pale green eyes watching her.

Miranda summoned her courage and met the stranger's gaze. She felt a trip in her pulse but ignored it. "You are staring, my lord." The lady did not hesitate to call him out for his rude behavior.

He did not appear embarrassed, rather the opposite. He braced his chin on a closed fist and openly continued his survey of her features.

Finally, he admitted the reason for his conduct. "When the King labeled ye as a widow, I had anticipated an elder woman." It appeared as though he searched for lines around her eyes and mouth, but there were none to be found. "Ye cannot be greater than twenty years," he guessed.

"Twenty and two years of age, to be precise," she said quietly. "Now, would you like to examine my teeth, or may we discuss the reason for your presence in my home?"

He sat up straight, his casual pose discarded. "By all means," he gritted.

Chapter 8

Crogan had been surprised to look down into this woman's vibrant young face when she greeted him in the bailey. His words had been no lie. The word "widow" evoked an image of a matronly female shrouded in black, her features aging, her stature hunched over time.

But Miranda Wilkes was nothing like that picture in his mind. She was a tiny little thing, petite in every sense of the word, with modest curves. But in spite of her small stature, she held herself regally. Her nobility announced itself in her graceful actions and precise mannerisms. She was a calm, quiet type, yet somehow her presence demanded his full attention. She could not be ignored.

The woman was not as beautiful as Dana, or even as lovely as his future bride, but she was certainly attractive. Her long raven-hued curls were pulled back into a plait, every last lock in place, but it was no leap to imagine them cascading over her shoulders in wild disarray. Her ivory skin was flawless, pulled taut over delicate cheekbones and a pert nose. Her mouth was shaped in a pouty pink bow, brows thin and finely arched.

But all of it paled in comparison to her eyes. Those eyes were the color of an approaching storm, wide and watchful and fringed with long dark lashes, yet they held a serene tranquility that was much like her nature, quiet and mysterious. He could not help but wonder what lay beyond them.

It was impossible to miss the matching gray smudges beneath her eyes. It announced that she lacked sleep, but he would expect nothing less from a mother robbed of her son. However, they were the only tell-tale signs that anything was amiss in the Wilkes castle.

She wore an invisible body of armor that kept outsiders from determining the thoughts churning inside her mind or the feelings stamped upon her heart. Was it possible she was as empty inside as she made it to appear on the outside?

Crogan wore his anger over Dana's death upon his sleeve, so it was a wonder to him that anyone could behave in any other fashion than outright outrage at the world for dealing such an unfair hand. It was possible her son would not return home alive. Lady Wilkes was certainly intelligent enough to realize that was a conceivable outcome.

So, his train of thought brought him back around to the question, did this mother truly hide her feelings so well, or was it that she simply did not care as much as she should?

With that thought in mind, he put forth the question, "Is the lad's nursemaid present? I would like all present who are close to the lad."

"The boy has a name; 'tis Edwin," she ordered softly, then followed up with, "and he was not in need of a nursemaid. I played every necessary figure in his life: mother, father, nursemaid, tutor, friend." Miranda's tone nearly broke.

"Edwin's aunt is a close figure in his life as well," Alfred pointed out.

Miranda immediately shook her head. "I will not rouse Rowena. She must rest."

Crogan arched a single auburn brow. "Is the lass ill?"

"The lady is exhausted in her concern over my son, milord. If she continues her conduct of late, aye, 'tis possible that she may take ill." She set the wine chalice on the table and placed her palms flat on the wooden surface.

"Nevertheless, 'tis important that I speak with her. I will need a full account of the castle's activities from all involved," Crogan commanded. His pale green eyes grew a deeper shade while his anger pulsed inside.

"If you feel the matter is so important, then you may speak with her when she is fully rested," Miranda stated in a quietly challenging tone.

"D'you take your son's abduction so lightly, my lady?"

Sparks ignited in her eyes. "Never again will you speak so crudely of my affection for my son, Lord Adair. Never. You seek to investigate within these walls, yet 'tis common knowledge that the man who has taken on this criminal act lives beyond them.

"The only account necessary is my own, and I trust 'twill be sufficient for a decision to proceed in securing the safety of my child." She had leaned ever so slightly forward, but she appeared calm and collected.

Crogan sat forward, which brought his face to within inches of her own, his voice hoarse and enraged. "The King has charged me with a duty, an' I will conduct this matter as I see fit. I do not seek your approval, nor anyone else's. My only concern is the welfare of your child. I will seek information when necessary, an' ye will cooperate fully.

"When I am not in need of information from ye, 'twill serve ye favorably to stay well out of my way. If ye impede my duty, an' the welfare of your child is given to risk, ye will have only yourself to blame. Do we have an understanding, lass?"

In spite of her obvious rage, she spoke in a monotone. "You are a vile man, Crogan Adair."

His smile was chilling. "I have been labeled much worse by many, an' not better by few."

Miranda stole another sip of wine and took a deep breath. "If we did not possess the same resolve for Edwin, I would have you ushered from this residence posthaste."

"But ye will not." He spoke with such confidence that her knuckles turned white as she clutched the metal goblet within her hand.

"Nay, I will not," she conceded as the servants served up trenchers of stew that overflowed with tips of roasted venison.

Miranda glanced at Alfred, who had simply sat there throughout their discourse, stunned speechless by the Scottish man's overbearing yet powerful display of presence.

"I will have your account while I dine, then I will sleep." With that stated, he dug into the meal with a voracity that spoke of his long journey.

The lady stared down at the stew. She suddenly appeared exhausted and weak, as though the fight had left her. Nevertheless, Crogan was surprised when she wordlessly obeyed his order.

Then she began her account. "Frederic Bishop has expressed his desire for the Wilkes lands on several prior occasions. However, his words were spoken in jest; therefore, they were not given the consideration they deserved. Initially, I accepted his civility at face value, but I quickly perceived an unsettling feeling about the man."

Crogan looked up from his savory meal. His eyes moved over her, pensive.

"When his jests transformed into veiled threats, I had thought to bar him from the premises, but, against my better judgment, I allowed him polite entrance in the hope that the man's compassion would outweigh his greed—"

Crogan's mouth opened.

Miranda instantly held up a hand. "—and, aye, I am well aware of the ramifications of that mistake, Lord Adair."

He simply gave her a curt nod, a light of admiration in his eyes.

"One morning, during an unannounced and unwelcome visit, he inquired of the whereabouts of my son. When I replied, Bishop's precise statement followed as such: '*I shall see him in time, 'tis certain…*'"

Crogan raised a single brow, intrigued, but he remained silent to allow her to finish.

"Following that visit, I increased the gatehouse and battlements guards in spite of my own assertion that I was being overly imaginative about the man's statement. But then I awoke not a fortnight prior to this night and found my son missing from his chamber.

"Men were sent out in search of Edwin, but he was not in the castle or the outlying grounds. I am certain Bishop has abducted my son, and 'tis only a matter of time before we receive word to evacuate these lands to secure his release," Miranda finished her account.

Crogan sat back in his chair, his trencher empty. He glanced at Alfred, then let his gaze settle on the lady at his left. "'Tis damning evidence, lass, I will grant ye that." As he stared at her, he realized she had not touched a bite of her food.

Perhaps he had been too hasty in his initial thought that she may be simply playing her duty as Edwin's mother rather than suffering the devastation of his disappearance. He had known too many parents of the nobility who entrusted the lives of their children to nursemaids, known enough of them to let that possibility affect his judgment, but clearly this woman did not fit into that category at all.

His gaze shifted to her slight figure. The loss of an appetite at that time would certainly not do her justice. She was already as frail as a twig. A strong breeze would likely throw her off balance.

"I have turned it in my mind again and again, but I cannot conceive of the best possible plan to assure my son's safe return," Miranda admitted in a whisper.

"We must appeal to your wisdom," Alfred spoke up.

Crogan pushed himself into a standing position, which forced his companions to rise as well. "'Tis a matter best left to a rested mind," he announced.

Miranda nodded in agreement. The lady looked at the servants awaiting command and called for an upstairs maid to show Lord Adair to one of the chambers prepared for the guests.

Crogan gave his hosts a parting nod then followed the young maid up the staircase and down a dimly lit corridor. She gestured to an open door, and he walked into a large bedchamber that appeared furnished for masculine taste.

The coverlet and mosquito netting over the large canopy bed were dyed a deep shade of forest green. On the oak bedside table sat a tray with a chalice of wine and a burning candle. A large Asian rug of black, red, and green accents lay on the floor at his feet. There was no need for heat in the midst of a warm summer, but the fireplace was massive and flanked by two heavy oak and leather chairs.

His squire had already dispensed his armor and personal effects to the corner near the fireplace. He turned to see a cherry wood tub filled with steaming water in the opposite corner and sighed gratefully.

"Would there be anything else you require, my lord?" the young maid questioned with blatant physical offering in her eyes and in her sensual inflection.

Crogan took stock of the alluring young woman with a full set of curves and a pretty face. Certainly, there was no need for him to deny the company of a lovely woman in his bed, but when he thought of the fact that it was his hostess's duty to provide such physical satisfaction for her male guests, he was struck with the unexpected thought that he would prefer to have the lady herself provide such physical gratification.

He frowned. He was not in the Wilkes castle to dally with the lady of the manor. He was there to retrieve her son.

"Nae," he said dismissively, sending her away.

Chapter 9

Miranda sat atop her beautiful snow-white mare, Spectrum, and gazed down at the Wilkes castle as dawn transitioned into day. The equestrian rider chose the east rise. She watched as the sun rose at her back, causing the light to touch the tallest tower of the massive structure. The darkness descended slowly, revealing every last stone that comprised her keep and her curtain walls.

While Gerald lived, those curtain walls had felt like a dungeon, raised to separate her from the true pleasures of life. But following his death, those walls became her security and an extension of her world. She loved her home. She loved her lands. But she would give it all up without a second thought if only to see her son again.

She was anxious to learn Lord Adair's plan, but it would be hours before he rose after his lengthy journey. Unwilling to wander the keep to await his appearance in the hall, she thought it would be best to take in the air. It was early, but the temperature already soared. The sky was cloudless. Thankfully, the humidity had dropped, causing the climate to be more bearable.

Nevertheless, there was a tangible feeling in the air. Her body was struck with a violent shudder, and the hair on her neck lifted upon an invisible force of energy that seemed to surround her. Instantly, she recognized it as a feeling that she was not alone.

Her eyes quickly scanned her surroundings. The wide expanse of her land appeared empty, with the exception of the forest to the south. A tense gaze settled on the dense growth of trees in the distance. The uneasy feeling lingered even as she saw nothing to cause alarm.

Thoughtlessly, she pulled on Spectrum's reins and turned toward the south. The pair spurred into a gallop as her gaze remained trained on the woodland before her. Hoof beats thundered against the earth. The breeze wrenched ebony locks from her tidy plait, and burgundy skirts bounced against the horse's flanks, creating a wondrous sight.

But as Miranda cut the distance between the woodland and herself, the feeling of being watched dissolved. When she acknowledged that change, she became more convinced that someone had been there, hiding amongst the trees.

Foolishly courageous, she charged into the shelter of the canopy and strained her eyes, looking into the dense foliage that seemed to beckon her within their shadowed depths.

Convinced that someone had been there, but uncertain which direction the person had fled, she decided against going farther. She simply sat there, pondering the situation. Was it possible Bishop had sent a man to spy upon their efforts? Nay, it was not possible; it was *probable*. Perhaps it could have been Bishop seeing to the task himself.

Miranda gnashed her teeth in anger, then kicked her heels, guiding Spectrum to return to the manor. The pair flew across the open English landscape in a flourish. When they arrived at the stables, Miranda was taxed and breathless, but her physical state did not dissuade her. She ordered the stableman to ready as many mounts as he could, then she broke into a sprint for the keep.

The petite figure burst through the double doors and immediately sought Alfred's figure. She spotted him seated at the dais in discussion with many of his men, patiently awaiting their guests' arrival in the hall.

Unwilling to waste time crossing the vast distance, her mouth opened, and her voice rose above the din. "'Tis an intruder in the woods!"

Instantly, the mass of men jumped into action. Miranda stepped aside as the hall virtually cleared. Chairs were overturned and mugs of ale spilled as countless soldiers rushed past her and out to the stables in search of any unwelcome trespassers upon the Wilkes lands. Before the double doors slammed closed, she heard Alfred's shouted commands in the bailey.

Miranda breathed a sigh of relief. If there was an intruder hiding in the forest, her men would find him, of that she was certain.

Unable to sit and wait for their return, the lady mindlessly climbed the stairwell with the intent to check on Rowena's slumber. But as she ascended the turn onto the top landing, she was brought up short to find Lord Adair descending. She halted and stared up into pale green eyes.

"I have heard a commotion, my lady." His voice was still husky with sleep, and his auburn locks were unbound and slightly mussed. The stubble on his chin appeared darker, adding to his disturbingly handsome countenance. But he was in full dress—a navy tunic and matching braies—and his gaze was vigilant.

"'Tis an intruder in the woods, my lord. The men have been dispatched," she whispered, far too aware that they stood alone in the meager space of the stairwell.

"An intruder?" He took a step toward her, bringing him close enough for her to reach out and touch. "Who?" His voice was harsh and demanding.

Miranda raised her head to meet his eyes. She could hear the blood rush in her ears. "I do not know, my lord; I did not see anything in the woods." She could hear the breathlessness of her words and masked a frown.

When she first met the man, she acknowledged the truth that he was marvelously attractive, but she refused to recognize her reaction to that truth because her son's welfare was first and foremost in her mind.

Now, as he hovered so near, she realized her heart hammered in her chest, and her knees had lost their strength. As she was able to smell the musky scent of his skin, her hands itched to comb through the auburn locks of his hair. As she stood before him, a quivering mass of vulnerability, she could not deny that she was physically attracted to him.

But to acknowledge it in such formal terms was an understatement. Miranda had been attracted to men in the past, but she had never been so overwhelmed with a feeling before. She felt as if she had been shoved into a stone wall, weakened and dazed as a result.

A smooth brow furrowed, and his head tilted slightly. "If ye did not see an intruder, how do ye believe one was present?"

Miranda shook off the haze in her mind and ignored the tremors in her body as she spoke. She needed to focus on the matter at hand. "I felt as though I was being watched."

"Ye sent the whole of your army out to track an intruder ye cannot prove exists?" His expression became thunderous.

Her defenses rose, and her voice was firm. "I believe someone was out there, Lord Adair."

Large, callused hands clutched her upper arms without warning. His action caused her breath to halt, and her eyes widened as she stared up into sculpted features.

"Your paranoia does not serve your son well, lass. Leave the matter to me," he ordered through gritted teeth.

Miranda took a much-needed breath to soothe herself. She did not struggle in his hold, merely gazed up at him and stated, "I do not succumb to paranoia. I have learned that a level head serves me best. I will not address my son's welfare on a whim."

She waited patiently for him to let her go, but he simply glared at her. As he held her arms tightly, she thought she felt an electric charge pass between them, but she passed it off as a battle of wills. It was a certainty that their wills had clashed since the first moment they met.

The seconds ticked by. Miranda fought to remain composed. She continued to ignore the hands that burned through the sleeves of her gown and stoically met the scowl that was clearly meant as an intimidation tactic.

He seemed not to realize that he held her so roughly due to his rage, so she finally requested, "Please release me, my lord."

His eyes fell to his hands, and slowly they loosened their grip. His arms dropped to his sides, and he stood to his full height. He seemed to take stock of their current situation, and his anger subsided.

"I cannot read the thoughts ye guard so well. It leaves me unwilling to trust in ye," he candidly admitted.

The lady's jaw clenched in frustration. "You have only to trust in my words, my lord, for they are the truth."

The fingers she could still feel upon her arms ran over the stubble on his chin, his expression pensive. "Perhaps. Only time will prove the honesty in that claim."

Miranda spoke without thought, a trait rather unlike her. "Do you always rise to anger so quickly?"

His gaze narrowed, and he crossed his arms over a mountainous chest. "Aye, it serves me well."

Miranda clutched her skirts in a firm grip. She was not dissuaded from continuing down a path best left unexplored. "You believe alienating those who surround you is the best course of action on a daily basis?"

His lips thinned, and instantly his hands returned to her arms. He held her in a biting grip and pushed her tiny figure until she felt the wall press against her back. "Ye seem adept at causing my rise of anger more than any other lass. Ye dare much in speaking to a virtual stranger."

Once again, Miranda did not struggle. To do so would be useless. He was far too strong for any meager attempt at physical retaliation. She gaped up at the large figure hunched over her own. He shot sparks at her with his eyes. She knew she had pushed him too far, but she was not frightened. Somehow, in spite of his unsettling behavior, she knew he would not raise his hand to her.

She gave a curt nod of agreement. "You are correct, my lord. I have overstepped my bounds. We are strangers brought together for the sake of Edwin's safety. 'Tis not my place to judge you."

Crogan's brow furrowed. He blinked and stepped back, obviously perplexed. "Ye have not raised your voice once in my presence, yet ye have succeeded in causing my head to spin in circles, lass. Your calm is maddening!"

Miranda clutched her skirts and moved from the wall. "My calm, my lord, is necessary."

His palm slid over the stubble on his chin. "Necessary?"

"Do you have children, Lord Adair?"

The question clearly caught him off guard. He merely shook his head from side to side as he watched her intently.

"When you have a child of your own, you will learn quickly that anger does not serve you well. Only patience, understanding, and tolerance are virtues best embraced by a parent. I stand by these words and my adherence to them in life."

Crogan took a step toward her, but the sound of approaching footsteps caused his action to halt.

Both their heads turned as Rowena appeared. A glowing pair of amber eyes shifted between the couple. She stopped before them and offered a graceful curtsy.

"Rowe, meet Lord Crogan Adair. The King has sent him to aid in Edwin's return," Miranda informed softly.

"Lord Adair, allow me to present Lady Rowena of the house of Clifton, my younger sister."

Miranda watched as their guest took her sister's hand and brought it to his lips.

Over the years, Miranda had accepted the truth that when she stood beside her sister, she became invisible to all male eyes. Even her own husband had forgotten her presence when Rowena was in the room. Gerald had been an unfaithful letch, but accosting Miranda's younger sister was one line he knew not to cross. The girl was an innocent and adored by every man in his army. If he had dared to force her hand in any fashion, he knew the masses would rise together and hang him for his crime.

Of course, that had not stopped him from trying to seduce her at every turn. But Rowena was wise to the man's faulty charm and miserable behavior toward his wife, and her loyalty was unfailing. She could not be swayed by him.

Men had tripped at Rowena's feet her entire life, but Miranda had never resented the girl for her beauty, *until that moment*. She felt a blow of jealousy strike her with such force that she had to look at the stone flooring at her feet. Shame instantly washed over her. Miranda knew she was attracted to Crogan. To deny it would be to lie to herself. But she also knew that attraction would fade in time; it was not an everlasting emotion. And it had no place in her life.

She had learned through experience that wanting a man only proved more trouble than it was worth. Initially, she had wanted her husband, but that emotion died as quickly as it had been born. She assumed it would be the same in this case. And in the unlikely event she was wrong, she would not harbor any hurtful feelings for Rowena simply because Crogan was as easily swept away by her beauty as any other man. Her love for her sister was unconditional, and she would not allow anything to intrude upon that.

"'Tis a pleasure to meet ye, my lady."

Rowena shamelessly clutched his hand to her bosom and stared up at him with wide, pleading eyes. "Please bring him back to us, my lord." Tears sprang into her eyes. "He is so young, so helpless."

Seeing Crogan's discomfort and speechlessness, Miranda spoke up, gaining her sister's attention. "Rowe, please believe me once and for all. Bishop has nothing to gain in harming Edwin. We will see his safe return, I promise you."

"But—" Rowena argued.

Crogan cut her off, "Your sister speaks true, my lady."

Amber eyes shifted between them. Finally, she nodded in agreement, but the desolate look on her face was heartbreaking.

Miranda put a comforting arm around her sister's shoulders and guided her down the staircase. "Now let us go below so you may break your fast."

Miranda watched over Rowena's progress as they ate the first meal of the day. Her own appetite was nonexistent, but she forced down several bites to offer the appearance of hunger for her sister's benefit. At first, her sister had merely stared at the food, seemingly unaware that two others sat at the table with her. Then Miranda urged her to eat, and finally she began to pick at the scrambled eggs on the trencher before her.

***

As Crogan ate, he thought back to the encounter on the staircase. Miranda had been so close. He had closed in on her intentionally. His gaze had moved slowly over her, from head to toe, intrigued by her squared shoulders and the proud set of her chin. He had anticipated that he would greet the lady after his short slumber, but to run into her in such a secluded place was a pleasant surprise.

Immediately he noticed that she remained in the burgundy gown with short tippets, and smudges remained under her eyes, but in that shadowed stairwell, he was able to see the windblown effect of her plaited curls and the blush of heat in her cheeks from her recent ride. The lady was a lovely sight so early in the morn.

But then she had caused him profound distress with her claim of an intruder. Crogan and his army had arrived not three hours prior, yet he already felt honor-bound to serve and protect all within the Wilkes castle walls.

And then that distress transformed into anger when she could not substantiate that claim. He had found himself within the whirlwind of a tornado: one moment he wanted to throttle her, and the next he wanted to sweep her into his arms to find out if those lips were as sweet as they looked.

And her everlasting composure was quickly working its way under his skin. He wanted to rip down those defenses and see the woman hidden within. Prior to his bath, he had decided that physical interest in the lady had no place during his service to the King. But her lavender scent was intoxicating, her petite figure and pretty face were more alluring every time he looked at her, and her mysterious eyes drew him in without effort. There was no denial on his part when he realized his interest had rapidly blossomed into genuine desire.

Her defense of herself and her confidence in that defense were a powerful display. She was certain there was an intruder. He had thoughtlessly taken a step toward her, uncertain of his intent at that time, but the noise of light footfalls stopped him.

As he popped a piece of bacon into his mouth, he realized he had stood close to Miranda's side in a protective stance without consciously acknowledging the act in that moment. It was simply bred in him to protect those he served or those who served him. Even though his sword and armor were in his chamber, he knew he was adept with his fists and could resort to using them if necessary.

At that point, he looked up to find a beautiful woman descending the staircase toward them. The lady's long raven curls were unbound, falling around dainty shoulders and a deep décolletage revealed by the square neckline of her pale yellow gown. She appeared rather young, but the set of curves concealed beneath that gown were that of a woman.

Dutifully, his hostess had introduced them, but he couldn't help himself from staring at Miranda. The tenderness in her tone as she spoke to the girl was telling. That observation had caused him to take stock of the women who stood before him. They did not look alike; there was much that differed between them, yet the raven curls and the same mannerisms announced their relation before Miranda could confirm it aloud.

As the Scotsman munched on a crumble of cheese, he was struck by a startling realization. Following Dana's death, Crogan had not been able to meet a staircase without thinking of her loss. That entire meeting had taken place, but he had been so distracted by the Wilkes ladies, he had not thought of his mistress once.

Guilt washed over him.

Chapter 10

Crogan silently observed Rowena's behavior, and at last he understood Miranda's decision not to wake the girl several hours prior. Clearly, she was not sleeping well; the shadows beneath her eyes were darker than Miranda's. And if her sister had not talked her into eating, she would have simply sat there, stewing in her own morbid thoughts.

Unable to help himself, he stared openly at the young lady. She was truly beautiful. Possibly one of the most beautiful women he had ever met in his life. And it seemed she was genuinely unaware of such truth. She was well-mannered, yet demure. And her impulsive personality announced her short years.

All in all, he labeled her as the perfect package. He could not imagine any man not wanting her. But for some reason, in spite of his own wordless summation, he was distracted by the silent presence at the head of the table.

He decided that speaking of Edwin and his disappearance while Rowena was present was not a good idea. So Crogan spoke of the first subject that came to mind.

He pinned Miranda with a stare and waited for her to acknowledge it. When she glanced up at him, he wondered, "So what was Lord Wilkes like?"

Was it his imagination, or did he hear the lady groan deep in her throat?

Her lips thinned for a moment. "I do not wish to speak of my husband."

Crogan shifted in his chair, not comfortable with the feeling that turned in his stomach as the lady spoke the words "my husband." "The memories are too painful?" he prodded.

"In a manner of speaking, aye, the memories are painful," she agreed and absently nodded her head.

His handsome features turned down in a frown. "In a manner of speaking?" Her reluctance to discuss the man who had sired her son caught his earnest attention, and he was unable to discard his desire to learn more.

Without warning, Rowena raised her head and said, "The man was a veritable letch."

"Rowe," Miranda chastised in a whisper. "Be respectful of the dead."

Rowena's gaze turned on her elder sister in obvious disbelief. "I cannot respect a man in death that I was not able to respect in life. And you, above all others, know I speak the truth. Do you deny it, Miranda?"

She met her sister's beautiful amber stare with unwavering eyes. "I cannot."

Rowena's gaze snapped to their guest, and she sat forward, displaying more life than she had since sitting down. "The man treated my sister in a deplorable fashion."

He stared at Miranda's regal figure as he put a question to Rowena. "A heavy-handed man?"

Miranda squared her shoulders and chose to respond for herself. She met his inquiring eyes with her own masked of feeling. "He never raised his hands to me in anger. Not once."

Crogan felt his insides sigh in relief. He could not stomach a man who used his greater size and strength as an advantage over a woman.

"'Twas not necessary for him to do so. He was adept at abuse without raising a hand—" Rowena's words were quickly interrupted.

"Please, Rowe, let us not air our dirty laundry before our guest." Miranda had voiced a request, but her tone was firm in its resolve.

The youth's features turned contrite. "I must apologize to you both. I spoke out of turn."

Miranda put a hand over her sister's, offering comfort. "Do not give it another thought."

Rowena provided a weak smile in return.

Crogan glanced back toward the vast hall of tables. He felt as though his presence was intruding upon a bonding moment only to be shared between sisters. The Scotsman saw that many of his men had entered to break their fast, and more continued to filter in, including his cousin.

Brodie glanced at the dais and caught Crogan's gesture to join them. With his long legs and purposeful gait, the man crossed the space at a rapid pace. He climbed the short staircase and breezed over to stand beside his cousin's chair.

All occupants of the table were able to see that his massive height matched Crogan's. He was also just as brawny. But contrary to his size, he possessed a pair of friendly emerald eyes. He sported a head of chocolate brown curls and a warm smile.

The trio at the table stood in polite greeting.

Crogan offered the proper introductions and watched as Brodie took Miranda's hand and brought it to his lips. As he observed the chaste gesture, he realized they bore personalities that would mesh well together. With Brodie's carefree outlook and marvelous humor, he could easily sweep the lady off her feet. And as a widow, Miranda was free to choose her next husband. Brodie had not yet chosen a wife.

Brodie was family, and Crogan felt it was his duty to point out the opportunity to be seen in their current situation, but something held him back. He could not bring himself to delicately point out the idea as a serving maid dispensed a trencher heaped with eggs and pork and fluttered away.

In fact, as he listened to their gracious hostess quiz Brodie about his accommodations and his comfort and noticed their instant rapport, he felt his temper rise.

Without a care for how his words would be received, he spoke in harsh tones. "Brodie an' I have much to discuss in terms of plans for your son. Leave us, ladies."

Clearly stunned by Crogan's rude interruption and sharp order, Miranda met and held his hard stare for several moments. Wordlessly, she asserted her disapproval of his crass behavior, then she turned to her sister.

"Let us take in the air, Rowe." With that, she grabbed her sister's hand, and they made a graceful exit from the dais.

Both men watched them until they disappeared through the doors of the keep, then Brodie turned to his cousin and wondered, "Have ye taken leave of your senses, Crogan? Ye ordered the lady of the manor from her own table."

"I do not wish to speak of the lass. We will speak of her son."

Chapter 11

With the whole of her army out combing the land, Miranda felt it was safe for them to walk the grounds without an escort. They crossed under the portcullis and emerged in the open countryside. The day was warm, but following Crogan's biting order, she was cold inside. She lifted her face to the sun in the hope that the heat from the rays would soothe her.

"Do you recall that day when Mama and Papa took us to the village market? We were still living at home, and 'twas the one time we shared a day as a family," Rowena asked quietly as she stared down at the grass.

Miranda nodded. "Aye, I do."

"I think of that day often."

The elder lady grew reflective. "'Twas a good day. I recall much laughter. Mama wiped tomato seeds from my chin. And I held Papa's hand." A small measure of tears burned at the back of her throat. For a moment, she felt hollow.

"'Twas the only time I felt their love. 'Twas the only time I felt loved by anyone, save you. Then you married, and you birthed that tremendous little boy. When he emerged into this world, I felt his love. I felt as though I had been gifted with that one family day, every day."

"You have not lost that, Rowena," Miranda stated with conviction as they continued to walk.

"Mama and Papa are lost to us." Silent tears rolled down the young woman's cheeks.

"Edwin is not."

Miranda gazed out at the open land for many moments. "One day, you will have a family of your own. You will have sons and daughters and a husband who loves you. And you will have us. You will always have us."

"Will you marry another, Miranda?"

Her brow furrowed, reminded of the horror of her first marriage. "Nay."

"You may find a good man."

She failed to see through her cynicism. Her smile held no joy, and her tone held no conviction. "Lord willing…"

Rowena brushed stray hairs from her vision. "Do you believe Mama and Papa will return from their adventures in the world?"

Miranda did not believe for a moment that they would ever see their parents again, but for Rowena's sake she heard herself say, "Perhaps."

Their conversation wore on as they walked the Wilkes land in the opposite direction of the woods. The time passed, and at long last, Miranda glanced at the sun's place in the sky. It was at its highest point.

"'Tis time we returned, Rowe."

Chapter 12

Miranda could hear the armies in drills as they drew closer to home. As she heard Crogan's voice rise above the din, she felt tension knot in her stomach. They passed under the portcullis once again and crossed to the opposite side of the curtain walls. Her gaze settled on the rows of men in armor, and a tremor of dread rolled down her spine. Adair's men were combined with her own, and they listened to Crogan's direction.

She turned to her sister. "Please go inside and rest, Rowe."

The Wilkes army spent hours a day in exercises, so Rowe wouldn't suspect anything out of the ordinary to see them break into pairs and draw their swords, Miranda thought. Her sister merely nodded and began toward the keep as the men closed their visors. The clang of hundreds of swords crossed and echoed off the stone walls.

Miranda did not hesitate to approach Crogan and Brodie while they faced off in mock battle. They held their weapons expertly; their footwork was flawless. But at that point, Miranda was too unsettled to take notice. She had no qualms about interrupting their swordplay.

She had to raise her voice to be heard over the noise of combat. "Lord Adair, I wouldst speak to you at once!"

Both men halted their action. They lowered their swords, raised their visors, and turned to face her.

"A moment, my lord," her voice was ice.

"I will join Alfred." Brodie offered her a smile, then left them.

Crogan clutched her arm none too gently and led her away from the men and their exertions. He rounded a corner of the keep and continued on until he could speak without having to shout over the noise.

Finally, he halted and let her go. He lifted his helmet away and braced it under his arm.

"Ye best have good cause, lass," he charged, his expression thunderous.

Miranda knew her minimal size was no threat to him. Nevertheless, she moved forward and glared up into his handsome face.

"You intend to siege, my lord?" she demanded perceptively.

If he was not wearing pounds of metal armor, she thought he would have casually shrugged as he announced, "A siege it must be. We depart at dawn."

Her fists clenched at her sides to maintain a semblance of equilibrium. "*A siege it must be*? The great Crogan Adair has devised a plan to siege to reclaim my son," she mocked distastefully.

Crogan glared down at her.

When he continued to stare without responding, she prompted, "Do you have anything to speak in your defense?"

Finally, he snapped from his reverie, and his eyes narrowed dangerously. "By all means, my lady, offer up a plan ye believe is superior."

Miranda blinked, caught off guard by his challenge. "I—" she stalled, unable to formulate a witty response. The truth was that she did not have a better plan, but she knew there had to be a better way than a siege. Edwin's welfare was at stake. To storm into Bishop's castle by force could not be the best way to retrieve him.

He nodded arrogantly. "I thought not." With that, he spun on his heel and walked away.

"You vile man!" she shouted at his back.

"Aye, I am aware!" he called over his shoulder with a smile in his voice.

As he rounded the corner, she realized her fists were clenched so hard that her nails dug painfully into her palms. She flexed her fingers and took a deep breath. When her heartbeat returned to normal, she recalled her dignity. With squared shoulders and chin held high, she followed the path around the keep. She ignored her bailey of men and sauntered into the Great Hall.

While she crossed the vast space to the kitchen with the intent to order up a much-needed bath, she was once again struck by the feeling that a pair of eyes watched her progress. Her petite figure halted, and she scanned the emptiness that surrounded her. The trestle tables were vacant. The serving maids in the kitchen were few and too busy with their duties to notice the lady of the manor.

Nevertheless, the feeling was distinct. She was unable to shake it off as she moved into the kitchen and directed a sweet young girl to have water heated and sent up to her chamber. Her eyes strained and delved into the shadowed corners, but there was no one there.

She knew she was not paranoid. The tingling hair on the back of her neck did not lie. But there was no way to explain such a feeling when the hall was clearly empty. Her lips turned down in a frown. She was forced to leave it in the realm of the unknown.

The feeling dissipated when she entered the stairwell and climbed to the chamber level. The slippers on her feet created a soft rustling when she walked through her sitting room, then she drew to a halt in her bed chamber. Miranda was an organized person; it was the only way to successfully manage a castle steeped with people and its surrounding villages.

Everything had its place, but on that day, she noticed that not everything was in its correct place. The door to her wardrobe was slightly ajar, and the contents of her vanity table were disturbed.

A ghost of a smile touched her lips. Rowena must have been searching for something. Generally, the girl respectfully asked her elder sister prior to borrowing anything, but in her current state of worry, she must have forgotten to do so.

Shortly thereafter, the water arrived for her bath. Winny helped her to disrobe and wordlessly exited as Miranda sat back in the wooden tub and closed her eyes. She welcomed the relaxation and warmth.

Widow Wilkes

She could hear the distant sound of swordplay in the bailey below and gritted her teeth against the irritation that stirred within. There had to be a better way to save Edwin.

She felt so incredibly helpless.

Chapter 13

Miranda did not linger at her bath. She cleansed her body in the lavender-scented water then recalled Winny to aid her toilet. Her figure was fitted into a lilac-hued underdress with floor-length tippets and a sleeveless violet overdress that molded her form to perfection. Damp raven curls were swept up into a silver coiffe, and her cheeks held a natural glow from hours in the sun. She presented a lovely picture.

She was mildly distressed when she checked in on Rowe but did not find her asleep as she had expected. The girl simply sat there, staring out the window embrasure as clouds approached on the horizon.

They chatted for several minutes, then Miranda left with a purpose.

First, she visited the kitchen to give orders for the evening meal. Then she wandered out into the bailey in search of Alfred. The battle raged on. Those who had hypothetically fallen had gathered around those who continued to fight, watching as though it were paid entertainment.

Alfred stood on the sidelines, calling out directives when necessary. She did not see Crogan amongst the circle of spectators, so she knew he was one of the few who remained in battle. Miranda acknowledged a moment of pride in his abilities, but she did not allow her thoughts to linger.

The lady summoned her captain from the crowd, and they moved toward the portcullis in a casual stroll.

"What have you to relay, Alfred?"

"I am afraid our search did not bear results, my lady."

She crossed her arms under her breasts and looked to the earth, disappointed. "I had assumed as much. If you had found an intruder, I would have been summoned with all due haste." Her eyes lifted to meet his curious gaze. "I did not imagine it, Alfred."

"I do not doubt your word." He gave her a smile of reassurance. "I have issued an order that the immediate grounds will be searched at dawn and at dusk until Edwin is safely in the manor once again."

She gave a curt nod of agreement. The lady ignored the urge to turn her head and watch the men in swordplay, one man in particular. They were shrouded in armor, yet she could pick him out without the least bit of trouble. Not only could she feel his presence, but the way in which he held his stature, so sure of himself and his abilities, drew him apart from the rest.

Miranda gave herself a mental shake. "Thank you, Alfred."

"'Tis my pleasure."

She gestured toward the bailey. "Please, join your men."

He executed a polite bow and sauntered back to the crowd.

She stared through the metal grating of the portcullis for a moment. The storm clouds drew nearer. A lightning bolt flashed in the distance. An ominous feeling washed over her, and a violent shiver shook her limbs. Then a warm breeze caressed her face, and she struggled to regain a positive outlook. Edwin was in the hands of a stranger, but she knew he had to be healthy and safe. He had to be.

With that, she spun on her heel to return to the keep. She had duties to tend to.

Chapter 14

After suffering through a tensely quiet supper and a fitful night's sleep, Miranda rose well before dawn. Outside, rain continued to fall. The thunder and lightning had receded deep into the night, but small drops continued to pummel the earth in a steady drum.

Without an appetite, she remained in her chamber. The lady paced until the sun kissed the horizon behind the cloud cover. When it was time for the armies to depart, she descended to the stables in split skirts and collected her mount.

She walked Spectrum around into the front bailey where hundreds of men awaited the rise of the portcullis. Many were on horseback, and even more would make the journey on foot. Moist drops bounced off the metal of their armor, creating a hollow drum that surrounded her figure and shook her insides.

She spotted Alfred near one of the tower gatehouses. He sat atop his warhorse, but he had not yet donned his helmet. Miranda ignored the water that dripped down her face and clung to her eyelashes. She moved toward the captain of her army.

As she approached, another mount joined Alfred, and she watched while Crogan took off his helmet and braced it under his arm. He pinned her with a hard stare, and an uneasy feeling formed in the pit of her stomach. Brodie also joined his cousin and observed her determined gait.

As three large men silently examined every step, she felt a dive in her courage. Raven curls had been drawn up in a lovely coiffe in the early hours of the morn, but now stray strands were limp and plastered to her head. The emerald gown with split skirts remained dry under her navy cloak, but the air was damp, and her figure felt muggy and sticky.

The smudges under her eyes were darker than ever. She knew she must look frightful, but she was not dissuaded from her approach.

Miranda gracefully climbed into the saddle and met Crogan's glare with her pride foremost in her visage.

"Have I kept you waiting?" she asked, hating the breathlessness of her voice as she felt his stare like a caress.

"Ye have not," he returned with an expression of disapproval. "I had not believed ye would see us off, my lady."

The uneasy feeling sprouted into a tremor of fear. "I have not arrived to bid you farewell. I have arrived to join the journey."

Between gritted teeth, he ordered, "Ye will not."

She squared her shoulders. "I do not seek permission."

"Ye will remain an' look after your sister."

"I have charged Winny with that task."

His jaw clenched, and he guided his warhorse closer. His massive form blocked out Brodie and Alfred at his back. "'Tis too dangerous."

Miranda clung to strength through her calm. "Danger be damned. 'Tis my only son."

His head shook in stiff negativity. "I forbid it."

Slender fingers clutched the reins with such ferocity that her knuckles turned white, yet her face was serene. "I care not."

The Scotsman's handsome features became thunderous. "Miranda."

She knew he chose to use her given name for the first time as a warning. And if that had not been enough, the harsh tone of voice had produced the same intended result. But in spite of his intent to instill fear through a word, she would not back down.

She summoned a deep tone of her own and returned the challenge. "Crogan."

"I fail to see the humor in your jest, lass."

"At last, we agree on one matter."

His hand shot out and grabbed her wrist in a firm grasp without warning. "Nae, lass, we do not agree a'tall."

"Crogan." It was meant to be a threat, but it sounded as an appeal.

"If ye continue your charade, I will be forced to have Brodie detain ye for the length of our absence."

Miranda fought to keep her mouth from dropping open in shock. "You jest."

He tugged on her arm, bringing her face within inches of his. "I do not."

She ignored the warm breath on her cheeks and the stall in her pulse. "I must go, Crogan, I must."

His lips thinned, and he sat back. "Ye have forced my hand, lass." His gaze remained fused to her face as he ordered over his shoulder, "Brodie, I must request that ye accompany the lass to the keep and detain her there."

The elder man moved forward to do his cousin's bidding without question. Before Miranda knew what had happened, two large hands clutched her waist, and abruptly, she found herself seated astride Brodie's horse. A thick arm circled her abdomen while she saw Crogan guide his mount into a backward step.

The space between them grew slowly. Finally, he turned away and shouted the command for departure.

With her insides twisted in frustrated knots, she was forced to watch as their arsenal of men filtered through the gates. Every last knight crossed under the portcullis, and when the final foot soldier was clear, the massive metal grate began to lower. The echo of metal on wood as it slammed shut sounded like a gavel of defeat in her ears.

Miranda fought tears that would have easily mixed with the rain. She pushed Brodie's arm from her waist and jumped down to the ground. She shot the elder man a glare meant to relay her feeling of betrayal, then marched toward the keep.

"My lady—" he implored, but she would not turn to face him.

With her skirts held tightly in her hands, she crossed the distance and sought refuge in the manor. Without pause, her petite figure climbed the staircase, and she hurried down the corridor to Rowena's chamber. She knocked politely on the door.

When no response was returned, she cautiously opened the heavy structure. A tense sigh escaped her mouth when she spotted Rowena knelt beside the bed, head bent, eyes closed, palms pressed together in fervent prayer.

On shaky legs, Miranda did not hesitate to charge into the room, climb the raised platform that supported the bed, and drop to her knees beside her sister. She prayed for the strength to endure her son's absence, she prayed for the patience to deal with the man sent to help them, but mostly she prayed for Edwin.

She asked for the Lord to watch over him in his time of need, to protect him from harm, and to return him safely to her arms.

It was only later when she realized that she had prayed for Crogan's safe return as well.

Chapter 15

Crogan looked to the sky. At midday, the rain finally ceased its relentless assault. He took a deep breath. Hours had passed, but he could not successfully banish the picture of Miranda's bedraggled appearance from his mind. He had left her in Brodie's charge, forced her to remain behind, but he would not let himself feel guilty for it. It was possible that they could march into battle, and battle was no place for a woman. If Bishop's army arrived to confront them, he could not assure her safety.

He knew his men would fight to the death for a good cause, but if they all fell in battle, she could die right alongside them. His concern that she remain behind in safety was just.

So why did the look in her eyes as they departed haunt him? As usual, her face had given nothing away regarding her thoughts, but there had been something in the depths of those stormy gray eyes that spoke in silence. The feelings there had been too many to label; nevertheless, he was beaten down by them. He knew she must feel helpless, and he was the cause. He knew she was angry, but there was no cure for that within his hands.

As she had stared at him, the weight of her trust pressed down upon his shoulders. Not only did he feel obligated to collect Edwin simply for the sake of saving the child's life, but he acknowledged a deeper need not to disappoint the child's mother. The lady had easily earned his respect. She had a fountain of strength that awed him. She was intelligent and kind. And there was no denying that she was beautiful. Inside and out.

While he had held her wrist, it had been difficult not to yank her into his arms for a taste of her moist lips. He had nearly given in to his desire at that moment, but then he recalled himself and the anger that instantly ignited because of her determination to ride into danger with them.

Crogan knew Edwin was her only concern, but he could not let the love for her son cloud her judgment over her own welfare. He also knew she did not realize it, but while he resided under her roof, he also held her life within his hands. That life had once been protected by another, a man she refused to speak of…

Curiosity prompted his eyes to shift to the rider at his right. "Ye have served Lady Wilkes in the years following the death of her husband, Alfred?"

If he was startled that Crogan abruptly inserted a question into the contented quiet, he did not show it. He simply offered a curt nod of acknowledgment without turning his head. "Aye."

"She has earned your trust?"

Another nod as he gazed off into the distance. "Implicitly."

Several moments passed as Crogan observed his companion's stiff regard, then, without warning, Alfred pinned him with a direct look. "If you wish to request information, extend your question, Lord Adair."

The captain's defensive attitude for Miranda was telling. He would not be swayed from his faith in her, not be amenable to words spoken against her. But Crogan was not wholly fishing for facts about the widow. He wanted knowledge of her husband.

"I have received the distinct impression that the lady of the manor does not mourn the death of her marriage. Gerald and she were contracted to wed?"

Alfred seemed reluctant to respond, but he said, "Aye, my lady was a mere girl of ten and five when they spoke their vows. My lord was a man of twenty and seven."

"'Tis a rather large gap for a girl so young," Crogan commented. He hoped to prompt Coombs to continue. It worked.

"Aye, in writing 'twas a smart match, but in reality…" He shook his head negatively. "I held the utmost respect for my lord, but in terms of his marriage, I witnessed a side of his character that I had not known existed."

Crogan's fists clenched on the reins. "How so?" The overcast sky seemed to hang low overhead. His gaze thoughtlessly searched the depths of the clouds, trying to remain detached from their conversation, yet unable to halt his desire to learn more.

"Gerald treated Lady Wilkes deplorably. The man was respectably loyal to his country and his army; he treated us well, but in his marriage, those traits were lost. He flaunted his liaisons in public, verbally assaulted her in front of his men, and humiliated her at every turn. As you have learned, my lady is demure, but she is a fighter." His voice grew soft and ponderous. "She suffered in silence. 'Tis my belief that Rowena and Edwin are the only reasons that she did not succumb to overwhelming despair in her life with him."

Crogan swallowed over his disgust with the deceased and thought of Miranda's claim that her husband had never raised his hand to her. Rowena had not voiced a confirmation to that claim, so he sought one from his companion in arms. "Did he ever resort to violence with the lass?"

Alfred wiped beads of perspiration from his brow with the back of his hand. "Nay. However, 'tis an incident that has lived in my memory for years. 'Twas an evening much like ours previous, thunder and lightning and howling winds, but there was revelry in the keep for my lord's birthday. The whole of the castle was well into their cups while music played, people danced, and the tables overflowed with a feast. The atmosphere was alive with joy.

"From my place near the fire, I observed my lord and lady in a distant corner, the scowl on his face and her stiff regard announced that they were clearly quarreling. She ignited his temper to such a degree that his arm rose with obvious intent to strike her, but she spoke, and he halted. His arm lowered. She walked away with great dignity and control."

He shook his head of dark locks. "I will never know what stayed his hand on that eve, but the following morn, the lady was particularly quiet. I believe he served his punishment for her conduct later that eve, whatever that punishment may have been." Alfred was silent for a moment, then he seemed to recall himself. He met Crogan's hard expression. "I have revealed too much. My lady will disapprove."

"'Tis not my intent to share our conversation with the lass."

Alfred merely nodded, and his gaze shifted to the horizon.

Once again, the Scotsman thought back to Rowena's words about Gerald being a veritable letch. It seemed her opinion may have been an understatement. He hated to think of Miranda in such a situation. It was true that their wills clashed upon occasion, and he was often prompted to anger because of her obstinate nature, but he would never wish such cruelty upon her, never.

She deserved a man who would respect her, a man who would treat her well, a man who would make her happy, but above all, a man who would love her.

Crogan's thoughts were interrupted when he spotted a lone rider on the horizon. They were nearing Bishop's lands, so he braced himself for the truth that it was likely one of Bishop's men.

He pulled up on his reins, and the remainder of his entourage followed suit.

From Alfred's place at his side, he strained to see across the distance. "The man is not familiar to me, but he wears Bishop's colors."

Crogan rested his hand on the hilt of the sword strapped to his hip and silently waited for the stranger to approach. The warrior within him was ready for battle.

Finally, the young man halted several yards before them. He did not appear to be much older than Rowena. "I speak on behalf of Lord Frederic Bishop."

"Your lord risks a life in sending ye alone," Crogan purred.

"My lord knows you will not murder the messenger."

Adair merely quirked an eyebrow at that. When the boy failed to continue, Crogan glared and spoke, which announced his leadership of their mass. "Continue before I grow bored, lad."

"I bring an oral message for the captain, and a penned message for the Lady Wilkes," he announced monotonously. "Sealed for her eyes alone."

Crogan felt his stomach tighten. He did not like it. But he did not say a word as he dismounted and moved forward, which forced the stranger to do the same. A hand lifted, palm up.

A rolled piece of parchment was placed in his hand. It was sealed and stamped with the symbol of Bishop's coat of arms. From his massive height, he stared down his nose at the youth. "And the oral message?"

The boy held himself stiffly, respectfully, as he relayed his master's words. "The boy will be slain if you attempt to surpass the curtain walls on this day. You are hereby ordered to vacate the Wilkes land posthaste."

Crogan reached out and clutched the boy's crimson and gold tunic in his fist. He gave him a sharp shake. His act easily instilled alarm that reflected in the youth's eyes. "What of Edwin's return?"

"The child will not be returned until Bishop is ready to release him."

Crogan growled dangerously. "The lands will not be vacated until the lad has been safely returned to his mother!"

Cautiously, the messenger removed Crogan's hand from his tunic. "Very well." With that, he pulled himself onto his horse's saddle and rode away.

A trail of epithets floated on the summer breeze as Crogan spun on his heel and threw himself into the saddle. He could not give the command for battle because the boy's life had been threatened. He was forced to return without Edwin; however, he was not empty-handed. He looked down at the parchment in his hand. *Sealed for her eyes alone…*

Chapter 16

There was a dusky horizon in sight as Miranda paced in the bailey. Unable to concentrate on anything of consequence for the length of the day, the lady had wandered the keep aimlessly. Servants had approached with questions for care of the manor, and she had answered thoughtlessly.

Finally, when the interruptions broke through her distracted state, she moved into the bailey to escape the curiously watchful eyes of her staff. She remained in her emerald gowns and navy mantle, which had dried during the course of the day. She was warm, but her mind was too preoccupied to acknowledge that minor discomfort.

Rowena was locked away in her bedchamber, lost in the comfort of her Bible. Miranda wrung her hands for the hundredth time, then a shout from the gatehouse caused her to freeze.

"Your army returns, my lady!"

From his place in the gatehouse, her guard had an unobstructed view of the land, so he was better able to see their concentrated approach.

Miranda moved to the portcullis and locked her tiny hands onto the hard metal. As she stared through the massive grate, she forced herself not to hold her breath, lest she swoon from lack of air. The moments ticked away like hours as she stood stock still, praying to see her son amongst the men.

However, as she waited, she could not deny the logic of her thoughts. Their return was too soon. They could not have secured a victory in such a short amount of time. Perhaps Bishop saw their numbers and released Edwin without a fight. Perhaps he had let go of his criminal intent.

She clung to her hope, but as the men entered her vision at long last, she knew Edwin was not with them. Miranda wanted to crumple to a heap there in the bailey and give in to her self-pity, but she simply retreated from the portcullis as it rose to allow the men entrance.

Her gaze immediately sought Crogan's figure. His helmet had been stowed, and that gave her an unobstructed view of his expression as he rode into the bailey. The sculpted jaw was set in hard lines, and his eyes were awash with rage and another emotion she could not define. She felt her mouth go dry.

He dismounted before her, and his squire was instantly by his side to aid in the removal of his hauberk. As the Scotsman shifted to his full height, she quickly moved forward.

"Where is my son?"

Crogan's handsome features finally softened. "Your assumptions were correct, Miranda. He desires the holding. We were ordered to vacate. An offer was not made to release the lad."

Miranda's strength dwindled. Her throat burned with unshed tears, and she looked to the earth at her feet. "I want my son."

A large hand gently touched her forearm to regain her attention. "And we have received a message for ye."

Miranda's gaze lit on the parchment in his hand. She ripped it from his fingers, tore open the seal, and vaguely noticed as a tiny leather flask that had been rolled neatly inside fell to the ground.

Crogan picked it up as she read the sloppy scrawl on the yellowed paper.

I anticipated a stalemate between us, Miranda. Now you must await further instructions for Edwin's return. Until then, open the flask and take that image to your pillow every evening.

Bishop

She looked up in time to see Crogan pour the contents of the flask into his hand. Horror struck her full force as the crimson liquid registered in her mind as blood. Her son's blood.

The lady's last thread of strength finally snapped, and emotion flooded her being. A panicked cry emerged from her mouth, and her features turned down in a harsh sob. The letter fell to the floor, forgotten.

Not quite comprehending her actions, she lifted her hands and began to pummel Crogan's chest. She desperately needed an outlet for her pain.

"My son! My helpless child! He's been hurt!" She continued to strike him and wail, unable to control herself as tears streaked down her cheeks. All she could think in that moment was that her sweet little boy had been harmed. His blood had been spilled.

Men surrounded them, silent and stupefied, as they watched their lady break. Many were empathetic, and many were stricken by the truth of the blood. More of them were openly shocked by the scene that had unfolded before them, yet, at the same time, they understood that it was long overdue for a lady buckling under too much pressure for one person to handle alone.

"You bastard, I want Edwin!" She wept as he allowed her to continue striking his mountainous chest with her little fists. "I want my son!"

Finally, the Scotsman caught her wrists and held them immobile. Without warning, the anger drained from her body and left her in a weakened state of grief. Her brow fell forward to rest against his chest, and deep, wracking sobs shook her figure.

He slipped an arm around Miranda's back, another behind her knees, lifted her into his arms, and swept through the crowd. Thoughtlessly, her hands circled his neck, and she buried her face in the crook of his shoulder as moisture continued to well in her eyes.

Crogan entered the keep and pinned the nearest servant with a stare. "Where is your lady's chamber?" he barked.

The maid stumbled over her directions, but he caught the complete response as he hurried to the staircase. His massive frame climbed the last step in seconds and moved down the hall.

"I want him back, Crogan," Miranda whispered into the quiet with a catch in her voice.

His head dipped to her ear, and he spoke in tender tones, "I understand."

Miranda was only vaguely aware as Crogan made the turn into her antechamber, breezed through the open space, and entered her bedchamber. There was no hesitation on his part as he moved to the bed and sat on the mattress with her in his arms.

Her heart hurt as he simply held her in the comfort of his embrace. Tears shimmered on her cheeks and dripped off her chin to wet his navy tunic. She wanted nothing more than to be holding her own child, offering the comfort of her embrace to him. She needed to feel him safe within her arms. He should be under her roof, not miles away, in who knows what condition he was living in at that moment. How badly was he hurt? Was he cold? Was he hungry? Did he have a bed to sleep in? Who was tending to him? Were they treating him kindly?

After several minutes, Crogan shifted Miranda's figure and stood. The instant she felt his eyes turn her way, she rolled over and buried her face in a pillow to hide her tears.

"Rest yourself, lass. I shall return in a moment." With that, he stalked from the room.

Miranda heard the soft click of the door and twisted onto her back to stare up at the mosquito netting draped over her bed. She suddenly felt so bereft. Crogan's abrupt absence was a stunning blow to her precarious emotional state. Through her pain, she had felt secure in his embrace; she welcomed the comfort and warmth of his body as he had held her close.

Now she was nearly devoid of any feeling at all. She was beyond the pain. At least she fooled herself into believing that for an instant, until the image of her son's wounded little body flashed in

106

her vision. A sob echoed in her stone chamber. The petite figure shifted to her side and stared out at the darkness through her window embrasure.

Night had fallen.

Unwillingly, Miranda imagined the worst. Her son could be lying on his deathbed with serious injury, and she was helpless to give aid. He could be in agony and uncared for, his wound left to the elements.

The lady shook her head. She needed to cling to hope; it was the only way to continue on. The amount of blood in that leather flask was minimal; the injury was certain to be minor and quick to heal. Slender fingers clutched her feather pillow. She needed to believe that theory as truth.

"I *will* see my son again. I *will* hold him safe in my arms." Miranda began to quietly hum one of Edwin's favorite melodies, and she prayed that somehow he could hear her voice despite the distance between them.

The lady did not acknowledge the creak of door hinges when it sounded; she assumed it was Winny to aid her nightly toilet. But she was surprised to see Crogan walk around the bed and seat himself on the edge of the mattress.

The Scotsman held what appeared to be a chalice of wine. "Drink this down," he ordered quietly.

Miranda decided the spirits would help to soothe her frayed nerves, so she accepted the metal goblet without a second thought.

After she rose to her elbow for leverage, she drank several sips of the red wine, then handed the glass to her guest.

She fell back onto the pillow and stared up at the curious sea-green eyes that gazed down upon her. "I must apologize for that outburst, Crogan. 'Twas uncalled for."

He shook his head, his features more handsome than ever in their softened state. "Nae, lass, 'twas long overdue."

Her humorless smile failed. "Perhaps in that regard, you are correct. But I should not have placed the blame at your feet."

A strong, supportive hand urged her back onto her elbow, and she took another sip of wine. "Love and concern for your child does not always include logic," he explained. The Scotsman revealed a compassion that caught her off guard.

"Your understanding is most unexpected, Crogan." She leaned back and stared up at the mosquito netting. Her mind spun in circles. Then suddenly she was struck by a stunning realization. She was alone with Crogan, in her bedchamber, on her bed.

Apprehension washed over her. In spite of her attraction to the man, she could not help but be hindered by past experience. Gerald had treated her terribly. His lack of affection in the bedroom had made her cynical and uneasy. Crogan sat so close, close enough to lean down and press his lips to hers if he chose to do so. She desperately wanted him to do so, but at the same time, the idea scared the hell out of her.

"I have duties to tend to," she mumbled and rolled away from him to the other side of the bed. The lady stood on wobbly legs and was abruptly assaulted by a wave of fatigue so heady that she nearly stumbled down the platform staircase.

Once she had regained firm footing, her head turned to find Crogan moving quickly toward her, an expression of startled determination on his face.

"What have you done?" she demanded in her groggy state. Her thoughts churned slowly; eyelids drooped.

"Ye need the rest, Miranda," he announced and reached out for her as her knees buckled.

"The wine…" her thoughts trailed off. She felt the security of Crogan's embrace an instant before she succumbed to a forced slumber.

Chapter 17

Miranda blinked open her eyes. She felt more rested and refreshed than she had in ages. Her head rolled to the side, and she was startled to see that the sun was at its highest point in the sky. The lady stretched contentedly, then the current truth of her reality broke through, and the tranquility of the moment crashed down upon her like a douse of icy water. Her body froze, and a miserable groan whispered past her lips.

Edwin remained absent and in unknown peril. And Crogan had deceitfully drugged her to sleep the previous evening. Her exasperation in that moment was staggering. She jumped up and rang for Winny. Edwin's safety was out of her hands at that time, but she could certainly deal with the second cause for her rage.

The lady took an abbreviated bath with the water in her washstand and Winny helped her into a clean cotte. Over the undergarment, a teal gown with floor-length tippets molded to her dainty figure. Raven curls were pulled back into a simple plait. Following the conclusion of her toilet, Miranda stalked from her chamber down to the Great Hall.

The masses had just finished with the midday meal. Many remained at the tables and absently chatted. Some had gone into the bailey for recreational activities. And a small handful of men sat in front of the lifeless fireplace, using the chessboards set up there.

Miranda spotted Crogan seated at a chessboard across from Brodie. Both men wore abstracted expressions as they stared at the board between them. They spoke quietly of inconsequential topics.

The lady crossed over to them and wordlessly halted beside their table. The men looked up, and Crogan met her glare as if he expected precisely that.

Suddenly, he grinned at her, which revealed even white teeth. "Did ye sleep well, lass?"

Miranda blinked, blinded by his smile. Heat fused her face, and words momentarily failed her.

When she simply stared at him without a response, his smile grew. Her dumbfounded gape dissipated, and she regained her glower.

She pointed an accusing finger at him. "You have deceived me through action, Crogan. How could you treat me in such a fashion?"

He rose to his full height and looked down upon her. "Ye may argue 'til ye are blue in the face, lass, but we are both well aware that ye were in desperate need of slumber."

Miranda crossed her arms under her breasts, needing the shield of her arms between his close, looming stance. She was aware that Brodie watched their discourse with avid curiosity, so she chose her words well. "I have misplaced my trust in you."

"I acted in your best interest," he defended, brow furrowed.

"You acted without my knowledge of your intent."

His eyes moved over her face, then pinned her to the spot. "'Tis true, but an apology will not be forthcoming. I stand by my decision to act on your behalf."

She peered up at him, wordlessly challenging him in a clash of wills.

Finally, he wondered, "How do ye feel?" His gaze made a sweep of her meticulous figure. It moved over her like a sensual caress.

Grudgingly, she admitted, "I am well enough." Her cheeks bloomed with a full blush as he openly admired her appearance.

"Ye look well enough," he drawled in his Scottish brogue.

The lady's heart thumped in her chest, but the fact that they had an audience allowed her to cling to her wit. "Your attempt to distract me with flattery has failed. I desire an apology, Crogan."

He crossed his arms over a muscled chest, his features schooled in seriousness. "Nae."

Her lips thinned in disapproval. "How will I trust in you?"

"'Tis your cross to bear. I will act in your best interest with or without your blessing, Miranda. Best ye learn such truth now."

The lady wanted to throw her hands up in frustration, but rather than act so foolishly before their guest, she simply frowned at him and walked away.

She was aware that everyone had witnessed her pathetic display the previous day, but she could not allow that to rule her actions. As the lady of the manor, she merely had to put the incident behind her and carry on as though it had not occurred. Her humiliation be damned.

Rowena was seated alone at her place on the dais, but it appeared as though she had not touched her food. She merely peered down at the trencher in what seemed to be a catatonic state.

A footman pulled Miranda's chair, and she filled it.

"You must eat, Rowe. You have grown far too thin," the elder sibling voiced as a trencher was placed before her.

Without acknowledging her sister's words, Rowe began to mechanically eat the stew in front of her.

Quietly, Miranda ate her bread while she observed the youth from the corner of her eye. She was far too pale and obviously sleep-deprived.

"You must rest yourself, Rowe. In the morn, we shall take in the air." It was a struggle, but she forced life into her voice.

"Aye, Miranda."

The elder lady covered her sister's hand in a protective gesture. "You must not put yourself through such torture, Rowe."

"'Tis rather hypocritical of you, Miranda, following that scene in the bailey." Rowena's gaze rose to meet her stricken stare.

"I am truly sorry you were witness to that momentary lapse. But I have recovered myself with renewed determination that we will see Edwin's return." She squeezed her sister's hand to give reassurance.

Noiseless tears began to slide down Rowena's beautiful face. "What if we do not see his safe return, Miranda? What if he is slain?"

She cleared her throat to relieve herself of the tears that burned there. "I will not allow such doubt into my home, Rowena. Hear me well, Edwin will return to us."

Her sister's constant state of doubt and grief were not welcome any longer. She fought for her own hope; to listen to such words of defeat only added to her misery.

Her tone was sharper than she intended. "Go rest yourself, Rowe." With that, she abruptly rose from the table and stalked away. Miranda loved her sister unconditionally, but her patience had met its end.

She did not realize her intent until she found herself in the stables. She waited while Spectrum was saddled, then tore from the grounds, moving beyond the curtain walls as if the devil himself blazed a trail at her back.

Wind whipped through her curls, which caused the pins to loosen and fall away. Her skirts flapped on the breeze, and her eyes watered from the sting of the air upon her face.

She rode Spectrum hard in an attempt to outrun her own anger and frustration. She needed a break from it all. From the manor and its obligations, from Crogan and his arrogance, and even from the sister she adored.

Miranda rode until her horse was winded and in need of rest. She slowed her mount to a steady trot and searched the landscape for the stream she knew ran north and south of her property. In the distance, the sight of a meager pond loomed near. Thoughtlessly, she slid to the ground and guided her horse to the watering hole. While the animal drank, she surveyed the landscape once again.

The pond was not familiar to her, and the stream she had assumed was nearby was nowhere to be seen. The lady frowned. She had not ridden long enough to stumble into unknown territory, had she?

A deep breath filled her lungs, and she slowly exhaled. There was no cause to worry, she assured herself.

Once Spectrum had regained his strength, the pair would search the land for familiar markers, and she would find her way home. The matter was easy enough to rectify.

Chapter 18

Crogan glanced at the keep entrance yet again, waiting for Miranda to breeze through the double doors. The dim light in the high window embrasures in the Great Hall announced the sun was setting. She had marched from the keep after the midday meal and not returned.

Crogan, Brodie and Alfred had gone into the bailey for some drills once their chess game concluded, and he asked after her return when they sought the evening meal.

He was startled to learn that she had not been seen in hours. Earlier, he assumed the lady sought some fresh air, but no such walk within the curtain walls could eat up such an extended period of time. Perhaps she had tended to some manor duties while she made her rounds. But when he saw the sun was beginning to set, his unease blossomed into genuine alarm.

The meal before him remained untouched while the others ate their fill. Rowena had not appeared; she had ordered up a meal to her chamber, a meal Crogan was certain the young lady would not eat as well.

"Your actions give ye away," Brodie observed. "Ye are concerned."

"She should have returned by now." He stood without warning. "I must speak with the guard in the gatehouse."

"I will join ye, cousin."

"As will I," Alfred chimed in.

The trio stalked out to the gatehouse. The beefy guard confessed, "The lady sought a ride beyond the curtain walls in the early afternoon hours, but she has not sought a return entrance."

Crogan wanted to beat the man senseless for not alerting them to her long absence. He actually stepped forward to do so, but Brodie halted his intent.

"Calm yourself, cousin. He was not given any such instructions to inform us of the lass's movements. The man is not to blame."

Crogan pinned the large fellow with a warning look. "If she has not fallen prey to some disaster, ye best beware that ye will inform us of her movements in the future, understand?" he ground out.

"Aye, my lord."

With that, Crogan spun around and hurried to the stables with Brodie and Alfred close on his heels. While in transit, he called a footman forward and barked orders for his men to be dispersed to seek the lady of the manor.

The Scotsman had given Miranda a hard time when she issued the premature order to seek an intruder on her land, but now that he learned she was missing, the possibility of an intruder was all he could think about.

***

The open landscape had faded, and she was swallowed up in the darkness of the forest. But was it the forest on her property? She could not be confident. While Spectrum slowly meandered through the trees in the darkness, she could not be sure of anything anymore. North, south, east, and west were merely words in that instant rather than a feasible reality. Unable to decide the correct direction, she allowed her mount to guide their progress.

A wolf howled in the distance. A violent shiver shook her limbs in spite of the warmth of the night. An owl hooted nearby, and she jumped in her skin. Miranda would not lie to herself; she was terrified. She also knew that if she was not so terrified, she would be feeling utterly foolish for getting herself lost. But there would be plenty of time for regrets later; first she needed to find her way home.

Her gaze turned to the sky. A ceiling of tree branches and leaves loomed overhead, but she could see small shafts of moonlight beyond that. It gave her very little visibility from her place on the ground, but she was grateful for any view at all. If it had been an overcast evening, she was certain she would not be able to see her hand in front of her face. As it was, she was surrounded by shadows and silhouettes.

Once again, Edwin's favorite melody sounded on her lips. But that time, it was not an attempt to soothe her boy; it was an attempt to soothe herself. Her voice sank into the trees on all sides while Spectrum continued to move forward.

An hour passed.

Then another.

Her throat was raw from her incessant singing, but she did not stop. It helped her to feel less alone. And her thoughts touched on her son so often that she worried she would not see him again, but not because of Bishop, because she feared she would not make her way out of the forest alive.

She scanned the shadows once again. Was it lighter than previously? Her gaze strained in the darkness. Was it possible she saw a break in the trees ahead? She urged Spectrum faster. As the mare moved forward, Miranda saw a large patch of moonlight up ahead. It was true; there was a break in the woodland.

She entered into the full white glow of the moon, with mixed feelings. The forest was at her back, but a wide expanse of unfamiliar land stretched out before her. Her fervent hopes were dashed instantly. The frustrated lady wanted to cry; however, she knew tears would serve her no purpose, so she sighed heavily and urged her mount into a steady trot. Once again, she allowed Spectrum to lead the way.

Exhausted from singing and from tension and apprehension, Miranda closed her eyes for a moment. She dozed off for a considerable length of time, but, miraculously, she had slumped forward onto the mare's mane rather than slide to the ground. When she opened her eyes again, she sat up to see a familiar sight. However, the sight did not cause her any joy.

Slender hands pulled up on the reins, and she jumped down to the ground. There was a sick feeling in her stomach as she slowly approached the same pond Spectrum drank from when she first realized she was lost.

Miranda sank to her knees in defeat, and tears welled in her eyes. Open palms covered her face. She prayed she was lost in a nightmare, but when they lowered once again, and she watched as Spectrum drank from the dreaded pond, she broke into a short bout of hysterical laughter.

Her laughter echoed on the wind and faded away as she sat back on her haunches and stared at the beautiful half-moon that reflected on the water. Her tears dried, and her heart felt laden.

She was half a day's ride from the Colvilles and half a day's ride from Bishop, but she had stumbled upon neither during her journey. If Miranda was one to believe in witchcraft, in that moment, she would have believed that a vengeful witch had placed a curse upon her.

Minutes crept past as she continued to stare at the still water of the pond. The day's breeze had died when the sun sank below the horizon. It left an eerie calm that was contrary to her trembling figure. The air was so motionless, she thought she could hear her heart drum in her chest, and it grew louder and louder. Then a vibration began in the earth beneath her legs and seeped into her bones.

Her imagination played cruel tricks on her. It sounded as if a rider approached. She looked up, and her eyes touched on a figure moving toward her far on the opposite side of the pond. The white glow of the moonlight gave the man's appearance a surreal quality, and that caused her to wonder if the sight was a mirage.

"Crogan," she whispered.

"Miranda!" The murderous expression on his face was certainly not a conjured image.

For an instant, she was overwhelmed with joy that he had found her, that she was not lost to the wilderness, but the fury he projected quickly stamped it out, leaving her uneasy. Her limbs were stiff as she stood to greet his approach.

The equestrian rider traced the edge of the pond and dismounted before her. He stomped up to her with such ferocity that she took a step in retreat. Callused hands gripped her upper arms in a firm grasp. "Holy hell, Miranda, I imagined the worst!" he shouted and gave her a rough shake.

"I—I—" she stammered, but her response died when he abruptly yanked her into his arms. When Miranda realized he was simply and silently holding her close, she rested her cheek on his chest and wrapped her arms around his lower back.

For a dizzying moment, the lady acknowledged the fact that his figure seemed to be a solid mass of impenetrable muscle everywhere, and he radiated a glorious heat that produced a wonderfully musky scent that was purely Crogan.

She felt so safe and secure that she never wanted him to let her go. Against her will, tears of relief sprang into her eyes, which she quietly allowed to course down her face.

"I feel so foolish," she whispered, trying to hold her voice steady.

He pulled back with the clear intent to upbraid her, but his gaze locked on the tears on her face, and his voice was softly accusing. "As ye should."

Miranda yanked herself from his arms and wiped the moisture from her cheeks with the back of her hand. "Thank you, my lord, for being so swift to point out the error of my ways."

His brow furrowed and eyes narrowed. "Ye could have been kidnapped, or worse!"

"As you see, that has not occurred. I merely fell prey to my own distraction." She clutched her skirts, squared her shoulders, and attempted not to notice that the moonlight played with the sharp angles of his face, which added to his stunning allure.

"I forbid ye to ride alone again."

Miranda's mouth nearly fell open in shock. "You jest!"

He took an intimidating step closer. "I do not."

"You do not possess the right to issue such a command!" she cried, unleashing her feelings with full force. Following the previous day's outburst, it was pointless to cling to her wall of reserved calm.

"I claim any rights I please, lass," he announced in a faintly deceiving tone.

Her stomach tightened when his gaze dropped to her figure. Thoughtlessly, she retreated another step. Then that glowing gaze settled on her lips.

"And I do not hesitate to take what I desire." He moved forward like lightning and yanked her into his arms.

Startled by his actions, her mouth opened to deny his intent, but words failed her. The man's kiss was an assault upon her senses. There was no time for thought. Desire instantly washed over her as his warm mouth moved against hers, hard and tender at once. Heat shot down her body; it weakened her knees and guided her arms to rise and clutch his tunic.

Her petite figure strained against him, and she lifted herself to her tiptoes in order to encourage their contact. His massive height bent lower, giving her access to wrap her arms around his neck while his hands slowly moved up her back. Callused palms gently slid over her shoulders and shifted to hold her face close.

His tongue ventured to taste her bottom lip, then delved inside.

Miranda heard a purr at the back of her throat as he deepened their kiss.

Tentatively, her tongue tasted his, not prepared for the jolt of excitement that traveled to the millions of nerve endings in her body.

She had never experienced such overwhelming desire in her life. She lost control of her thoughts, her logic, her reasoning. Gerald had never treated her to a like kiss during the entire course of their marriage. He had never inspired her to respond with such uninhibited fervor. Her husband had treated her like a whore. He took what he wanted from her without giving anything in return.

She had birthed a child, yet she felt as though she were experiencing genuine desire for the first time in all of her two and twenty years. It equally awed her and created a hint of bitterness in her subconsciousness.

But somehow, through the veil of passion, a warning signal sounded deep within. Miraculously, she conjured the strength to rip her mouth from his and back away several steps in order to regain her reasoning.

"I cannot do this," she breathed in a hoarse voice. "Not while my son's well-being hangs in the balance. 'Tis wrong."

Crogan stared at her, his breath labored. His hands rose to comb through mussed auburn locks. His mouth opened to speak, but nothing emerged.

Miranda nearly smiled. She had never seen him at a loss for words before. To see him thusly was quite disarming and endearing. It took all of her willpower not to walk back into his arms to continue that heart-stopping kiss. Her insides still trembled; her lips still tingled.

"We must return," she said decisively.

He nodded absently, and Miranda turned to collect her horse.

Their journey to the manor was made in tense silence.

Chapter 19

When they arrived at the castle, the guard in the gatehouse emerged. He looked up at Miranda's place on her mount in the moonlit bailey.

"I am pleased to see you have returned fit and unharmed, my lady. I shall send riders to retrieve the men in search of you."

"Thank you, Abrams." She began to urge Spectrum forward, but the guard halted her movements.

"My lady, you have guests."

Miranda's features pinched in confusion. "Guests?"

"Aye. One Lady Alice Farraday has arrived with her entourage."

A muttered oath sounded nearby, which gained Miranda's avid attention. Her eyes shifted to Crogan as an unsettling wave washed over her. "An acquaintance of yours?"

His eyes shone brightly under the white glow of the moon as he stared at her across the distance of several feet. "The lass and I are contracted to wed upon the arrival of the New Year," he revealed.

Miranda felt a knife of jealousy twist in her stomach. Betrayal and disappointment slapped her hard across the face. Such knowledge changed everything in an instant. She no longer had the right to desire him; he belonged to another. And he had kissed her with the full knowledge that he was betrothed.

It seemed the trait of a letch could be applied to Crogan as well as her deceased husband. She could not look at him in the same light, and it made her want to run to her chamber, throw herself on her bed, and cry until there were no more tears left to shed.

But her pride was quick to intrude on her sadness and compensate. Her wall of strength erected itself, and a composed curtain lowered over the lady's lovely features. She gazed at him through a mask of stoicism, but it was impossible to keep the accusation from her voice. "Of course you are." With that, she kicked Spectrum into motion and left Crogan in her dust.

She jumped down from the snow-white mare in the stables, ignored the Scotsman's entrance, and headed for the keep.

"Miranda." He grabbed her wrist, and she felt as if she had been scorched.

She ripped her arm from his grasp and reacted on instinct. Stormy eyes spit fire at him, yet she spoke in quiet tones. "Carry out your assigned duty, and leave me in peace." If she continued her dignified tirade, she would give herself away and choke on the tears that swiftly rose in her throat, so she whipped around and stalked to the castle, biting back emotion.

During the walk, she managed to regain a semblance of calm and prepared herself to meet Adair's betrothed. She pushed through the double doors and immediately spotted the young lady seated alone at the table on the dais. At such a late hour, the Great Hall was virtually empty.

Clearly Alfred and Brodie had not concluded their search because she knew they would be there awaiting her safe return. And the lady's entourage would have been escorted to the servants' quarters for refreshments following their journey. One of the manor's maids had placed a trencher of food and a chalice of wine out for their unexpected guest, but they had not been paid any heed.

Miranda's fists clenched in her skirts of their own volition. Even across the distance of the large chamber, she was able to see that the girl was quite young, and unbelievably stunning in her beauty.

Her shiny blond curls had been swept up into an impeccable gold coiffe that complemented large chestnut eyes. She was seated, but Miranda hated the fact that she could see the youth was well endowed and possessed a waist nearly as small as her own.

The cut of her lavender gown was marvelously flattering to her figure, and that only added to Miranda's hurt irritation. *Of course his betrothed would be young and beautiful,* she thought bitterly.

She continued to discount Adair's presence at her back, but even if she was not acutely aware of his proximity, the way Lady Farraday's eyes lit up when she looked in their direction clearly announced that he had entered the Great Hall.

The girl stood and flew down the abbreviated staircase, swept past her hostess, and threw herself into her betrothed's arms. "Crogan, I have missed ye so!"

Miranda silently observed as he gently disentangled her arms from his neck and pinned her with a questioning stare. "Alice, what brings ye to England so *unexpectedly?*"

Now that the young lady was on her feet, Miranda noticed she stood close to five inches taller than her own petite frame. She hated their easy exchange, yet she could not force herself to look away.

"Grandmamma passed." Her expression was dramatically grief-stricken, but tears did not accompany it.

Rather than pull her into his arms and offer heartfelt condolences, his gaze shifted to their spectator. "Alice, I must introduce Lady Miranda Wilkes, our generous hostess." His eyes lingered on her face as he gestured to the girl. "Miranda, I present Lady Alice Farraday."

Chestnut eyes settled on the shorter female. They clearly picked up on his informal use of their hostess's name.

"Crogan's betrothed," Alice quickly added, then went through the polite motions of a curtsy, prompting Miranda to do the same.

"I must apologize that I was not here to greet you myself. I hope you were well received by the staff." She wore her hostess mask to perfection despite her mixed emotions.

Alice presented a sickeningly sweet smile that did not reach her eyes. "Aye, Lady Wilkes. Your servants were most gracious."

Miranda nodded her approval, unable to summon a smile, even a fake smile. "You must be exhausted following your journey. Would you like to have a bath ordered up, or shall I show you to your quarters posthaste?"

"Aye, my lady, I desire slumber."

"Of course, please follow me." She sent Crogan a curt nod, which dismissed his presence.

"Let us catch up at daybreak, darling," Alice purred quietly.

Miranda did not miss the covert wink his betrothed presented to him before standing on tiptoes to place a kiss on his cheek. She turned away and began toward the stairwell without waiting to see if her young guest followed.

Without acknowledging her reasoning for it, Miranda chose a guest chamber in the opposite wing of the castle from her own rooms. She gestured to the luxurious space and watched as Alice entered. The youth gazed around her temporary residence.

"I hope this will be sufficient," Miranda spoke mechanically.

A forced smile was sent her way. "Aye, thank ye, Lady Wilkes."

"Please ring if you need anything. One of the maids will be prompt to attend to you. I shall retire now. Sleep well." Miranda did not wait for Alice to reply; she simply turned and hurried away.

Her steps did not halt when she entered her bedchamber. She immediately began to pace. Restless and aggravated over recent events, she could not sleep in such a state.

Alice was clearly a spunky young chit, intent on staking her claim over Crogan when any woman walked near. Miranda could not deny that she was envious, but more so than her jealousy, there was simply something about the girl that made her skin itch with dislike. There was an instant impression of vain superficiality that reflected off her big eyes and bright smile.

She shook off such thoughts. Alice was not her concern.

And neither was Crogan; nevertheless, her hands clenched in indignation. He had not disclosed the news that he would be married with the New Year. She told herself to stop right there as she shook her head from side to side.

The man did not owe her any explanations. He was present for one task: retrieving Edwin. So why did she feel so betrayed that he failed to tell her? Because he kissed her, that was why. They had crossed that line... *He* had crossed that line.

She wanted to throw her hands up in the air in defeat. It was just as well anyway; she could not allow herself to be distracted by inconsequential issues while she waited for Bishop to make his next move. So, she convinced herself that Alice's arrival was a blessing in disguise. The girl's presence would help her desire for the man dissolve quickly and without regret. But it was going to be difficult to forget that incredible kiss.

Miranda's pacing stalled as the hair on her neck tingled and stood on end. She glanced up and scanned the large space of her bedchamber. There was nothing. Swiftly, she spun around and looked at the door. It stood slightly ajar. She was certain she had closed it. Her stomach twisted in fear. Without wasting a moment, the lady rushed forward and pushed the door open.

Her gaze delved into the shadowed interior of her antechamber. There was no movement to be seen. She dismissed the room and charged through it, then through the open doorway into the corridor beyond, while her heart hammered in her chest.

She took in the sight of a massive man turned with his back to her, drifting away, but she had gained such momentum at that point that she could not stop herself from slamming into a solid frame of muscle and bone.

Her petite body bounced back into a stumble, but there had been so much force from the collision that she could not maintain her footing. Her hands uselessly clutched the open air at her back as she landed hard on her derriere. A whoosh of breath escaped her lungs, and she felt a painful jar followed by an unpleasant pins and needles sensation that surged through her limbs. Delicate palms scraped the stone flooring.

Through the haze of discomfort, turbulent eyes rose in time to see Brodie whirl around and take in the sight of her fallen form.

"My lady! Are ye hurt?!" he demanded, his expression shocked and contrite.

She shook her head in the negative, which prompted him to hurry forward and offer his hand.

While he helped her to stand, she wondered, "Did you see someone take flight from my chamber?"

Brunette brows furrowed in confusion. "My lady?"

"An intruder. There was an intruder in my chambers," she spoke quickly. "I did not see a soul, but I know someone was just there."

"I saw no one exit into the corridor, lass," he assured.

At that moment, her cynical side kicked into gear. The panic faded, and she felt her suspicion rise. "Brodie? Did you seek me in my chamber?" She knew the question was daring, but it needed to be asked.

He appeared taken aback. "Nae," the Scotsman returned emphatically.

Her sharp mind was quick to pick up on the glaring truth that his chamber was not located in that wing of the castle. Her eyes narrowed upon him. "Your quarters are in the south turret, Brodie. What brings you here?"

Clearly, he tried to mask an expression of guilt. His mouth opened, and it appeared his mind worked at a rapid pace. "I must have executed a wrong turn. I fear the corridors in the manor are rather similar. 'Twas my intent to retire."

She wanted to believe him, but the uneasy feeling in the pit of her stomach did not subside. What could she do at that point? She had no proof that the man had been watching her. And in the unlikely event she was wrong about the surveillance, it would be a tremendous insult to accuse him of such immorality.

Miranda hated to do it, but she would have to dismiss the incident, just as she had the previous times she felt she was being observed but was unable to locate a culprit.

"I must have been mistaken. My day has been rather trying, and I am fatigued."

"Of course. Please seek your slumber, lass." He gave her a handsome smile.

She turned and pointed toward the south hall. "And, Brodie, your chamber is in that direction."

"Aye, thank ye." His massive figure moved past her, and she watched until he disappeared from sight.

Was she simply being overly skeptical due to the abduction of her son? It was likely just a coincidence.

Unable to stamp out her unsettled feelings, Miranda decided it would be best to check in on her sister's slumber. She made the short journey to Rowena's door and cautiously opened it. The bed was empty. Her heart stopped.

But in the next breath, it began to beat again when she located the girl seated before an unneeded fire in the fireplace. Tears glistened upon her ivory cheeks as she stared into the biting flames.

Miranda padded into the stiflingly warm room. "Rowe?"

Amber eyes lifted, and, despite her tears, Rowena offered a demure smile. She gave a soft giggle and wiped at the moisture on her face. "I desired the soothing effect of a fire."

Miranda felt herself laugh for the first time in weeks. "The sweltering heat is soothing?"

A slender hand pointed to the fireplace. "I wanted to watch the flames."

The elder sibling slowly approached. "Do you mind if I join you?"

"Certainly not." She patted the empty space beside her as an invitation.

Miranda seated herself next to her sister on the white linen chaise and settled herself comfortably. They watched in contented silence for so long that eventually both of them dozed off in spite of the temperature.

Chapter 20

Miranda's eyes cracked open. The fire had long since dwindled into ashes, and dawn trickled through the open shutters in the windows, which created long shadows in Rowena's bed chamber.

Her sister paced quietly nearby. The elder sibling could not help but smile as she observed such graceful movement, a mirror trait to her own penchant for pacing. Something was on her mind.

She blinked away the blanket of sleep. "Rowe?"

Her sister's gaze settled on her. "I have learned that we have guests."

Miranda nodded as she felt the sharp reminder of Alice. "Crogan's betrothed."

Rowena halted and faced her sister. She watched her closely. "His betrothed?"

Another nod.

She approached and knelt before her. The girl's voice was tender. "You have feelings for him, Miranda."

Her eyes dropped. Her sister knew her too well. "I cannot."

A beautifully understanding smile was sent her way, and she brushed a raven lock of hair from Miranda's eyes. "Your mind does not guide your heart. 'Tis obvious in the way you look at him. What will you do?"

"The attraction is in its infancy, Rowe. I will do what I must. I will learn to let it go." She stated it as fact, then pushed herself to her feet.

"Miranda…?"

The concern in her voice only seemed to magnify the elder woman's emotions. She ignored Rowe's question and presented one of her own.

"Will you be joining us to break your fast?"

Rowena grinned. "I would not miss it."

Miranda ordered up a bath. It was her duty to be present for meals to play hostess to her guests, but her most recent guest caused her to procrastinate. She had no desire to go below. She had no appetite. But obligation forced her to rise from her bath and ring for Winny to aid her toilet.

The day was much cooler than expected for the last day in July, and the wind howled outside, which caused the window shutters to rattle as she waited patiently for the lady's maid to sweep her locks up into a silver net. As a navy gown was pulled down over her head, she could feel her stomach knot with tension.

The velvet fabric complemented her petite figure, and the silver trim on her tippets gave the effect of wealth and power, but in that moment, she felt far from powerful. Her confidence waned; her pride was cracked.

She descended the staircase with a regal posture and a serene expression that belied the feelings at war inside of her. Miranda immediately noticed that she was the last to arrive. Brodie, Rowena, Alfred, Crogan and Alice all watched as she crossed to the dais. Slim hands lifted her full skirts to allow her to climb the small staircase with ease.

She sent a nod toward her guests and seated herself in the chair a vigilant attendant pulled for her. Without pause, the servants bustled about to serve their meal.

While everyone began to eat, Miranda realized she could not look directly at Crogan, or at Alice. She was quite adept at concealing her feelings from the world, but that morning she feared she was failing at her practiced skill.

Her eyes remained downcast as she addressed her unwanted guest. "I trust you slept well, Lady Farraday."

Alice's eyes settled on her bowed head, which forced Miranda to discard the feelings biting at her insides and raise her chin. Her gaze rested on the young girl. Once again, her appearance was impeccable.

"Aye, thank ye, Lady Wilkes."

"I must express my condolences on the passing of your grandmamma, my lady," Brodie inserted politely.

Alice gave him a sad smile. "Aye, she will be missed. But I am eternally grateful that I do not bear my grief alone." She looked at Crogan and patted his hand in an intimate manner that was extremely telling.

Miranda decided in that moment that the couple had visited their marriage bed prior to the marriage. The rapport they shared was not that of acquaintances, of that she was certain. Had Alice visited his bed the previous evening? Had he visited hers? She sat back and pushed her trencher of food away in disgust, which gained her sister's curious gaze.

Miranda had a feeling that Rowena had picked up on her own silent thoughts when her sister suddenly joined the conversation. "On that thought, I must say congratulations are in order."

Alice looked at the younger, more attractive lady, and there was a visible fire in her eyes. "I appreciate your sentiment, Lady Clifton."

"Have you set a date for the joyous occasion?" Rowena probed.

"January the first," Alice replied with great pride and an underlying possessiveness that was not lost on Miranda. Crogan simply sat there, following the conversation as a spectator would observe the theatre, his features set in stone.

"Ye are all most certainly welcome to attend." The girl continued, "King David will be in residence. 'Tis truly an honor."

"The King?" Alfred seemed most impressed. "'Tis quite an honor indeed."

"My cousin and I know the leader of our country well. David initiated the betrothal at Crogan's request," Brodie chimed in, and that caused his cousin to pin him with a glare.

"Is that so?" Rowena's rhetorical question was a smokescreen. Miranda could see her sister's thoughts churning, prompting Brodie to continue on, almost as if they were putting on a production.

"Crogan was brave enough to put such a decision in our King's hands," the elder cousin revealed.

"It certainly appears the King chose well, as it seems the two of you get on famously. But what prompted such a move?" Rowena put the question directly to their Scottish guest.

Crogan shifted uncomfortably in his chair, and for some reason, he looked at Miranda. Her heart tripped, but in the next instant, his words revealed why his gaze had settled upon her.

"I lost someone close to me."

She thought of the danger in losing her son, and her heart immediately went out to him. She had to fight to maintain an expression of polite curiosity.

Alice quickly intervened. She touched his hand, which effectively regained his attention. "Oh, Crogan, I was not aware."

"Dana Dillingham was a remarkable woman," Brodie offered. "I would have been proud to welcome her into the family." He glanced at Alice for a moment, and the look in his eyes told everyone at that table that he did not possess such feelings for the lady currently betrothed to his cousin.

Miranda watched in morbid fascination as Rowena sat forward in her seat, clearly intrigued. Her sister instantly picked up on Brodie's veiled insult and realized she had an ally in Crogan's entourage. The production continued with greater drama as the two played their parts in defense of their family.

"Please excuse my rudeness, but what has passed to create such a turn of events?" Rowena tested.

"An unfortunate accident. If Dana had not slipped in the stairwell, causing her death, I believe Crogan would be happily married to her as I speak."

The only thing that saved Miranda from crying on Adair's behalf in that moment was the fury on his face as he glared at his cousin. She wanted to voice her sympathies, but Alice was right there with her contrived compassion, swiftly reminding Miranda that it was not her place to offer her feelings to him.

"Crogan," she crooned.

His eyes narrowed on his betrothed. "I do not wish to discuss it, Alice. Not now, not ever."

She made no attempt to hide her hurt feelings. "Very well."

Rowena must have felt that it was her turn to introduce a topic to continue to needle at their unwanted guest. "Forgive me, Miranda, but I must admit some remarkable similarities in all of our lives. My sister was contracted to and wed a man I found most disagreeable."

If the subject of Dana had not been so tragic, Miranda would have almost been amused by Brodie's and Rowena's conniving interaction, but now that the topic had transferred to her own state of affairs, her body grew rigid with tension.

"Another also taken in death?" Brodie offered up the expected rhetorical question.

Apparently not willing to take their veiled innuendos without a fight, Alice loaded her arsenal, but it was not Brodie or Rowena she struck with the weapon of words; it was Miranda.

"I must convey my sincerest hopes and prayers for your son, Lady Wilkes. Crogan told me of his abduction. 'Tis truly terrible." Her words were so sugar-coated that Miranda felt a turn of nausea in her stomach.

"I appreciate your concern," she answered appropriately. And with that, she had had enough. Her eyes shifted to her captain. "Now I must apologize in advance for my absence, but Alfred and I have duties to tend to. Please excuse us."

Crogan rose along with them. "Duties, what duties?" he demanded.

Patiently, she explained, "As lady of the manor, I have an obligation to look in on my people personally. I make my rounds on the last day of every month." She began toward the staircase, which prompted Crogan to cross around and block her path. Her head lifted, and their gazes locked.

"Under the current circumstances, I believe 'twould be best to send a surrogate in your stead."

"I will not." Unwilling to quarrel with him in a room packed with people, she decided to make a small concession. "However, if you feel 'tis necessary, you may join my entourage to oversee the matter."

He gave a curt nod in acceptance.

"I believe a ride is in order," Alice announced in a sweet voice, inviting herself along.

Brodie simply stood up, wordlessly stating that he would join them as well.

Rowena rose with a stunning smile on her face. "We shall all go."

Chapter 21

On their way to one of the surrounding villages in her charge, Miranda found herself riding between Alfred and Rowena. Brodie, Alice, and Crogan rode at their backs. A third row of six men-at-arms rounded out their entourage.

Miranda made her best efforts to ignore the virile presence that rode directly behind her while she and her sister chatted about castle details: changes that needed to be made in the weaving room, the desire for an additional laundress, a reprimand for one of the members of the kitchen staff, necessary stock for the pantry, tapestries that were long overdue for a cleaning. The list was endless.

As they shared their casual conversation, Miranda was greatly relieved to see a mild spark of life in her sister's eyes. The haze of panic and concern had shifted, which had allowed a semblance of normalcy to return.

In no way was Edwin forgotten. Their worry and their tension remained in the pits of their stomachs, but they continued on, because they had to. They clung to their routines to the best of their abilities in order to stave off the madness that would accompany constant fear, concern, and an idle mind.

The wind whipped at her skirts and her coiffe, freeing many strands of raven hair, and the overcast sky threatened rain, but Miranda would not allow the weather to dampen her spirits. Her days visiting the villages were her favorite out of the whole month.

It gave her a chance to check in on the people whom she depended upon, and who depended upon her. And with the current circumstances in her life, she needed it on that day more than ever.

She was the overseer of three separate communities in Yorkshire. She visited on a rotating schedule, to ensure that she set foot in each one at least four times in a year. Miranda had cause to visit on more occasions for many reasons, but she never wavered from her schedule.

As they approached the south village, the hustle and bustle of its workers could be heard at a distance. The noise of the blacksmiths and silversmiths rose over the din of the shoemaker, cloth makers, candlemakers, bakers, grooms, tanners, and butchers. Farm hands and herdsmen were in the distant fields. They tended to their animals and crops.

A trio of giggling peasant girls walked along the worn path they traveled on, carrying casks of flour. When they heard the horses approach, they politely stepped aside and offered smiles of welcome for their lady and her companions.

When they reached the outskirts of the village, Miranda turned to Crogan and Brodie. "Wait here if you like." With that she, Alfred, and Rowena dismounted.

The cousins did not share a decision. They simply dismounted as well.

Too pompous to mingle with commoners, Alice announced, "I shall wait here with the men-at-arms."

"Very well," Crogan stated and turned, leaving her to pout in silence.

As Miranda and Rowe led their group of escorts through the dirt-covered streets, the villagers took notice of their arrival. Men, women, and children flocked to them in hoards, abundant smiles lighting up their faces.

***

Brodie, Crogan and Alfred stood back and watched the conduct between the ladies of the Wilkes castle and their people.

Adair could not help but admit that he was awed by the scene presented to them. The women were received with welcome embraces and laughter, jokes, and heartfelt stories, but above all, respect.

Most men ruled through fear. It was difficult for a man to rule and earn respect. As he continued to observe, he saw that Miranda did not treat them as meager peasants; she treated them as equals, worthy of her time and energy, worthy of her friendship. And friendship bred trust and loyalty. For a woman to reign over many thousands of people and earn their respect, trust, and loyalty, that was truly an awesome feat.

And Crogan had seen Miranda smile on many occasions; he was able to admit she had a lovely smile. However, with the constant worry over her child, it never seemed to reach her eyes. But in that moment, when he saw the look of fulfillment upon her face as she grinned down at a toddler who had tugged on her skirts, he found himself mystified by an abrupt and acute reaction to sweep her off her feet and carry her away in his arms.

To where and to what end? It did not matter. All he knew was that he wanted her in that instant more than he had wanted anything in his entire life.

He did not love her; he could not love her, because he would never allow himself to feel that way toward another woman as long as he lived. But it scared the hell out of him to acknowledge the fact that he could not recall ever wanting Dana with the intensity that he felt for Miranda in that moment.

Unable to help himself, he had thrown caution to the wind the previous evening and kissed her with all the passion she inspired. And what a kiss it had been. She had ignited his desire to stunning heights, then pulled herself from his arms, leaving him dazed and confused.

Following that lapse in judgment, he swore to himself that he needed to maintain his distance. He had no use for a relationship at that time in his life. Certainly not while her son was in the hands of a criminal. And certainly not while he pined over the loss of Dana.

The fact that he was betrothed was of little consequence to him for the simple fact that he had very little care for the sanction of marriage and all that it entailed. The only matter for his betrothal was for the purpose of gaining an heir.

Then Miranda learned of Alice's arrival and her status as his bride-to-be. The accusation in her tone when she had said "*of course you are*" clearly relayed that she felt betrayed by him, and for some reason, that did not sit well with Crogan. It did not sit well with him at all.

For some foolish reason, he meant to explain his side to Miranda in the stables, but she brushed him off like an insignificant gnat, and it was then that he decided he must harden his heart against the woman. She was too easily slipping past his defenses, and what made it worse was that she was not making any attempt to do so.

He would retrieve her child, leave her in peace, and go on to be married in order to obtain his heir. It would be as simple as that. But he had to remind himself of that plan once again as a woman handed a baby into Miranda's capable arms.

She gazed down into the giggling little face and let out a throaty laugh of her own. The sound flooded into his blood, heating it several degrees, then settled in his groin. Against his will, his eyes were drawn to the graceful curve of her neck as the echo of her laughter faded away. His lips tingled as he imagined pressing his mouth to that satin skin. Then the tingle transferred to his fingertips as the fantasy continued and his hands slid around that tiny waist to cup that luscious little backside and press her against his—

Suddenly, his cousin's voice ripped him from his carnal thoughts. "The lass is truly wonderful with those people," Brodie observed.

"Aye, I have always admired her for winning them over so completely," Alfred added. "'Tis not like anything I have ever witnessed in all of my years."

"The 'lord' of many lands, wealthy beyond imagination, respected by her people, and rather lovely in appearance. Why are men not flocking to the widow in droves?" Brodie put a voice to a question Crogan had silently asked himself many times already.

"They have," Alfred confirmed, "but when she refused every last one, eventually the visitors in search of a wife stopped arriving on our doorstep."

Brodie's brunette brow furrowed. "Why do ye believe she refused them all, Alfred?"

"Following a joyless marriage, I do not believe any woman hastens into another."

"Aye, 'tis logical." Brodie's gaze shifted to his cousin, yet he spoke to Coombs. "I have yet to take a wife myself…"

Crogan's eyes narrowed as a blinding fury erupted inside of him. Without realizing it, his hands balled into fists of rage.

Brodie smiled in return.

"Do you wish to ask for the lady's hand?" Alfred asked directly, clearly caught off guard by the notion.

"Do not concern yourself, Alfred." The Scotsman turned from his cousin and clapped the man on the back in a friendly manner. "'Twas merely a passing thought."

Crogan's eyes rose to the sky while he gnashed his teeth together. It was then that he noticed the darkened clouds on the horizon.

Wordlessly, he weaved through the crowd and put a hand on Miranda's arm to gain her attention. She looked up into his face, and her smile faded.

"We must hasten away, Miranda; storm clouds grow near."

The lady nodded, disappointment turning down her lovely features. She reached into her voluminous skirts and dispensed the coin she had available. With that, she grabbed Rowena's hand and headed for the edge of the village where their horses awaited.

They pushed their mounts hard, but, unfortunately, they did not beat the rain. They were soaked through in moments, forced to ride the remainder of the distance while the cool drops chilled them to the bone.

Chapter 22

When Miranda woke well before dawn the next morning, she acknowledged what could not be denied any longer: she was exhausted, mentally and physically. The hours of lost sleep and the constant drive to keep herself busy had finally settled deep within her.

She lay there for quite some time, willing sleep to claim her, uncaring that she would need to rise for breakfast eventually. But she could not drift away into the contentment of nothingness. Thoughts of her present situation kept her awake. She thought of her son, of Rowena. She thought of Crogan…

Still angry at the man in spite of the logic that she should not be, violently she threw the covers aside and rose to greet another grueling day.

Miranda ignored the fatigue in her limbs while Winny aided her toilet, then she descended the staircase to find the Great Hall nearly empty. Most of the castle would still be in slumber at such an early hour. Her petite figure, encased in a lovely wine-colored gown, trudged across the vast space and ascended the dais.

She pulled her own chair and seated herself. Miranda still felt as if a shroud of sleep blanketed her mind and body. Rather than wait regally for the remainder of her breakfast companions to join her or rise and seek the pantry to take long overdue inventory, she gave in to the need to prop her forearms on the table and rest her cheek on them. Her eyes closed of their own volition, seeking the rest she required.

It was the sound of a chair scraping the floor beneath her feet that jolted her from an unconscious state. She sat up in a sharp, jerky motion. Her gaze lifted to see Brodie smile at her from his place at the table.

"Please, do not let me disturb ye, lass. Ye must be in much need of rest."

Daintily, she rubbed the sleep from her eyes and gave him a modest grin. "I appreciate the offer, my lord, but I fear 'twould be a grave insult to my guests if I slumbered through a meal."

As she spoke her words, Miranda realized her suspicion of two evenings previous had dissipated. The conversation he shared with Rowena for their last breakfast had won her over without question. The position he revealed in terms of Alice and the contract to wed his cousin was just a bonus on top of his charming personality and good looks.

Footsteps approached and shifted her focus.

Alfred bowed politely to his lady and took his rightful place at the table.

Miranda looked out over the crowd of men who occupied the trestle tables below. She had slept longer than she realized. The hour grew late. Her eyes touched on the empty chairs at her right. Crogan and Alice had failed to appear. And Rowena was also absent.

One likely excuse for Crogan and Alice's vacant seats was prompt in her thoughts. An image of the pair entwined together amongst rumpled bed covers flashed in her mind. The handsome man bestowed a kiss upon his bride-to-be with a passion equal to the kiss he had given her. A red haze passed over her vision, and physically she shook her head against the idea.

Such ideas would not serve her well. She banished them in the hopes that they would not visit her again.

Her gaze shifted to Rowena's chair. She had missed numerous meals since Edwin was kidnapped, but Rowena had fought through her self-imposed solitude and began to join them in the recent days.

Miranda glanced toward the stairwell, uneasy. Was it possible the girl had undergone a backslide into her catatonic depression? Perhaps she simply overslept?

Following Edwin's abduction, Miranda was not willing to overlook any such feelings of concern. Contrived or not.

With her meal untouched, she looked down the table at its occupants. "Please excuse me, everyone." She rose with great dignity to conceal her tense state.

To her great misfortune, she lifted her gaze to find Alice descending toward her on the staircase, halfway between the first and second levels. The ladies halted, almost as if they were subconsciously facing off.

"Good day, Lady Farraday," Miranda submitted politely even though she could not stop herself from wondering if the girl had just come from her betrothed's arms.

The corner of Alice's mouth barely twitched with a smile. "Good day, Lady Wilkes. Your direction is at fault if ye intend to break your fast."

Miranda did not try to laugh off the lady's remark. She pinned her with a passive stare. "I seek my sister," was her simple response. She certainly did not owe her guest any explanations.

A head of unbound blond curls tilted to the side; her expression grew serious. "Ye do not seek my betrothed?"

Rather than succumb to Alice's blatant attempt to spark her anger, Miranda smoothly wondered, "Do you intend to draw me into a quarrel, Lady Farraday?"

Alice crossed her arms under her breasts. From the excessive height of a higher step, she looked down her nose at the elder woman. "Ah, a resourceful evasion to my request. Ye are clever, I must admit."

Miranda felt her hackles rise. Clearly the girl had discarded any pretense of courtesy. "What do you seek, Alice?"

She pushed her curls onto her back, descended a step, hunched over, and leaned in close. Lovely features transformed into an ugly mask of possession. "Crogan is *mine*, Miranda. Ye best not forget that." With that, she sent her a sickeningly sweet smile, then pushed past her tiny figure and continued on down the stairwell.

She watched Alice disappear, rather stunned that the girl had the audacity to threaten her hostess in her own home. Miranda had believed Alice to be an unexpected inconvenience, but their most recent exchange elevated her opinion into that of genuine annoyance.

She shook her head in utter disbelief and restrained anger, then turned to continue with her intent to check in on her sister.

Distracted by the words ringing in her ears, her eyes were on the stone staircase near her skirts when she turned the corner onto the top landing.

"Miranda."

The familiar voice caused her head to rise without thought. She found herself abruptly staring up into Crogan's mesmerizing sea-green eyes.

Miranda was already irritated as a result of the turbulent scene with Alice, but that feeling only grew when she concluded that the timing of the couple's descent was far too coincidental. They had been sharing their morning in each other's arms and chose mere minutes to stall for time so they would not arrive in the Great Hall together.

And on top of all that, Crogan was disturbingly handsome with his auburn locks pulled back in a loose queue and his large muscular frame accentuated with an emerald tunic, belted at the waist, and black braies. With his broad shoulders and ruggedly masculine features, he seemed massive and intimidating.

With the theory of where he spent his morning locked in her head, her self-imposed comment erupted more sharply than intended. "Blast! I must use an alternative route to navigate between levels."

Rather than introduce a conversation, she simply stepped to the side with the resolve to dismiss his presence and continue on, but he moved to block her path.

Their gazes locked. Miranda fought to keep the emotion from entering her eyes as he searched their depths. Silently, she allowed him to try and read her expression, her body language.

When he merely continued to stare at her, seemingly pondering his thoughts, she spoke, "Let me pass, Crogan."

He took a deep breath, and his features softened. "I believe we need to have a discussion."

Her head automatically swiveled from side to side. "Nay, a discussion is unnecessary."

"I owe ye an explanation." He moved closer.

Instinctually, Miranda longed to stay within arm's length of the man, but she took a step back, telling herself that it needed to be done. She tried not to smell the woodsy scent of him or feel the tremor in her limbs that his proximity caused. "Nay," she voiced, quietly but firmly, "you owe me nothing."

He claimed another step, forcing her to retreat once again. The cool stone wall was at her back. "I believe ye to be avoiding me at every turn, Miranda."

She took a deep breath. His close presence numbed her razor wit. "I believe you to be delusional, my lord."

He cursed into the silence. Then two bulky arms rose, and his palms pressed to the wall beside her shoulders, imprisoning her within his stance. She could feel his warm breath caress her face while his eyes narrowed upon her.

"I do not condone this," he growled angrily.

Her brow creased. "I fail to understand your meaning."

"Ye have withdrawn, Miranda. Ye condemn me for my future marriage, and I will not have it."

She stared up at him, flabbergasted, but she maintained her calm and faced her honesty. "Nay, Crogan, I condemn myself."

A light of understanding shone brightly in his eyes. "Ye condemn yourself for your feelings for me."

Her fingers threaded into her skirts. She clutched them tightly because she knew he was right. She could not find an adequate response, so she continued to stare up at him in pregnant silence.

"Ye desire me, and it terrifies ye," he declared as his expression grew tender.

For the first time, she noticed he had incredibly faint lines at the corner of those beautiful sea-green eyes—smile lines. His lashes were long, which only accentuated his gaze more. Those dark brows were thick, yet finely arched. The sharp cut of his cheekbones added to his sensual, masculine allure. He was clean shaven, his jaw all hard angles, but his skin appeared incredibly smooth. That full, tempting mouth, dear lord, she wanted that mouth on her, everywhere.

Miranda took a deep, trembling breath. "I—" But a witty response was not forthcoming.

"Tell me ye feel nothing when I touch ye," his voice was a whisper as his hand moved to slowly trail a finger down her cheek.

"I—" The best thing to do in such a situation would be to tell a whopping lie, but her moral center would not absolve her, and her body would most certainly betray her if he called her bluff.

He drew her into his arms, held her against the hard wall of his torso, overwhelming her with sensation. "Tell me ye feel nothing in my arms, Miranda." His voice was pure velvet.

She was drowning in his steady gaze, melting in his words as the tone of his voice wrapped around her like the arms holding her close. "Crogan, I—"

"Tell me, Miranda," he whispered near her ear.

A shiver shot down her spine. "I cannot lie, Crogan, I do feel an attraction to you, but logic must guide me—" she spoke breathlessly.

"Logic be damned." Then his lips found the parted invitation of her mouth.

His kiss was hungry, demanding. Miranda felt as though he was branding her as his, despite the circumstances, despite the obstacles that stood between them. But in that moment, she cared not. Her mouth clung to his, drinking him in, meeting his passion equally.

Thoughtlessly, an arm rose to hook around his neck while her free hand slid into the silky locks of his hair. Her fingers combed through them, dislodging his queue.

He held her tightly, nearly forcing the air from her lungs with his strength. One arm was locked around her back, his hand splayed over the ribs at her side, and the other was hooked around her shoulder. His palm supported her neck as he pressed closer, deepening their kiss.

Miranda's body was in flames. She had never experienced the ultimate pleasure of passion, but instinct kicked in. She nearly considered lifting her skirts for him then and there as his tongue ravaged her mouth, but in the back of her mind, she knew it was wrong. Some unknown force allowed her to break her mouth free and gasp for air.

"Crogan, nay," she croaked. "You cannot seduce me while your bride-to-be sits at my table." Her hands clutched his tunic, and she pushed her body away from him. The warm sensations coursing through her body only caused her emotions to spin out of control.

She was overcome by bitterness with herself for allowing him to kiss her again, and frustration with him for putting her through such torment. With tears threatening at the back of her throat, she swore at him with a respectable calm. "Damn you, Crogan. Your actions lock you into the same faithless category as my husband."

With the sight of his startled expression burning in her eyes, she pushed past him and ran down the corridor to her sister's chamber.

Miranda paused before the door, in desperate need to catch her breath and regain her solid composure. Crogan had caused her to unravel, and she was not comfortable with that. So easily he had drawn out a confession of her feelings for him. So easily he had crawled over her wall of logic and ignited a physical display of her verbal confession with that kiss.

She wanted to hate him for it. She wanted to hate him as she had hated her husband. But the desire he provoked within her with his presence muddled the line between truth and consequence. The truth was that he would be married in the not-too-distant future, but he courted her desire, and, consequently, she would suffer the pain of his loss if she acted on her feelings and let him into her heart.

She could rationalize everything away simply to justify the fact that she wanted him like she had never wanted any man in her life. But she would not. She could not give in to the temptation he presented. And that was what she must continue to remind herself to maintain her logic.

Miranda sighed miserably and forced her thoughts to shift. She raised her eyes to the door before her. Delicate knuckles rapped softly on the oak structure leading into her sister's bed chamber.

Silence.

Her unease in the Great Hall returned full force.

Miranda thoughtlessly bit her lip as she pushed open the door. Her eyes scanned the room. Rowena was not instantly visible; however, the bed curtains remained closed. She rushed over to the platform as quickly and quietly as possible. As she held her breath, she pushed the sheer white material aside and looked down upon her sister's sleeping figure.

A sigh of relief floated upon the air. Miranda gazed down at the younger woman, and a hint of a smile touched her lips. She would never consider waking her. The youth needed the rest even more so than herself.

As she continued to watch the girl in her blissful dream state, her smile began to wane. Rowena was still. Too still. And her breathing seemed dangerously shallow.

Her relieved state instantly flipped over into panic. She was suddenly desperate to wake her.

"Rowe?" She gently but firmly patted a pale arm. She received nothing, not even a flicker of an eyelash.

Her voice rose an octave. "Rowe?"

Two palms cupped the girl's face. Miranda's heart stalled as the feverish heat from her sister's skin seeped into her hands. She peered more closely and noticed the tiny beads of perspiration on a smooth brow.

"Rowena, I need you to awaken," Miranda nearly shouted, but her sister remained unresponsive.

The elder sibling wanted to break down in tears of frustration, but she bit back her emotion and jumped down from the bed. She broke into a sprint; slim legs hastily carried her down to the Great Hall. Ignoring the heads that swiveled in her direction, she crossed the massive space with a purpose, climbed the dais and pinned Alfred with a hard look.

"Rowena's ill. Send for the physician immediately," she ordered in a sharp tone.

"Oh, Lord," Alfred breathed, clearly troubled by the news.

Miranda knew Alfred cared for the girl. She caught his covert looks of longing when he thought no one was paying attention. She picked up on his subtle gentleness toward her, and his overprotective attitude when she was involved. But he never seemed willing to admit his feelings, not to anyone.

Miranda would not press him for a confession. If and when he chose to speak up on the matter, she would be prepared to listen.

"Aye, my lady, I will send for the physician at once," he spoke to her back as she turned away, not waiting for a reply. She called to the nearest kitchen servant to have fresh water sent up and hurried back to the stairwell, too distracted to realize that an audience had observed her efforts.

Chapter 23

Miranda paced the corridor, too distracted to care that Alfred, Brodie, Alice and Crogan milled about nearby. Silently they watched her progress while the doctor tended to Rowena. Inside, she was a wreck, despairing for her sister's health, but outside, she appeared composed and a bit sidetracked by current events.

She had remained close to Rowe's side as she waited for the physician. The lady cooled her fevered skin with damp cloths and spoke of idle matters, allowing the unconscious figure to hear her voice. But when the moderately attractive middle-aged man with a bag of medicine and first aid supplies stepped into the bed chamber, he pointed to the door, wordlessly telling her he would not diagnose the patient while a concerned family member looked on.

So, she was forced to continue biding her time. The tenacious woman desperately clung to her endurance, but in those long minutes of limbo, she acknowledged an unwelcome vulnerability.

Unable to help herself, she glanced in Crogan's direction. Casually, he leaned against the wall, arms crossed over his chest, his eyes following her figure as she paced. She avoided meeting his direct gaze.

Miranda wanted to throw caution to the wind and hurl herself into his arms. She yearned for the strength, security, and comfort his embrace would provide. But she did not have the right to act on the idea. Alice stood at his side, watching over him with vigilant eyes.

Hastily she looked away, hiding the tears that instantly blurred her vision. A single drop slid down her cheek, but she refused to wipe it away as she allowed her dormant temper to overcome her sadness. Damn the fates for striking down Rowena while Edwin remained in unknown peril. Damn Bishop for putting them all through hell.

The volume of emotion she had been subjected to on that day abruptly came rushing in upon her all at once, adding to the weight on her shoulders. Her tiny, exhausted figure was near its breaking point, and she knew it, because the fatigue that abruptly swept over her was threatening.

Aware that her legs would not hold her slight weight for much longer, she moved to the wall near Brodie, pressed her back to the cool stone, and slowly slid down into a seated position. She pulled her knees up to her chest, propped her forearms on her knees, and dropped her head to her arms.

"Miranda, are ye well?" Brodie did not hesitate to query.

Searching for aid from any avenue at that point, she stared up into the Scotsman's concerned eyes. "Please, Brodie, tell me that Rowe will be fine. I need to hear it."

He knelt down beside her, and despite the impropriety of it, two beefy arms curled around her hunched figure. Her head dropped to his shoulder, grateful for his offer of support. "She will be perfect, Miranda. We all fall ill occasionally; 'tis simply one of those times."

The lady allowed his words to seep into her being, and it gave her the power to tap into unknown reserves of strength. She raised her head and gave him a smile steeped with optimism and hope. "Thank you. Thank you for that."

He grinned back, causing his eyes to crinkle at the corners. "Always pleased to help, lass."

She gave a throaty laugh and shifted. Determining her intent, Brodie offered his hand to help her stand. The two of them joined the line of people awaiting the doctor's appearance. They ignored the shocked looks they received for the display they had just put on. Alice's mouth had fallen open, and she was rather tardy in closing it. Alfred's eyes were wide. And Crogan's features were set in hard lines of fury.

As the minutes ticked by, Miranda became aware of the scathing looks Alice threw her way, but every time she turned to meet the girl's pinched expression, she smoothly shifted her head away. Unwilling to play such games, Miranda finally decided to stare at the young bride-to-be, lying in wait.

At last, Alice sent her another hateful look, but when she found Miranda watching her, prepared for the wordless attack, she visibly jumped in her skin. Of course, the outspoken chit did not flinch away. She issued a silent challenge, refusing to back down. Their gazes clashed.

Without warning, Rowena's door opened, and the doctor stepped out into the corridor. Miranda rushed forward and stared up at him expectantly.

He gazed down at her from his moderate height, and the corners of his mouth turned up. "Rowena will mend."

Miranda let go of the breath she held as relief flooded her mind and body. She sent the physician a smile that blinded. "Thank you, Doctor."

His expression grew solemn. "Do not thank me yet. Your sister is extremely ill. Her health is flailing in exhaustion. She will need extensive care to regain her health. She needs rest and must not do anything to exert herself. Her diet is priority, and her mind needs to be free of stress."

Miranda's determination faltered at that. She could do everything the doctor ordered with the exception of relieve her stress.

"Of course, 'twill be done," she assured, unaware that her words were a little shaky.

"She awoke, but I have sedated her to aid her rest through the fever. Watch over her carefully; she will seek a familiar face when she wakes. I shall return in a fortnight to monitor her progress."

Miranda nodded as the alleviation began to overwhelm her to such a degree that her throat burned.

"And do not tax yourself to see to my exit, I will show myself to the door." He gave her a reassuring smile and turned and walked away.

She could not acknowledge the spectators at her back. Silent tears coursed down her cheeks. Without a word, she hurried into Rowena's antechamber and swung the door shut in hopes of shutting herself from the world. Once she was alone with her tumultuous emotions, a sob escaped her. It was followed by another. And another.

***

From their place on the opposite side of the door, Brodie and Alfred exchanged empathetic glances and walked away. Crogan remained glued to the floor. He stared at the door. The sound of Miranda's tears on that occasion were no less unsettling than the first time he had been witness to them. She clung to her strength and hid her feelings so well that a glimpse of her sadness was like a fist to the gut.

For a moment she had seemed to falter while waiting for the doctor's diagnosis, but she sought proximity to Brodie rather than himself. And that had enraged him. When he saw her within his cousin's arms, he had wanted to drag the elder man out to the bailey and beat him bloody.

Alice had grabbed his hand and gave it a squeeze.

And now he heard the widow in tears.

Thoughtlessly, his hand rose to the door handle with the intent to act on his impulse to comfort her, but a palm on his arm gained his attention.

Alice's features were softened in sympathy. "Let us leave her in peace, Crogan."

With teeth on edge, his hand fell from the door handle. He pinned Alice with a heavy stare. "I wouldst speak with ye."

Chapter 24

Miranda was unable to stop herself from pacing at the foot of Rowena's bed for the duration of the day. She was fatigued, but that fell second to her tense restlessness. When she was not pressing cool damp cloths to a feverish brow or telling comedic stories to her sister's sleeping form, she was pacing and praying.

The doctor had assured the lady of the manor that her younger sister would make a complete recovery, but a shadow continued to hover over them. Miranda was not convinced that everything would be all right. The two people she loved most in the world were not safe and healthy, and it frightened her more than she wanted to admit.

Her helplessness weighed heavily on her conscience. She knew she was in a poor state mentally, but perhaps she was in a worse state physically. Miranda could feel the weakness in her quivering limbs, which meant it was sheer willpower that gave her the strength to fight through each day. She wanted to cry, and she wanted to scream in anger, but she found that pacing was her only outlet at that point.

A knock sounded on the door.

"You may enter," she called in a fragile voice.

A kitchen server glided into the room with a tray of food. She cast a woeful glance at the pale figure in the bed, then curtsied to the lady of the manor and wordlessly exited the room.

When the door opened, Miranda glanced out into the antechamber and noticed Alfred's stiff figure also pacing, clearly concerned over Rowena's health. He looked up, and their gazes met for a brief instant before the door swung shut.

Two days and nights passed. Rowena slumbered on, and Miranda and Alfred continued to pace in their separate rooms. Miranda would have welcomed the captain's company, but it would be improper to invite the man into her sister's bedchamber. So, they suffered in silence.

At dawn on the third day, Miranda dozed on a chair near Rowena's bed.

"Miranda?" a gravelly voice wondered.

Gray eyes popped open, and she sat up despite her lethargy. An amber gaze had settled on her slumped figure.

"Rowe?" She pushed herself from the chair she had placed on the platform and shifted to the edge of the mattress. A palm moved to the girl's brow. The fever had finally receded. "Oh, thank you, Lord in heaven," she whispered as tears sprang into her eyes.

"What has passed, Miranda? Why do I feel so thick?"

She wiped away the moisture on her cheeks and presented a serious regard. "You have been dreadfully ill, Rowe. But you will mend. You need a great deal of rest."

Rowena's eyes moved over the features on her sister's face. "You appear dead on your feet, Miranda."

She gave the girl the brightest grin she could muster in her weakened state. "I will be fine; you must not concern yourself, Rowe."

A hint of a smile touched the girl's lips, but it was most evident in her eyes. "Thank you, Miranda, for watching over me." With that, her meager strength had waned, and she drifted off to sleep once again.

Miranda lovingly brushed a strand of hair from her sister's cheek, then picked her way down the platform staircase. The door felt incredibly heavy when she pulled on the handle and met Alfred's gaze as he halted his pacing and looked up.

"I thought I heard Rowena's voice," he spoke almost frantically.

Miranda nodded and leaned against the doorframe for support. "The fever has broken."

His frown transformed into a relieved grin. "'Tis wonderful news."

Miranda clutched her skirts and slowly moved toward the corridor.

"My lady, are you unwell?" His words momentarily halted her progress. "You can barely stand," the captain observed with a note of unease.

"I will be fine, Alfred, thank you." She continued forward and paused to lean against the doorframe once again. "Please fetch a servant to bring Rowe sustenance. She is in slumber, but her appetite will be fierce when she awakens. And also, please have a bath ordered up for myself. I shall retire to my chamber to rest while awaiting its arrival."

"Of course, my lady." With that, he hurried off to do her bidding.

Miraculously, Miranda made it the length of two corridors to her chamber. She trudged into the sitting room, and as she crossed to the bedchamber, she felt a familiar presence silently observing her.

Her eyes scanned the space and halted with a jump in her pulse when she saw Crogan seated on one of the chaises, his gaze locked on her.

"Crogan," she drawled slowly as she felt her fatigue closing in. "'Tis highly improper for you to enter my private quarters."

He stood and walked over to stand before her. "How does your sister fare?" His smooth brow furrowed as his gaze moved over her figure.

"She is on the mend…" Her knees chose that moment to fail her, and blackness momentarily hazed over her vision.

Crogan easily caught her swooning figure against his large frame. He stared down into her white pallor as her eyes blinked open.

"I—" she whispered.

"Hellfire and damnation, Miranda!" he swore and swung her up to cradle her in his arms. "Ye have taken on far too much!" He carried the tiny figure to her bed and gently deposited her there.

"I will be fine, Crogan. I just need to rest for a moment," she assured as she stared up at him with wide eyes, startled by his raised voice.

The Scotsman stood up and began to traipse back and forth beside her bed like a caged animal. He paused and pinned her with a glare. "What if ye had been in navigation of the stairwell? Ye could have fallen to your death!" He resumed pacing.

She sat up, defensive. "But I was not in the stairwell."

The massive man halted once again and threw her a scowl. "But ye could have been."

Clearly Dana's death haunted him, but in no way did the circumstances of the lady's death apply to her. Slightly dumbfounded by his behavior, she asked, "How must I respond to such logic?"

"Ye will not respond," he issued furiously. "Ye will rest."

"But I have ordered up a bath. And I must return to Rowena shortly," she announced, her voice firm in its resolve.

His handsome features grew pensive for a moment. Finally, his gaze settled on her, his expression determined. "Ye will have your bath, then ye will share quarters with your sister until ye have both recovered adequately. And ye will follow my orders, if I have to guard ye myself, Miranda."

"But, Crogan, I am not in need of recovery," she argued.

He stomped up to the bed and loomed over her with his great height. "Not a word, Miranda." Two callused palms clutched her shoulders roughly and pushed her back onto the pillows. "Rest yourself." Then, contrary to his arrogant demeanor, he grabbed the patchwork coverlet folded at the foot of the bed and draped it over her petite figure.

With that, he trudged from the room and slammed the door shut.

"Well, I never—" she trailed off, too tired to be angry.

She slept straight through the line of servants who entered with buckets for her bath. In fact, she slept through the whole of the day, and the night as well.

When her eyes blinked open at dawn of the following day, she was stunned to see a familiar face smiling at her.

Disbelieving the sight, she sat up and rubbed the sleep away.

"Reissa? Am I dreaming?"

Her neighbor laughed. "Nay, Miranda. Your eyes do not deceive you." The lady sat next to her bed, the picture of perfection. She wore a beautiful gown of royal blue, and her shining straight strawberry blond locks were unbound, falling around her trim figure.

"I thought you to be at court." She accepted the glass of water her guest handed to her and drank slowly, wetting her dry throat.

"Viktor granted my request to return. I worried for your son. I could not stay." Reissa took the glass and placed it on the bedside table. "I have watched over Rowena through the night. Her spirit is tremendous. She is recovering in leaps and bounds."

Miranda closed her eyes for a moment, digesting the unlikely turn of events. When she looked at Lady Colville, there were tears of gratitude in her eyes. "I am ever so grateful you are here, Reissa. You are the answer to my prayers."

She patted Miranda's hand and sighed heavily. "'Twould seem not answer enough. Edwin remains in the hands of that criminal."

A head of raven curls nodded dejectedly. "Aye, we are forced to wait for Bishop's next move."

"My husband and Lord Adair have spoken at length on the matter. They are in agreement. Aye, I fear we must wait."

Miranda wondered hopefully, "You and Viktor will stay with us until my son has been returned?"

"Aye, of course, if you do not mind."

She grinned. "You are welcome to stay as long as you wish."

"A visit is long overdue; however, I wish our cause was not so unfortunate. 'Twould seem I have worried in excess for nothing. Lord Adair has the matter well in hand." Reissa grinned with a twinkle in her eye.

"Viktor would have reacted in kind to Bishop's messenger?"

She brushed a stray strawberry blond lock from her vision as she nodded in agreement. "Aye, Viktor has commended the Scotsman for his restraint. Many men would have stormed the keep in spite of Bishop's threat." Reissa tilted her head and grinned at the woman who was her junior by two years.

Confused by the lady's suspicious smile, she asked with a furrowed brow, "Reissa?"

"Lord Adair is handsome, intelligent, and he makes an attempt to hide it, but he has been mad with worry over you, Miranda."

A blush bloomed in her pale cheeks even as the idea of his concern warmed her heart. Then her thoughts settled on Alice, and the warmth dissolved. "And 'tis impossible not to overlook the beautiful blond clinging to his arm. The beautiful blond he is betrothed to."

Reissa's brow rose for a moment in concession, but she added her opinion to the matter, "A beautiful blond he barely tolerates."

The conversation had quickly grown deeply personal, yet Miranda had no qualms about admitting her theory to the other woman. She was so easy to talk to. "They have already experienced the marriage bed. And continue to do so."

Her neighbor's serene face grew thoughtful, with a hint of disbelief. "You are certain?"

Miranda had no direct proof to back up her statement, but she trusted her feelings on the issue. "Fairly certain." Uncomfortable thinking about such happenings between Crogan and his future bride, she threw back the patchwork blanket and shifted to the edge of the bed.

Seeing that Reissa was about to chastise her intent, she voiced, "I must stretch my legs, my lady."

Miranda stood slowly, not completely trusting her strength. Her legs were shaky, but they held her erect. She walked over to the washstand and splashed some water on her face. "I would like to check in on Rowe."

"I apologize, Miranda, but I cannot allow that. Lord Adair has strict orders for your welfare. You must continue to rest."

Her eyes pinned her guest with a purposeful gaze. "That man is not my husband, nor my father, nor my brother. I will not be ordered about by him." Even as she spoke the words, she could not help but feel the fatigue settling upon her once again. Perhaps she should rest for a while longer.

Reissa rushed over and threaded their arms together, offering support. "Back to bed, Miranda."

"Aye, I concede."

Reissa helped her climb into bed, then stood back.

"You must be in need of rest yourself if you watched over my sister all night," Miranda decided, even though the lady appeared fit and lucid.

"I was able to sleep for several hours at your sister's bedside. I am quite well, Miranda. I will have a fresh bath ordered up for you and some broth to aid your strength."

Miranda was asleep before Reissa had cleared the doorway.

Chapter 25

Crogan had been wiping the shaving cream from his face when he heard a sharp cry that abruptly cut off in shattering silence. Clad in only a pair of navy braies, he sprinted from his chamber with the sound of a scream ringing in his ears. Not caring that his feet were bare and chilled on the stone flooring, he rushed to the stairwell at the end of the corridor. He bounded down the steps two at a time, but a tragic sight halted him in his tracks.

A broken figure lay on the staircase. Fire-red waves cascaded over her face, hiding the identity of the lady he already knew it to be.

With his breath stalled, he carefully stepped over the figure, descending below her position. He turned and fell to his knees, scraping his shins on the corner of a stone step.

"Dana, nae," he choked. A callused palm brushed the silky locks from her face.

His jaw dropped open. The vacant stare was not Dana's.

"Miranda?" His thoughts spun, refusing to believe it. "Miranda?!" Auburn brows furrowed in shock. "Miranda, nae." He reached out and pulled her limp little figure into his arms, unable to comprehend the situation even as tears began to stream down his face. A tormented sob echoed up the stairwell.

"Miranda."

Crogan's eyes blinked open in the darkness. His body was drenched in perspiration. Immediately, he sat up; the confusion of his dream lingered in reality. He had suffered that nightmare on many occasions, but the change of the victim was entirely new.

As his mind spun, he jerked the coverlet aside and jumped down from the bed. Clad in nothing at all, he crossed to the washstand and splashed tepid water onto his face in hopes that it would wash away the memory of his nightmare. But it was still fresh in his mind as he ran a hand over his wet face.

Crogan braced his palms on the wooden structure and stared down into the disturbed water in the porcelain bowl. In the darkness, all he could see was a distorted silhouette of his head, but he was distracted from the sight.

He had grown to expect the unconscious reminder of Dana's death, but to see Miranda's corpse so vividly, that he had not been prepared for at all.

Damn that woman for the burgeoning desire he could not temper. Damn that woman for crawling into his subconscious, the one place he could not banish thoughts of her. And damn that woman for affecting him in so many unexpected ways.

He wanted nothing from her. He was on the King's assignment, then he would return to Scotland and live his impulsive life. He would follow whatever path presented itself, bed any woman he desired, and pass on his fortune to his children when he passed on.

Crogan was not asking for much, and he certainly was not asking to lust after a woman who already bore the badge of marriage and mothered a child not of his own.

At one point, he had thoughtlessly given himself the license to discard the hands-off rule, but he needed to re-evaluate the logic of that decision. His intense desire for her was muddying the waters. And even as he reminded himself that he would not allow his foolish infatuation to guide his actions, he was beaten down by an overwhelming need to seek her out, to touch her skin, taste her lips.

He had gone to her chamber several days hence with the innocent idea that he wanted to ask after her sister's welfare following two days of Miranda's absence, but when he was honest with himself, he knew he simply wanted to see her. He wanted to be near her. Hear her voice.

Outrage spurred him. Callused hands picked up the porcelain bowl, and he hurled it into the darkened fireplace. Water splashed onto himself and the floor. Porcelain shattered, creating a deafening noise, while the impact caused a plumb of ashes to rocket into the air and created the billowing effect of smoke.

"I will not succumb to this. I will not," Crogan decided. He was not ignorant enough to think he could turn off his hunger for the woman, but he could certainly turn off his reaction to that hunger.

He would not worry over her health any longer. He would not wonder at her feelings for his cousin. He would not let his eyes stray for the sight of her. He would not let her opinion of him affect him in any way. And he most certainly would not kiss her again.

Chapter 26

After sleeping through another full night, Miranda rose to greet the day, declaring herself fit enough to venture from her chamber. Without pause, she padded down to look in on her sister.

She found Rowena sitting up, laughing at a comment Reissa had made from her place beside the bed. Much of her color had returned, her brow was dry, and the light of her spirit was visible in her eyes.

The sight produced a smile in response.

"Miranda," Rowe welcomed, lifting her arms for a greeting embrace.

When she wrapped her arms around her sister's full frame, she was startled to learn how much weight the girl had lost since Edwin's abduction. Merely looking upon her in recent days had not relayed how much she had wasted away. Her voluptuous figure was nearly as slim as her own.

Her eyes shifted to the bowl of oatmeal in her sister's lap. "I hope you are eating," she mentioned as she seated herself on a second empty chair that had been placed near Reissa's on the platform.

"Aye, Lady Colville has been instrumental in my recovery. I am most grateful to her. And I am overjoyed to see you in good health once again, Miranda. You had watched over me so vigilantly. I feared you would fall as ill as I." The guilt was evident on her face.

180

"I was merely in need of rest, Rowe, and I have received it. Have I missed anything in my absence?" Miranda quizzed, primarily thinking of her son.

As if she had read her sister's mind, Rowena confessed, "Nay, we have heard nothing of Edwin."

"We continue to bide our time," Reissa added, offering an encouraging smile.

The ladies chatted for close to an hour, then they excused themselves to allow Rowena to rest. Reissa decided she would ask her husband to join her for a ride in the countryside, and Miranda chose to order up the bath she had not been able to partake in prior to her spell.

Less than an hour later, the servants filed out, and she stepped into the tub of warm water. Assured that Rowena was mending well and Reissa had temporarily shouldered her duties in the manor, Miranda granted herself the luxury of a leisurely bath. In fact, she dawdled so long that she dozed.

Due to the heat of the summer, the water remained comfortable, so Miranda ended up sleeping for several hours in the tub without disturbance. Finally, her stiff neck recalled her to wakefulness. With skin that resembled prunes, she climbed from the wooden basin, well rested for the first time since Bishop stole her son.

Winny helped to aid her toilet. She swept damp raven curls back into a tidy plait and buttoned her slim figure into a modest wine-hued gown. She stepped out into the corridor and took a deep breath. It was near the hour to sup, and she would join her guests for the first time in days.

With head held high and skirts clutched in hand, she descended the shadowed staircase. Near the mezzanine, halfway between levels, a tiny figure moved from the shadows, causing her to give a startled cry.

Miranda stared down at the boy and took in his wasted appearance and smudged face. He could not have been greater than eight years of age. And the imploring expression on his face was heartbreaking.

"Please, my lady, I am starving," he rasped.

The sound of footfalls rushed toward the staircase and climbed to see who and what had caused a scream to drift down into the Great Hall.

"Miranda?" Viktor's voice was heard, diverting her attention.

She looked up to see Colville's expressionless face. Crogan stood at his side. Alfred, Brodie and Reissa brought up the rear in the narrow passage.

"The boy surprised me is all," she explained as her gaze returned to the child. Her slight figure bent forward, which brought them eye level to each other. "Are you alone?"

He nodded.

"Where are your parents, sweetheart?" she tested in a soothing tone.

"Mama is dead, and Papa ran away," his voice quivered in fear.

The missing pieces of the puzzle began to fit together in Miranda's mind. "Have you been hiding in the castle?"

Another nod as a tear rolled down his soiled cheek.

At last, that explained her feelings of being watched. She felt more weight spontaneously lift from her shoulders.

"You need not have been afraid of us, sweetheart."

He sniffled loudly.

"What is your name?"

"Miles, my lady."

Miranda stood to her full height and gave him a sweet grin. "I would be honored if you would join our supper this evening, Miles." With that, she held out a hand in offering.

The crooked smile he bestowed upon her in that moment nearly brought her to tears. He took her hand, and the pair continued down the staircase together.

Everyone in that narrow stairwell silently stood to the side, allowing the lady of the manor and the orphan to lead their party to the Great Hall.

Miles was seated at the family table along with Miranda's many guests. Several towels were placed on his chair to aid his small stature. His large blue eyes widened in awe as the servants began to dispense the meal. The platters steeped with food were a remarkable sight for a starving child.

Miranda peered down the table at her small guest and smiled when she saw his amazed expression. Surrounded by empathetic people, Miles simply watched as several hands reached for the food on the platters and quickly filled his trencher until it brimmed.

He gaped at the trencher and paused as if trying to decide where to start, then finally he chose a turkey leg and tore into it with gusto.

Miranda would not distract him with talk. Clearly, he needed to eat. So, she looked around the table. Viktor sat at her left hand, and Alfred was one chair down on her right. Beside Viktor were Reissa, Miles and Brodie. Beside Alfred were Alice and Crogan.

First, the lady of the manor was struck by the glaring fact that her sister remained in her chamber. The girl's absence was impossible to ignore. The empty chair at her right seemed to shout its vacancy. It would be days before Rowena would be up and about, but Miranda soothed such thoughts with the truth that her sister was on the mend.

Then, against her better judgment, her eyes settled on Crogan. He stared at Alice as he related a story about his parents, but he must have felt her focus, because his gaze shifted.

He glanced at Miranda for an instant. Her jaw tightened. The look he gave her was undeniably chilling. His gaze abruptly returned to his betrothed, which left Miranda shaken. Her eyes dropped to her trencher, attempting to collect her composure.

Miranda had not been prepared for Crogan's about face in his demeanor toward her. In the short amount of time she had known the man, she had been witness to many facets of his character: arrogance, anger, intelligence, logic, and passion. But she had never experienced his cold indifference.

Initially it was painful, more painful than she could have imagined, but that pain was quickly replaced by a numbing sensation that she welcomed wholeheartedly. She had told herself she would have to move past her feelings for him; she would have to ignore what she felt. His behavior would only help to serve that purpose.

Miranda raised her gaze and looked at the man to her left. "Viktor, 'tis a pleasure to see you again. I must thank you for granting your wife's wish to join us. She has been an angel to watch over us." She had to force her voice to be steady.

Even though the man was handsome beyond belief, she continued to feel intimidated by him. Authority and menace seemed to ooze from his presence, yet when he interacted with his wife, there was a human quality that could not be overlooked.

Unexpectedly, he gave her a sly grin. "I must admit I did not possess any personal desire to remain at court."

Reissa gave a soft laugh. "Aye, 'tis true. Clearly, he was miserable, but we were weighted down with the truth that Edwin's abduction must take precedence over the King's wish for our presence. Edward was most gracious when we requested to aid in your cause."

Miranda tilted her head in wonder as she thought of the Colvilles' children. "Where are Fulton and Maisie?"

Viktor put a hand over his wife's. "They are visiting with their Uncle Collin and Aunt Moira."

"You must miss them terribly," the lady of the manor decided as she felt the hollow spot in her heart for her son.

"Moira has longed for their visit for quite some time," Reissa offered gently. "She and Maisie share a tremendous rapport despite the lack of bloodline."

Her gaze rested on her female guest. "I admire your sister-in-law's tremendous spirit. She will speak her mind at any cost. I believe I have much to learn from her."

Viktor's eyes touched on his wife in a playful manner. "I believe Reissa has already embraced many such lessons from Moira."

The little woman gave her husband a suffering gaze, but the twinkle in her eyes revealed laughter. "I have learned the value of speaking my mind, sir."

"To my great dismay." He breathed an exaggerated sigh.

Reissa gave him a playful slap on the arm, and, as a result, he broke into laughter.

Miranda watched their scene, awed by the traits Reissa's presence revealed in a man who seemed as hard and unyielding as stone. Such a thought caused her mind to touch on Crogan.

The man was large and intimidating. Easily angered. Had he behaved in such a fashion prior to Dana's death? Was there another side to the Scotsman she had been denied because of his broken heart?

The lady stopped herself there. It simply did not matter. He had been sent by the king to retrieve Edwin, and he would go on to marry Lady Alice Farraday. Miranda had no right to ponder such thoughts. She was not part of the equation.

Without warning, the noise of a trumpet sounded in the bailey outside, announcing the impending arrival of guests. Miranda felt her insides pinch in confusion. No one was expected. Who could possibly seek entrance to their gate now?

Viktor's eyes pinned her with a direct stare. "Do you anticipate guests?"

She felt the whole of the table look her way; Crogan's eyes felt heavier than the others. "Nay." Her gaze shifted to the messenger crossing the Great Hall. Thoughtlessly, she rose to await his arrival.

Could it be Bishop? Could it be in relation to her son? She prayed that was the case.

She watched as one of her most trusted guards bounded up the dais and moved to stand before her. "A Lord and Lady Clifton demand entrance, my lady."

Miranda's knees momentarily grew weak. She had to focus on standing strong and erect in front of her guests. The news was no less than a shock.

Her parents had arrived.

The lady took a slow, deep breath. She had convinced herself she would never see them again. It had been seven years since they said their dry-eyed goodbyes. Why were they here? And why now?

Her gaze met the guard's questioning stare. "Of course. Please see them into the bailey."

He gave a curt nod. "Aye, my lady." With that, he was gone.

Miranda waved a servant over to give the order to set places at the table for two additional guests and to have another bed chamber readied. Once the bubbly young girl had gone, Miranda was forced to address the curiosity of her companions.

"Your parents, Miranda?" Alfred's expression was obviously perplexed.

"Aye," she confirmed. "Amherst and Dell Clifton have returned from their adventures."

"'Tis most unexpected," the captain spoke her thoughts aloud.

"Aye," the lady agreed wholeheartedly.

"Am I speaking out of turn, Miranda, or do I sense that happiness is not overflowing within you as a result?" Reissa tested quietly.

"Our history is—" she paused as she searched for the correct word, "indifferent." She glanced at the entrance, then she peered at her guests. "Please excuse me."

The lady's petite figure descended the dais and crossed the Great Hall. She walked into the moonlit bailey to see two familiar figures moving toward her. A guard led away the horses at their back.

"Papa, Mama, welcome." Her words were perfunctory, her tone flat. The couple drew near, and Miranda immediately noticed their aesthetic changes.

Dell Clifton had always been a beautiful woman with shiny raven waves and gray eyes, but the years had not been kind. She had deep stress lines around her eyes and mouth. Gray streaked her dull waves, and her eyes lacked the luster that had once thrived there.

But her father was worse. Much worse. Once upon a time, he had been a strapping man with dirty-blond waves and amber eyes. Now his tall figure was stooped and wasted, cheeks sunken, eyes extremely bloodshot. Amherst Clifton had always enjoyed an excess of ale with his supper. Perhaps he had enjoyed more than his fair share in recent years?

They halted in front of their daughter. Dell looked her up and down. "You're too thin and pale, Miranda."

"Why is your sister not here to greet us?" Amherst demanded in a hoarse voice, but then he pulled his wife along without waiting for an answer. He walked past his eldest daughter and continued into the keep.

"Always a pleasure," Miranda spoke in a softly sarcastic tone to no one in particular as she followed after the couple.

Chapter 27

As Miranda took her seat at the table, she dreaded raising her eyes to see her parents seated amongst the crowd of guests. They had been placed beside Crogan, which meant she had to stare past him to speak with her parents.

Amherst did not bother to speak to any of the other guests, including his daughter. Without pause, he began to eat the food that had been heaped onto his trencher. Although, as Miranda silently observed his actions, she realized his hands were shaking, and his bites were tiny.

Dell tried to covertly wipe a crumb from his chin, then lifted her gaze to take stock of her surroundings. Gray eyes that matched Miranda's settled on Rowena's empty chair. "Why has your sister failed to join us?"

"She is resting, Mama."

"She cannot rouse herself to greet her parents?" Dell demanded, obviously insulted.

"The girl has recently taken ill, but rest assured, she is on the road to recovery, my lady. She needs her rest," Crogan inserted in a firm tone.

Dell looked at the man seated beside her. "And who are you, young man?" Technically Crogan was only seven years her junior, but the woman had gained an air along with the Wilkes fortune.

"Lord Crogan Adair, a guest on behalf of the King," he responded smoothly.

The elder lady lifted her chin and looked down her nose at him. "A Scotsman to boot?"

"Aye."

"On the king's behalf? Why?" she wondered in a raspy voice.

Crogan's gaze touched on Miranda, which caused her racing heart to stall. "Perhaps the matter is best left for your daughter to explain."

Her mother's eyes drilled into her. "Miranda, have you taken another husband?"

She nearly choked on the port she had been in the process of swallowing. It went down like a stone in her throat. Rather than provide an answer to a topic best left untouched, she presented a question of her own.

"What brings you here, Mama? Have you and Papa tired of traveling?"

Dell looked at her husband with a cool stare. "Your papa is wasting my dear. In the final stages. Contracted from any of the number of harlots he dallied with during our trip 'round the world."

Several gasps erupted, and this time, Miranda did choke on the red port in her mouth. She coughed and heaved, struggling for air.

"Miranda?" Crogan wondered, rising from his seat.

"Dear Lord, she's choking," Reissa breathed.

Taking note of her trouble, Viktor swiftly leaned over and gave her three hard pats on the back. She instantly felt beaten and bruised by his rough handling, but he had also managed to dislodge the bubble of wine stuck in her esophagus.

She sucked in a deep breath and let it out, immensely relieved. "Oh my, Viktor, I must thank you for your aid. 'Twas rather alarming, unable to breathe."

He gave a curt nod as if it was something he tended to on a daily basis.

Reissa grinned in hope of lightening the atmosphere. "The man is useful upon occasion."

With her emotions running high, Miranda could not help but laugh at the lady's little jest. After that startling experience, it felt good. But she was instantly assaulted with mixed emotions.

Her father was dying. And her mother had no qualms about telling the world why. Dell had always been somewhat outspoken, but during their time away, that characteristic had apparently grown in leaps and bounds.

Just then, her father broke into a horrible fit of hacking. He dug into his pockets to cover his mouth with a handkerchief as he turned away from the table.

Miranda watched his difficulty, trying to analyze her feelings in that instant. The man had sired her, raised her. True, they had not shared a father-daughter bond in all of her life, but there had been some good days when she was young.

192

There had been rare glimpses of affection within him. But yet, as she stared at him, she realized it was not enough. His death would not be a tragedy in her eyes. How could she mourn a man who had never really loved her? A man she had never really loved either? That lack of feeling between them was the tragedy in itself.

When his coughing spree ended, Miranda eyed him and offered the proper sympathy. "I'm sorry to hear of your difficulties, Papa."

He stared her dead in the eye, his expression troubled. "When's dessert?"

She gave him a forlorn smile and humored him. "Shortly, Papa."

"So where is my grandson?" Dell's voice sounded. Edwin had never met his grandparents.

Following the news of Amherst's illness, Miranda could not bring herself to admit more bad news, so she fabricated a small story for her parents' benefit.

"He is visiting with friends, Mama." She felt several stares turn in her direction, wondering at her fib, but her eyes fell to her trencher, unwilling to address any of them with a wordless response.

Mindlessly, her hand returned to the silver chalice beside her trencher. She sought the numbing effect of the port. She had not been prepared for Dell and Amherst's arrival. Her insides were a jumble of nerves. And her parents' outrageously rude behavior in front of her guests only caused the knots in her stomach to tighten.

"Send for him, Miranda. I want to see my grandson," her mother dictated, then finally turned to the meal before her. Daintily, she picked up a piece of bread and began to eat.

Miranda simply nodded, unwilling to admit her lie. "Aye, Mama."

There was a tense moment of silence. Then Brodie spoke up, changing the whole of the heavy atmosphere with a simple question. "So, you and your husband have seen much in your travels. Where have you visited?"

Dell smiled at the handsome man on the opposite side of the table and then launched into an animated lecture about where they had been and the amazing things they had seen. She told her stories so well that everyone at the table was enraptured, with the exception of Miranda.

The lady of the manor was not listening at all. She was lost in her own miserable thoughts, chalice in hand. She missed her son terribly. She prayed for Rowena's quick recovery. And she realized that she resented her parents' sudden return.

If her father remained in good health, they would still be out seeing the world with Gerald's fortune. They had not sought the Wilkes property because they genuinely missed their daughters; they sought a home base for Amherst to live out the remainder of his days.

Ever so slowly, the spirits helped to aid her endurance for her present set of unwanted circumstances. She pasted a fake smile on her face and gave the appearance that she was avidly listening to her mother's words and the sporadic comments and questions extended from the audience, but her mind was not present.

All eyes were on Dell, respectfully listening, but suddenly Crogan's head turned slightly, and those sea-green depths shifted to Miranda.

Their gazes locked.

His expression was hooded and unreadable. There was still that chill she felt earlier, but there was something else too. Miranda wanted to break the connection, but she couldn't find the willpower.

When he continued to stare, she was given the impression that he was trying to read her thoughts, trying to figure out how she was faring now that her parents had settled into supper in their daughter's home.

She summoned as much indifference as she could manage, but the wine impaired her silent response. Genuine curiosity shone in her stormy gray depths. The lady wanted to know what he was thinking as he looked at her. She was left to continue to wonder because he abruptly broke the stare, and his gaze moved back to Dell.

Eventually, people began to excuse themselves to retire for the evening. Viktor and Reissa were the first couple to exit.

"'Twas lovely to meet you, Lord and Lady Clifton," Reissa offered politely. Then she turned to their hostess, her eyes steeped with empathy. "Sleep well, Miranda."

She nodded politely and watched them go. She ignored the feeling of warmth in her veins from the wine.

"I believe I will also retire," Brodie chimed in. "Would you like me to show our little guest to a room?" he questioned, referring to Miles.

"Thank you, Brodie, 'twould be greatly appreciated," Miranda accepted with a smile. "Please ring for Winny to ensure he is well looked after."

His head bobbed in confirmation, and they were off.

"Show us to our room, Miranda," Dell ordered abruptly and rose from her chair.

Miranda waved over an upstairs maid. "This young lady will show you and Papa to your room." She knew it was unforgivably rude not to personally show her parents to their quarters, but with the help of the port, she was beyond caring at that point.

"Miranda," Dell chastised.

"Go, Mama," she returned in an inarguable tone.

Her mother gave a sigh of exasperation and allowed the servant to show them to the chamber level.

Only Crogan and Alice remained, and a majority of the men-at-arms in the hall had also adjourned to their quarters, so that left the vast space virtually empty.

"Your parents are gems," Alice said with thick sarcasm. With that, she turned to her betrothed. "Please walk me to my chamber, Crogan."

His eyes hit the girl with an irritated glare, but clearly, he had no desire to remain with their hostess. Wordlessly, he rose, gave Miranda a curt nod, and accompanied his betrothed to the stairwell.

Miranda would not allow herself to watch them go, but once she knew they had passed beyond view, she gave a painful sigh. Alone at last, the intelligent lady was aware that she should also retire, but an hour later, she continued to wallow in spirits, plagued by thoughts of the past. She stared across the distance to the kitchen fire and watched it burn down into ashes.

Miranda recalled the morning when Rowena spoke of that day with their parents at the market. Her sister had been thinking of them, and without warning, they arrived on her doorstep. Subconsciously, Rowe's thoughts must have picked up on their father's illness.

She must have felt them nearby. The idea was alarming. Miranda worried her sister would not accept the news as calmly as herself. But, like it or not, Rowena must accept it, because her father's death was imminent.

As she stared at dying flames, she felt a subtle shift in the air, and within minutes, rain began to pour beyond the shelter of the keep. A clean scent drifted through the high window embrasures, tickling her nose. She breathed it in and slowly exhaled, welcoming the change in weather.

Her husband had hated the rain, or, to be more precise, thunder and lightning, which would likely explain her penchant for welcoming it with open arms. The man had been fearless, but the one thing that had caused him to tremble in apprehension was a fierce thunderstorm. Miranda had never known why, but she considered the possibility that he believed it to be God's wrath seeking him out for his sins. And he certainly amassed enough sins for ten men.

Miranda could not help but recall a particularly crude evening with her husband. When it stormed, he seemed to be harsher in his behavior, as if he sought her as an outlet for his fear.

Gerald had picked a fight with her because he caught her smiling at one of his knights while the man told a comedic tale on behalf of his lord's birthday. Her husband had dragged her from her place before the fire. Rather than seek a secluded room to chastise her, he simply moved into a corner where anyone could have overheard them.

"Whore!" he had shouted.

Gerald flaunted his liaisons in public, but if he was witness to an innocent display of affection in Miranda for another man, then he was quick to call her out for adultery.

"I provide marriage, a roof over your head, any luxury you desire, and you dally with my knights!" Gerald had charged outrageously.

"'Tis untrue," she denied wholeheartedly. "I have not lain with another."

"Whore," he rasped furiously.

In that moment, something inside of her had snapped. Her pride announced itself, and she unleashed her anger. "Whore? You deem me a whore?" Her eyes took on the light of the storm raging outside. "You, my dear husband, are the whore!"

Miranda's insides cringed as he raised his hand, but the words sounded in her mouth despite her terror. "I will give you an heir, but you will never earn my respect."

His hand had halted.

She walked away with her head held high, but Gerald continued to simmer over their quarrel for the remainder of the evening.

Miranda retired early with the hope that Gerald would continue in his cups and forget she had attacked his pride.

She had hoped in vain.

The slamming of her bed chamber door woke Miranda from a fretful sleep. She sat up as the bed curtains were yanked open, revealing Gerald's sneering face.

"Out of bed, Wife!"

"Gerald?" she tested, her heart jumping to her throat.

"Now," he growled.

At a snail's pace, she rose to stand before him.

The beautiful man stood back and crossed his arms over his chest, his expression domineering. "Disrobe." White-blond curls shone brightly in the candlelight; teal eyes possessed a malicious glow. His tunic had been removed, leaving him clad in black braies.

Miranda's limbs began to quiver. "Gerald?"

"Disrobe, Miranda, or I shall be forced to put your sister on the auction block," he threatened with a villainous grin. "With that pretty face and virtue intact, the wench would fetch a fortune."

She knew her husband was capable of anything. And she had learned through previous experience that he did not make idle threats. If she did not obey, he would follow through with that heinous act; there was no doubt in her mind. Miranda would not risk her sister's welfare, not ever, not even to save herself.

"Very well," her voice was a whisper. With trembling fingers, she untied the laces of her white cotte.

Up to that point in their marriage, Gerald had seen her in many states of undress, but he had never seen her completely bared. Her husband had not taken the time to disrobe his wife and love her properly, not even on their wedding night. The man was always so eager to seek his pleasure that a majority of the time he had simply lifted her skirts.

Miranda made her best attempt to hide her humiliation as the silky material slid down her arms. The proud lady held her head high as she dropped the garment to the cool stone flooring. Then she pushed down her drawers and stood in front of her husband, naked.

"You may be a disappointing wife, but I cannot deny that you are beautiful in your natural state," he complimented and insulted at once.

"I could speak the same of you, Gerald," she admitted.

His hands dropped to his sides, and he moved closer. "And what of my knight? Will you speak the same of him?"

"I will speak nothing of him."

"Beautiful *and* intelligent, yet equally disappointing," he drawled, then without warning, he bent over and pulled down his braies. With a sweep of his foot, the garment was discarded. Her husband was as bare as she.

Gerald was a glorious specimen of manhood, but his actions caused her insides to cringe. She merely had to look at him to know he was ready to take her. The realization caused nothing but apprehension. "Carry on with your punishment and leave," she dared.

"Punishment? Making love to your husband is punishment? A dutiful wife would not believe so."

Miranda thought he would strike her in that instant, but rather than strike her, he guided her back toward the hard stone wall. He clutched her leg, raised her knee with his forearm underneath, then entered her with one hard thrust.

The lady gasped in pain even though she had braced herself for his intent. She turned her head and closed her eyes as he mercilessly drove into her again and again. His breath was warm on her neck, harsh and labored. The cold stone bit into her back as he pressed against her. She did not deny him; she did not fight.

He shuddered and let out a grunt of satisfaction, then stepped back.

Despising her husband, Miranda did not make any attempt to shield her expression and stared him straight in the eye. Her spine was rigid with false strength, but inside, her limbs continued to tremble.

"That spirit will be broken when I am through with you on this, the eve of my birthday." He pulled on his braies in one graceful motion. "I shall return."

And he did. He visited three more times in the next few hours, and on each of those three occasions, he treated her to the same, unfeeling, raw assault.

When he slammed from her room for the final time that eve, dawn was near. Miranda's body felt thoroughly used and bruised. At long last, her head had bowed, and she wept.

Miranda returned to the present. The fire had died down to embers that glowed, and rain continued to fall outside. Just the thought of that horrible evening caused her to feel as used and unwashed as she had at that time.

The woman did not feel comfortable in her own skin. She needed to move. She needed the rain.

Miranda set down the chalice, rose clumsily, and crossed the keep. She threw open the double doors and stood there, with head back, eyes closed. She allowed the brisk wind and rain to accost her.

The rain was chilling in its effect, but Miranda welcomed the cool drops on her flushed skin. Wind tore at her skirts, and liquid clung to her lashes, but she noticed none of it. She focused on the feeling of the rain and the night, cleansing her body of the unwanted memories, cloaking her in shadows.

Impetuously, she walked out into the bailey, where strong arms banded around her waist and yanked her back toward the open doorway. She immediately began to struggle as a shock of panic sped through her veins.

"Have ye taken leave of your senses, Miranda? Ye will catch your death out here!" Crogan roared near her ear as he dragged her back to the keep.

The fact that it was Crogan did not halt her rebellion. She continued to fight against him, unwilling to return inside.

"Let me alone!" she shouted desperately.

Something in her tone caused him to halt. He turned her to look up at him through the wind and the rain.

"Let me alone," the woman repeated in a whisper, attempting to mask her expression through her inebriation. The world was spinning. Fatigue was settling upon her with all due haste. It had been years since she consumed so much port.

***

"Gladly," he returned grimly as raindrops slid down his chiseled cheeks. With that, he spun on his heel and marched to the keep entrance.

A sickening thump sounded at his back.

Crogan whipped around to find Miranda lying on the cobblestone walk in a crumpled heap, unconscious.

A curse floated onto the breeze. The massive man rushed forward and knelt at her side. Fingers delved into raven curls, searching for any possible head wounds from the fall. When he determined she was uninjured, he breathed a sigh of relief.

Easily, he lifted her into the security of his arms and returned to the keep. Without difficulty, he kicked the doors shut and journeyed to Miranda's chambers.

Adair's mind had been closed off in relation to this lady; he would not allow it to open. The Scotsman placed the unconscious woman in her bed, then turned and marched from the room without looking back.

Chapter 28

Crogan paused in Miranda's antechamber as a thought occurred to him. The lady's gown was soaked through; there was still the risk that she could catch a chill if she slept in damp material. She had just recovered from her exhaustion, and her health would remain precarious for days, which only added to that risk.

Miranda's gown needed to be removed. And he could not summon Winny to tend to the task because the young maid would never be able to lift her lady's unconscious frame.

He closed his eyes and muttered an oath. The large man turned and paused prior to opening the bedchamber door. He took a deep breath, blocking the images the idea invoked, then entered the room.

His eyes settled on her serene expression. In slumber, she appeared younger than her two and twenty years. She appeared untouched by trouble, untouched by her son's abduction, and untouched by marriage. The latter thought caused a barrage of images he could not fend off.

Miranda had been married; her husband had known her intimately. Another man had touched that silken skin, tasted those soft lips, and taken pleasure from her female form. Without realizing it, his hands clenched into white-knuckled fists. There was no denying such thoughts; her son was irrevocable proof that she was not an innocent. Why did that knowledge tug on his temper?

He had successfully banished her from his mind, but his body refused to oblige his mind. A tremor of desire shot through his veins. Who was he kidding? He hadn't successfully banished her from anything. She was all he could think about. And his desire only seemed to grow in leaps and bounds. As he stared at the beautiful woman lying atop the bed, he realized that disrobing her would not be the best approach. A second, more feasible idea flourished.

***

A firm, persistent patting sensation upon her cheek caused Miranda to surface through her unconsciousness.

"Miranda?"

Her eyes snapped open to see Crogan hovering near while his fingers tapped the side of her face, clearly attempting to wake her.

The last she could recall, she had been out in the bailey, in the rain. She looked down at her damp clothing and became aware that she lay in bed. A glassy gaze shifted to Crogan in question.

"What happened?"

"Ye swooned." The handsome man frowned down from his seated position at her side.

Miranda was pleased that the spinning had subsided, but she remained rather intoxicated. Her reasoning and judgment were slack.

Crogan was so close, but her previous apprehension was absent. She gazed at him without restraint, her thoughts fuzzy and elusive.

His eyes shifted away, and quickly he stood. "Ye need to summon aid for that wet gown, Miranda," he ordered in a stern voice.

Guided by her state, Miranda's brow furrowed, her feelings easily surfaced. "You treat me to a chilling disposition on this eve, and now you dare to order me about, Crogan Adair?!" In a violent motion, she pushed herself from the bed and pounded down the platform staircase less than gracefully.

Mindlessly, her hands lifted to the buttons at her back and struggled to open them. "You retired for the evening. I did not request your presence in the bailey," she pointed out with a note of irritation.

He gave her a scowl and growled, "I should have left ye to your devices?"

"Aye!" The lady shouted as her fingers worked on the buttons, too preoccupied with their quarrel to realize that she was succeeding.

"As experience has proven, ye cannot be trusted when left to your own devices!" he shouted furiously, taking a step closer.

Gradually, the last button broke loose, and her tired arms dropped to her sides. She paused to shoot him a glare. "My sister was ill, damn you; she needed me."

"I will not quarrel on the matter, Miranda. Ring for Winny." With that, he spun on his heel and marched toward the door.

"Of course, Alice must be waiting." She failed to conceal the sarcasm in her tone as she reached for the neckline of her gown and yanked it down, revealing the form-fitting bodice of a white cotte. Her inhibitions were lost; her jealousy soared.

Crogan halted and threw her a direct stare. "Excuse me?"

"You heard me!" she shouted as she stepped out of the gown and threw it at him in a fit of rage. "Alice awaits!"

The Scotsman snatched the gown from the air and stomped over. He peered down upon her from his great height. "Ye are too bold, lass," he growled darkly in reference to her assumption and her scantily clad figure. Crogan stared directly into her eyes.

"Perhaps, but you cannot chastise me for dishonesty." She glared up at him, head held high, chin up, shoulders back.

"Where I spend my evening hours is not your concern," he returned in an inarguable tone.

"You are correct," she agreed, her words clipped. Slim hands reached for the gown he held between them. "'Tis not my place to pass judgment. Please leave my chamber." Miranda pulled on the gown, but Crogan refused to release it.

He glared down at her, a challenge written in his eyes.

Her lips thinned. She exerted more pressure.

As did he.

Miranda abruptly yanked so hard, she thought the gown would tear into two, but at the same time, Crogan chose that instant to let go. The momentum coupled with her slowed reaction time caused her petite figure to lurch backward. All she could do was close her eyes and pray that her behind took the brunt of the fall.

But suddenly two arms miraculously banded around her waist, saving her from the misery and humiliation of her clumsiness. With the gown clutched to her chest, Miranda opened her eyes to find Crogan gazing down at her intently, contrary to their recent clash of wills. She felt weightless and breathless in his arms.

He continued to hold her off balance, certain to monopolize her attention. "That lesson was meant to teach ye not to assume anything in relation to me." His hold tightened, almost in a punishing grip. "I have not bedded Alice under your roof, Miranda."

She released her grip on the gown and curled her fingers in Crogan's tunic with purpose. "Forgive me if I do not believe your claim."

He grunted angrily and swept her off her feet. His action caused Miranda's heart to jump up into her throat. Without ceremony, he dumped her onto her bed and stormed from the chamber, not sparing her a backward glance.

She stared at the door. Was it possible she had made a mistake? No, she had not misinterpreted the rapport between Crogan and Alice. She could not fathom why he would assert such a fantastic lie.

Chapter 29

Miranda's eyes snapped open, then immediately closed as daylight caused a fierce streak of pain to pass across her eyes. She groaned miserably, regretting her indulgence. In an attempt to numb herself to her parents and memories of the past, she had consumed more than her little body could handle, and she had behaved abominably as a result.

She recalled the scene with Crogan, and she groaned emphatically. She had argued without logic, condemned him for bedding Alice, and stripped down to her cotte without a second thought.

"Miranda, what have you done?" she demanded out loud, disgusted with herself.

She sighed and accepted the fact that she could not alter the past. She would endure, as she had for most of her years.

Dainty feet touched the platform, and she rang for Winny. After she gulped down a glass of water, her first order of business was a bath.

The steam and the warm water greatly helped her dehydrated condition. She dallied for some time, then finally stepped from the wooden tub and drank down a second glass of water. Winny aided her toilet. Her figure was clothed in a beautiful jade-green gown with silver trim and floor-length tippets. Raven locks were pulled back into a simple plait.

With only a dull ache remaining as a reminder of her foolishness, she entered the shadowed corridor beyond her chamber. Miranda did not hesitate to seek her sister's quarters.

She knocked softly.

"Enter!" Rowe called in a strong voice.

Miranda passed through the doorway and ground to a halt, pleasantly surprised to see her sister seated at her vanity, pulling a silver-handled brush through shiny black curls. Rowena grinned at her through the large oval mirror atop the vanity table.

"How are you feeling?" the elder sibling wondered with a smile of her own.

"Fabulous. If I was not aware that I had been ill, I would never be able to surmise that I had been," she continued to brush through her locks.

Miranda moved to stand at her back and stared at her sister's reflection. "Perhaps you will break your fast with us on the morrow?" she questioned.

A beautiful face fell, clearly disappointed. "I had hoped to break my fast with the masses this morn."

"Please rest another day, Rowe. I do not wish for you to strain your health too quickly." She implored with her expression.

"Very well," Rowe reluctantly agreed. She placed the brush on the vanity and looked at her sister through the mirror expectantly.

Miranda knew Rowe was aware that she had news. She could not hide anything from her. Something in her eyes must have given her away. Slim fingers touched the exquisite curls, then began to comb through them, taking on the task of plaiting the girl's hair rather than summoning a maid.

"What is it, Miranda?"

She sighed heavily and met her sister's gaze in the mirror. "Mama and Papa have arrived."

Rowena's features locked in shock.

"Papa is on the path to death, and Mama is clearly bitter."

Amber eyes fell, and her brow wrinkled. "Papa?"

"Aye." She began to braid the three thick ropes together.

Rowena was reflective for many long moments, then her gaze rose. "I am uncertain of my feelings, Miranda."

"I received the news equally."

She looked at her own reflection. "I have longed for their return for years, but now I must admit, I do not possess any compulsion to see them."

Rowena's eyes sought her sister's gaze. "Why do I feel so, Miranda?"

The lady paused to give the girl her complete attention. "They have failed us, Rowe. We have not received the love we deserved, the love we were entitled to as their children. In response, we do not feel any obligation to give it in return."

The beautiful youth nodded sadly. "Aye. You speak true."

Miranda finished off the plait and secured it with pins. "I have not spoken of Edwin's abduction. They believe he is visiting with friends."

Once again, Rowena nodded. "You have such weight on your shoulders, sister; you do not need their judgment of Edwin's state falling upon you as well."

"Thank you for understanding."

The youth grinned, giving support. "You know I will stand in your corner, Miranda, even when I believe you to be wrong. I am your sister; 'tis my duty."

The elder woman leaned over and curled her arms around Rowena's shoulders, showing her gratitude with a quick embrace.

She stood to her full height and suggested, "Perhaps you should rest, Rowe. The news of our parents is rather draining."

"I will not argue that token."

The youth was slipping back into bed when Miranda quietly exited the chamber.

Chapter 30

Miranda suffered the morning meal in silence. Everyone spoke around her, as if nothing was out of the ordinary, including her parents. Amherst and Dell continued to speak of their travels. Brodie and Crogan revealed tales of childhood antics. And Viktor and Reissa spoke of their children. Miles and Alfred listened with avid curiosity. Alice simply sat there with a sullen look on her lovely face.

Miranda was surrounded by people, but in that moment, she could not have felt more alone.

Finally, after she choked down several bites of bread, Miranda excused herself and strolled directly out to the stables. Ignoring the repercussions of her previously reckless ride into the countryside, she blazed from the stables and into the summer sunlight.

She stretched Spectrum's legs beyond the curtain walls, but she had learned from her mistakes. The lady took stock of her position on the property at all times. She indulged in an energetic ride but remained grounded enough not to allow herself to get lost.

Without realizing why, she retraced her steps to the pond that had witnessed Crogan's first kiss. Her petite figure dismounted and approached the meager shore. She stared down at an unfamiliar reflection in the water.

Miranda's appearance had not transformed in recent weeks, but she felt as though she gazed upon a lady she did not know. The lady in the water was helpless to save her son. The lady in the water was sad, jealous, and bitter. And the lady in the water had fallen hopelessly in love with Crogan Adair.

The stunning realization nearly knocked her on her behind. For a moment, she thought she could not breathe. Miranda retreated several steps and took a deep, calming breath.

She dropped to her knees, and her head fell to open palms. Heartbroken, she gave in to the need to weep quietly. How could she have allowed herself to fall in love with him? A man betrothed to another, a man haunted by a ghost, a man incapable of returning such sentiment.

Once again, Miranda found herself lost, but this time geography had nothing to do with it.

She looked at the tranquil picture of the still pond. Trembling fingertips wiped the moisture from her face. She closed her eyes, let her head fall back, and welcomed the warmth of the sun's rays.

As Miranda had told herself a million times since her son's abduction, she would endure because she had to. There was nothing to do but carry on. She could put her faith in the hope that she would see Edwin again. But the fact that Crogan was as good as married, she could not put any hope in that. The idea was defeating, deflating, and difficult to suffer. But she bit back the tears that threatened a second time.

She would endure.

Miranda stood and shook off her unwanted thoughts. Impulsively, she threw caution to the wind. The petite frame wriggled from her jade green gown and stepped from a standard white cotte and drawers. Nude, she waded into the pond up to her ankles. The days of cool weather had taken its toll. The water was refreshing in its chilling state, but that mattered not to Miranda. She dove in without a second thought.

The pond was surprisingly deep. It allowed her to sink to the depths before breaking through the surface with a feminine grunt.

***

The forest was not three hundred yards from the pond. The ceiling of branches created a distant shroud of shadows and mystery. Concealed amidst those shadows was a figure.

Silent.

Still.

Watching…

Chapter 31

Unwilling to sit at the supper table with Crogan following her epiphany at the pond, Miranda took her meal in her sister's chamber.

"Miranda, you are quiet on this eve," Rowena observed.

A ghost of a smile touched her lips. "I am generally quiet, Rowe."

"True," she agreed. "But your quiet is extended."

"I am merely fatigued."

Rowena's head tilted in thought. "Nay, 'tis a lie."

Miranda's head lifted; her expression was a stone mask. "Please, Rowe, let us share our meal in contented silence. I ask this of you."

"Mama and Papa?"

Miranda said nothing.

"Edwin?"

Still nothing.

"Crogan?"

"Please, Rowe," she pleaded quietly.

"Very well," the girl conceded.

They shared the remainder of their meal in polite silence.

The hour was late when Miranda kissed Rowena's slumbering brow and entered into the shadowed corridor.

A startled breath escaped her when she was brought up short to find Lady Farraday waiting for her outside of the antechamber door.

"Alice."

The voluptuous blond crossed her arms under her breasts and threw daggers at the elder woman with her eyes. "Do ye dabble in curses an' spells in the night?"

With her stoic mask in place, her guest was not able to see the confusion swirling inside. "Excuse me?"

"Ye have bewitched my betrothed."

Miranda nearly snorted in disbelief. "You could not be more mistaken."

Alice's eyes narrowed. "Ye do not see it."

"There is nothing to see, Alice."

Her hands fell to clenched fists at her sides, and she took a menacing step closer. "*I* see it." She took a deep breath. "*I* see the way he looks at ye when he believes no one is watching."

Miranda stood to her full height. She felt dwarfed by the taller woman's frame. "I assure you, Alice, you are mistaken."

"Witch. Ye have cast a spell upon him, ye dowdy, emotionless spinster."

Through clenched teeth, she said, "Perhaps 'twould serve you well to retire."

The lady exploded in fury. "I warned ye, Miranda." Without warning, a palm cracked across her face, catching her completely off guard.

Shocked and pained by the assault, Miranda retreated a couple steps, her head turned from the impact. A hand immediately rose to soothe the smarting flesh of her cheek. Her mind spun, stunned, angered and insulted. From her wounded position, her gaze rose to see Alice hovering over her, fury emanating from every pore.

Instinct told the lady of the manor to react in kind, to defend her honor, her integrity. But logic and reason swept over her instinct. She would not allow herself to sink to the brat's immature level. She would rise above it. She would take the higher ground.

Once again, Miranda rose to her full height, her palm lowered to her side. "You are not welcome in my home, Alice Farraday. You will pack your belongings and depart at dawn," her voice was steady and firm. She had to bite back a grin when her guest appeared taken aback.

"B-but—" she stammered, clearly not expecting such a result.

"And 'twill not do you any service to appeal to Crogan on the matter. *I* am the lady of the manor, and *I* reserve the right to decide who departs, and who remains."

Alice stamped her foot like a spoiled little girl. "I hate ye, Miranda Wilkes." With that, she marched off.

Miranda watched her go. When she turned from sight, the lady gave in to the need to palm her smarting cheek again. She was irate. She had been assaulted in her home by a guest. By an irrationally jealous guest. Crogan's guest.

Crogan had brought that girl into her life. And she could not wait to inform him that his betrothed would be leaving them. If he felt that it was necessary to depart with her, then so be it. Viktor had joined them; she had all the help she needed to retrieve her son.

Anger guided her down the corridor, directly to Crogan's chamber. She did not bother to knock; she simply slammed open the door and scanned the room for his presence.

He looked up from his stance before the fireplace. He had been staring down into the cold, empty pit. His massive figure was clad in a pair of black braies and nothing else. But Miranda would not allow his disrobed state to enter her thoughts. She was in a snit, and she would unleash hell on him.

"My patience has met its end, Crogan," she growled.

His brow furrowed as he drew closer. His gaze traveled over her appearance, then finally settled and narrowed upon her face. "What happened to your cheek, Miranda?"

"I have been struck—" she growled.

"Who?" he interrupted in a harsh demand.

"Your charming betrothed has voiced her emphatic opinion one time too many, Crogan. I have asked her to leave," Miranda stated in a matter-of-fact tone.

Her eyes unwillingly slipped to his chest, and her heart tripped. A fine mat of hair announced a virility that was overwhelming. And the mountain of muscle there was impressive; it continued into the span of his arms. The volume of his biceps made the line of his veins overtly visible. A mix of trepidation and attraction swept down her spine in a violent shiver.

His expression transformed into one of skepticism. "Alice? Alice has accosted ye?"

Her gaze lifted, stunned by his reaction. "You disbelieve?"

"Why would she strike ye?"

"The reason is irrelevant. She will depart at dawn." With that, she spun on her heel with the intent to leave the room. Their proximity was beginning to affect her physically. The space felt stifling. She needed an escape. But a hand on her arm stalled her efforts. He walked around to face her.

"Ye do not react on impulse, yet the reason has caused ye to storm into my chamber unannounced, Miranda. 'Tis certainly relevant," he charged with a furrowed brow.

"I was angry and reacted without thought," she spoke logically. But the warmth in her body was far from logical.

"An' ye continue to avoid me at every turn," he confessed. "Which is why your abrupt visit in my chamber is cause for question."

His words triggered her temper. She stepped dangerously close and glared up into his handsome face. "I avoid you? You dare such when you look at me with cold eyes?"

"I do that which is necessary," he stated through gritted teeth. The eyes that traveled over her figure were scathing, almost punishing.

Feeling insulted by his look, she rasped harshly, "As do I. Which is why Alice will depart at dawn."

"Ye take daring liberties, lass," Crogan grated, clearly irritated.

"She does not serve a purpose here."

"She is my betrothed," he declared. Yet he did not deny her decision or defend the lady.

"She is merely a distraction. You have been requested to retrieve my son, not dally with your future bride." Miranda fought hard to keep her jealousy in check as she spoke the words.

Once again, his eyes traveled over her figure, but the menace was gone. His gaze was an invisible caress. "Nae, Miranda, Alice is not the distraction. *Ye are.*"

"Excuse me?" she squeaked.

He took a step forward.

She took a step back.

"I have been fighting it, but to no avail." Without warning, he reached out and dragged her up against the hard wall of his body. "I want ye."

His penetrating look disarmed her, and his admission only caused her resolve to weaken. "Crogan, I—" she whispered, but lost the will to escape as she welcomed the feel of his arms banded around her.

"Let go of your inhibitions, Miranda," he whispered.

She felt his warm breath on her face. The soothing timbre of his voice settled over her like a warm blanket. The lady of logic and reasoning let go of everything that had been holding her back. She threw her arms around his neck, rose to her tiptoes, and pressed her mouth to his.

Crogan responded instantly. His hold tightened, and his lips moved against hers.

Feeling his response, a being inside Miranda sprang to life. Her passion exploded, and she let it guide her. She gave him a kiss that sent tingles of pleasure down to her core. She tasted him, touched him. Her hands moved over his shoulders, marveling at the feel of his skin beneath her fingertips. Her body pressed against him, wanting him close, closer. But it wasn't enough.

Abruptly, she broke free and stepped back, out of his arms.

His brow creased, and he reached out for her, but she slapped his hand away and gave him a licentious smile.

He arched a single auburn brow, obviously intrigued, waiting for her next move.

Her hands rose to the buttons at the back of her gown. With deft motions, she opened the closure of her garment, all while watching Crogan's eyes move over her figure, taking in every curve, every hollow. Then their gazes locked, and an electric charge passed between them.

The lady knew in that moment that there was no going back. But in that moment, she simply did not care. Instinct alone guided her, and she listened to it eagerly.

Slender hands pulled the gown down her arms then pushed it over her hips, letting it puddle at her feet. Then, without a moment's hesitation, she reached for the laces at the front of her cotte. She gave a little tug, and the knot pulled free. The material separated with her guidance, then that garment, too, fell into a puddle at her feet. With a quick push, her drawers slipped to the floor.

She stood before him, naked, but she did not feel ashamed, or frightened, as she had with Gerald. She felt the power of her female form as Crogan drank in the sight.

"Ye are even more beautiful than I had imagined," his voice was hoarse with desire. "An' I have imagined it many, *many* times." Once again, he stepped forward, and she did not deny him.

In fact, she reacted in emphatic welcome. She threw herself into his arms, lifting her feet off the floor to wrap around his midsection so she wouldn't have to fight against her meager height to meet his lips. They shared another explosive kiss while Crogan reached down and kicked his braies off, then moved over and took a seat on the bed.

With her backside supported by his thighs, Miranda pulled him close and deepened their kiss. She pulled him against her with the strength of her arms and the legs that remained wrapped around his waist. She heard a purr in her throat and heard his soft groan in response.

Miranda felt like she was on fire. Her body throbbed in a way it never had before. She broke contact with his lips and kissed the stubble on his cheek, then his hard jawline.

Without warning, a hand moved to cup her breast, and that caused a sharp intake of breath. Her head fell back as a shock of pleasure shot through her body. Warm lips pressed to the column of her neck as his hand moved over her, testing the weight of her meager chest, drawing out her nipple with the flick of his thumb.

A whimper sounded, but she wasn't aware that it was her own. She was completely lost. Then she felt his mouth shift to replace his hand. Her palms fell back to press against the mattress as her chest arched toward him, giving him unlimited access to taste her.

When he had stimulated her to the point of madness, she locked eyes with his and gave him another sly smile. With a palm to his chest, she pressed him back until he lay on the bed. She straddled his hips and looked down upon a figure that was ready and waiting for her, a figure that, admittedly, was more impressive than her husband's had been.

She watched as the plait of raven locks that had fallen over her shoulder caught his attention. He began to pull the pins from her hair and finally released the long tresses. He combed through them with his fingers, then cupped her nape and pulled her face down so he could claim her mouth with his own.

Miranda indulged in the seductive kiss for many moments, but finally broke free, unwilling to wait another moment for the unfamiliar release she sought. She positioned her tiny figure above him, then lowered herself, sheathing her body on his silken shaft.

Her innocence had been lost long ago, but this experience was new to her. She had never known such pleasure. The feel of him inside of her was exquisite. A moan escaped her, and Crogan sat up and wrapped his arms around her, crushing her chest against his. A hungry mouth claimed hers once again.

Miranda wanted to devour him, her tongue pressed to his as her fingers slid over the stubble on his cheeks, then buried themselves in his soft auburn locks. They continued back to cup his scalp, but as she felt his pulse inside of her, her fingers curled into fists in his hair.

His large work-roughened hands slid down her back, gripped her hips, and ground her against him, causing them to rip their mouths apart and groan in unison.

She gazed at the beautiful man in the guest room bed, and he stared back. The intensity in those sea-green depths took her breath away. His desire for her was clearly written there even though he wore a sleepy, sexy expression. It spurred her on. Her palms caressed the power in his shoulders, then moved lower, pressing to his chest.

Miranda pushed him back, so he lay on the bed once again. In spite of such new territory for her, her body knew what to do. The

226

woman reacted, moving against him as his hands continued to grasp her hips. She felt a tightening deep inside of her. It continued to grow as her breath labored.

For the second time, her hands shifted to the mattress beside Crogan's thighs. For an instant, she stared up at the bed curtains overhead, but her eyes squeezed shut as that tight ball of tension finally snapped.

She was tossed into a whirlwind of sensation that rocked her to the core. She floated upon a crest of wonder and awe, at last knowing what Gerald had felt when he sought the use of her body.

Somewhere in the distance she heard her a deep, male groan.

Eventually, the ebb subsided, and she was left with a perspiring glow. As she tried to recapture her breath, she smiled up at the ceiling, and at last, the satisfied woman looked at Crogan.

His eyes were also shining with the light of repletion. He gave her a crooked grin. "Miranda—"

She pressed a finger to his lips, cutting him off. "Shh."

Abiding by her wishes, he remained silent. Fatigue was settling upon her, so she was pleased when he wrapped an arm around her, pulled the sheets back, and settled them into a comfortable position. With a muscled arm thrown over her waist, they drifted off into a deep, contented sleep.

Chapter 32

Miranda's eyes snapped open. She could feel Crogan's figure tracing her back, his breath fanning her naked shoulder. Night was still upon them.

The first thought that struck was the truth that he had given her one of the single most wonderful experiences of her life. But a second, more logical thought followed.

Dear Lord, what have I done? 'Tis wrong, 'tis so wrong. Edwin is in the hands of a criminal, and I have dallied with his rescuer. But that was not all; Crogan did not belong to her. He never had. He was betrothed to another. And haunted by the ghost of a woman he had truly loved, a woman she could never be.

She squeezed her eyes shut for a moment, stunned by her own lack of forethought when she had willingly jumped into his arms and into his bed. Hell, she basically initiated the whole bloody scene.

Crogan had merely told her that he wanted her, and she had been unhinged to the point of insanity. Overcome by the need to flee, she gingerly slipped out from under his arm and inched toward the edge of the bed.

"Going somewhere?"

Miranda jumped out of her skin. Without turning around, she confessed her reason with brutal honesty. "Attempting to escape my mistake." With great dignity, she rose in her nude state and walked over to the garments that remained in a pool on the stone floor.

"Mistake?"

"Aye. A mistake for so many reasons." Gracefully, she shrugged into her cotte and tied the laces.

"I do not believe that." He jumped down from the bed and approached.

With the knowledge that he was not wearing clothing, Miranda refused to lift her eyes. "Please return to bed and allow me to walk out of here, Crogan." She reached for her gown.

He clutched her forearm in a firm grasp, forcing her to raise her eyes to meet his. "Do ye deny what has passed between us?"

"I do not."

"Then why do ye seek escape?" he demanded, continuing to clutch her arm.

"Edwin is, and will always be my first priority, Crogan."

He scowled down at her. "I see the lady of logic an' reasoning has returned with all due haste."

"The lady of logic and reasoning is who I am," she defended coolly.

"Nae, she is who ye choose to hide behind."

Her temper flared, but she maintained her calm. "You are betrothed, Crogan. Do you deny it?"

His gaze narrowed. "I do not."

"For years, I watched Gerald parade his dalliances in front of my eyes. I will not be one of those *other* women, Crogan." With that, she yanked her arm from his grasp, and with her gown held in her hands, she rushed from the room.

Clad in only her cotte and drawers, Miranda broke into a flat-out run in the shadowed corridor. Fearing that someone would witness her unclothed state, she hurried into her antechamber and swung the door shut at her back. However, she did not hear the resounding sound of the door banging shut from the force of her action. Confused, she turned to see the cause.

Crogan stood there in the open doorway. He had not paused to don a single garment; he had simply followed her in his nude state.

Miranda's jaw dropped open in shock. "You—" she choked on her words, "you—" Finally, she shouted quietly, "You're mad!" She hurried around his figure, pushed him further into the room, and closed the door.

"I simply needed the assurance that ye did not seek to challenge a flight of stairs in your haste to leave me," he revealed in an accusatory tone.

In that moment, Miranda felt an overwhelming urge to break into tears, despite his obvious irritation. He had worried she would traverse the stairwell to the main level and fall as a result of her speed. He had feared she would follow the same tragic route as Dana. He had acted in care of her in spite of himself and the possible consequences of being seen.

But she did not allow tears to appear. She quickly collected herself and responded in a contrary calm, "As you see, I have sought the refuge of my chamber."

He crossed his arms over his chest and looked down his nose at her. "Aye, I see."

Miranda took a deep breath and stepped into her gown. "I will return with your clothing." As she slipped her arms into the sleeves, she pinned him with a look meant to be an order. "Please wait here."

He simply stared at her in response. Without glancing back, she swiftly returned to his chamber, collected his braies from the floor, pulled an emerald tunic from the wardrobe, then made the reverse journey to her antechamber.

It appeared that Crogan had not moved during her absence. She threw the garments at him, then continued on into her bedchamber and shut and locked the door behind her.

Chapter 33

Dawn had arrived.

Still rather unsettled after the night's activities with Crogan, Miranda had not returned to bed after she locked herself in her chamber. She had watched the sun approach the horizon while she fed on her guilt for giving in to her desires. And that guilt only increased when she acknowledged the truth that she would not erase that time with Crogan if given the opportunity to do so.

It had been a monumental mistake. But at the same time, she could not regret it. She loved the man. And she would have to carry that one night with her for the rest of her life, because he would be married to another.

The lady shook off the depressing thought and approached the door. Miranda had decided it would be best to escort her unwanted guest out. She needed the assurance that the despicable lady was well and truly gone from her life.

After arranging for transportation, she summoned Alice with a knock on her door.

When the structure opened to reveal the beautiful young woman, Miranda braced herself for anything. But Alice simply looked at her expectantly.

"'Tis time, Lady Farraday."

Her lovely face turned into a vivid mask of anger. "Crogan will not allow this, ye horrible wretch."

232

"Crogan will not deny my decision," she spoke confidently.

With that, Alice opened up her lungs and bellowed for her betrothed, "Crogan!"

Aware that she could not stop the headstrong girl, Miranda merely stepped back and allowed the girl to indulge in her tantrum.

She continued to call for him, waking the whole of the castle in the process. Doors along the corridor opened, and heads poked out. But Miranda remained steadfast in her decision.

Finally, Crogan turned down the hall and marched toward them, his handsome features set in lines of fury as he took in the scene of Miranda waiting idly by while Alice shouted his name.

Seeing his approach, Alice moved into the corridor and took his hand, appealing for aid. "That horrible woman is forcing me out of her home. Please, Crogan, tell her ye will not allow it!" She stared up at him with imploring eyes.

He pulled his hand from her grip and pointed to the ugly bruise on Miranda's cheek. "Ye are the cause of that, Alice. Aye, Miranda has every right to do so. Ye have behaved deplorably."

Alice's mouth fell open. She looked from one stone face to the other, both of them obviously standing against her. Then she pinned Crogan with a glare and laughed humorlessly. "Ye have bedded her. Ha! The witch has pulled ye into her clutches at last." She pointed a finger into his chest and hissed, "Ye heartless beast."

"We have yet to speak our vows, Alice," Crogan's words confirmed the girl's suspicions.

Flashing eyes turned on Miranda. She gave an ungodly screech and lunged for her with claws bared, but Crogan quickly stepped in, catching her wrists in an iron grasp. "Ye will not lay hands on her a second time."

"Very well, Crogan, defend your whore. But I will not stand for this." The blonde yanked her wrists from his hold, spun on her heel, and stalked toward the staircase.

Alfred appeared before them in the corridor. He looked at Miranda and Crogan as they followed Alice down the hall. "May I offer any aid, my lady?"

She nodded. "Please fetch the lady's belongings."

"Aye." With that, he moved past them to do his lady's bidding.

Alice continued to the Great Hall and pushed open the entrance doors with furious gusto. At long last, she turned back to face Crogan.

Miranda was stupefied when she saw the girl's livid expression melt into tears. Without warning, she threw her arms around Crogan's neck and sobbed.

"I forgive your indiscretions, darling," she wept into his shoulder. "I love ye, and we will be married as planned."

Miranda's head spun from Alice's changing moods. She looked to Adair, wondering at his thoughts, but his expression was inscrutable as he allowed the girl to cling to him.

Then, as quickly as she had sought his embrace, Alice turned and ran from the keep as tears zigzagged down her cheeks.

Crogan stared at the closed doors that swung shut in her wake.

Miranda, unwilling to play any further part in the man's affairs, turned and walked away.

Finally, Alice had departed. But the girl's absence did not grant Miranda the approval to court Crogan. The marriage would stand. The King had stamped his blessing upon them, and nothing could change that. Such an idea was daunting.

The man would remain close at hand, but she could not reach out for him. She could not seek his secure embrace. With Edwin in Bishop's care, she needed to feel such security more than ever.

During her journey toward the kitchen, the lady was brought up short to find her mother rushing toward her. Her weathered features were pinched with a modicum of concern.

"Mama, what has passed?"

"Your father has taken a turn for the worse, Miranda. He cannot rise to meet the day. I believe 'tis only a matter of hours," the elder woman estimated.

"I will send for the physician immediately."

"He is beyond the aid of a physician now."

Rather than consider her own feelings on the matter, she immediately thought of her sister. "Rowena will need to see him, Mama."

Clearly rattled by the turn of events, Dell was rather amiable in reaction to her daughter's order. "Of course, my dear. We must all speak our farewells before 'tis too late to do so." Then her head bowed in an attempt to collect herself.

Miranda offered her hand in solace. Dell took it. She gave her mother's cool limb a squeeze. "Go to him. He needs you now more than ever."

The elder woman lifted her head, and Miranda was startled to see regret in the depths of her gray eyes. "Your father has never really needed me, Miranda." With that, she retraced her steps to the stairwell and disappeared.

She left her daughter staring after her, perplexed by the departing statement.

"Is there anything ye need, Miranda?"

The lady jumped, unaware that Crogan stood nearby. Rather than face him, she simply shook her head from side to side. "Nay, thank you." Then she followed her mother's lead and headed for the second level, leaving Crogan to stare after her.

Chapter 34

Miranda entered Rowe's chamber to find her seated at her vanity table, brushing through damp raven curls. She had already bathed and dressed. The elder woman moved to stand at her sister's back. She dreaded being the bearer of bad tidings, but she did not hesitate to speak when those amber eyes looked at her reflection in the vanity mirror expectantly.

"Papa is in his final hours, Rowe. We agreed that your confinement has met its end. Go to him. Seek what you must."

Rowena's expression was much like her own when Dell revealed Amherst's precarious state in the hall: indifferent, then confused by such an emotionless reaction. To feel indifferent toward their father when he seemed larger than life and invincible was understandable, but to maintain such feelings when his time was growing so short was not so easy to understand.

At last, she nodded. "Thank you, Miranda. I will go." She gazed into the mirror for a moment, taking stock of her reflection. Satisfied that she presented an immaculate figure, she rose from the wooden bench and turned. Their gazes locked. "Will you see him?"

It was Miranda's turn to nod. "Aye, I will see him. Then 'tis certain I will need a ride to clear my head."

"I would love to join you."

"Do not overexert yourself on your first day rejoining civilization, Rowe," she warned softly, then smiled, offering comfort. She knew her sister was nervous about seeing her parents again. But to see Amherst on his deathbed was more than she had asked for. The doctor had ordered Rowena to avoid any undue stress, but in this situation, there was no help for it.

Rowena's eyes were wide. "I would request that you join me to give moral support, but I believe 'tis time I stand on my own two feet."

"You are certain?" Miranda wondered softly.

She nodded and gave a genuine smile of confidence. "I am."

"If you need me, I will be outside that door."

Rowena's slender arms curled around Miranda's waist, showing gratitude without words.

At long last, the siblings hooked arms and traveled the corridor to their parents' chamber. Rowe spared her sister one final glance before going on into the room, alone.

The resounding clang of the door swung shut. A shiver rolled down Miranda's back. She feared more for her sister's well-being upon facing their father than she feared for his dwindling life.

Without realizing it, the petite figure began to pace. A parade of thoughts preoccupied her to the point of lost time. She thought of Edwin; always, she thought of Edwin. Prayers were sent to the heavens for his welfare, and for news that he would return to her soon. When would they receive details for their next step? When would she see her son again? The days felt like weeks. The weeks felt like years.

Miranda knew she had passed the point of constant worry and transitioned into a state of partial numbness. And that was the only thing that saved her from continual hysterics.

Then images of the previous evening invaded and replaced her concern with guilt and heartache. What a wonderful mistake it had been. She believed she had alienated Crogan by admitting her feelings about their night, yet, contrarily, he had aided Alice's departure from the manor. It was a small victory. But the New Year would see his wedding day, and that knowledge was heart-wrenching.

At that moment, she knew Crogan Adair could not continue on in such close quarters. Loving him while he was within arm's reach, but unable to express her feelings, was excruciating. Miranda needed to take some action, but her mind was too bloated with feeling over her father's condition that she could not figure out a solution to her dilemma.

Until her mind kicked into gear, and she could think clearly again, she would simply avoid him.

Suddenly, the chamber door swung open, and Rowena entered the corridor. Her eyes were red-rimmed and grief-stricken, but she managed to give Miranda a sad smile. She did not have to say a word; the resolution was written clearly on her face. She had made her peace with Amherst, and she had said her goodbyes.

Rowena lightly touched Miranda's upper arm. "He waits for you now."

She nodded slowly.

"I believe I shall go below and join our guests to break my fast." With that, she was gone.

She watched until her sister had disappeared from sight, then her gaze shifted to the structure that stood between herself and her father. A tiny knot of tension began to form in her stomach. That was most unexpected. She had assumed she would be able to see him and hold on to her indifference like a safety net. She was wrong.

Miranda took a deep breath and pushed open the door.

Chapter 35

The shutters remained closed, and the fireplace was empty, casting her parents' room in shadows. There was a chill in the air, but Miranda could not decide if it was real or imagined. Through the slits in the shutters, she could see sunlight beyond, and, for a moment, she longed to be outside, drinking in the warmth of the sun's rays.

Dell sat at her husband's bedside. She had leaned forward in her chair to hold his hand. Her face was a blank slate.

Her father appeared weak and subdued, but as he stared at her approach, there was no denying the glow of life that still shone in his eyes. A thin coverlet was pulled up under his arms and spread across his chest, his blond curls were tousled, and his cheeks were pale and sunken.

While she stood there peering down upon the man's dying figure, she realized she was not inspired to speak. There was nothing in her heart that she felt needed to be said. A shiver coursed through her body.

Their gazes held, and the silence stretched.

After what seemed to be an eternity, Amherst's mouth opened, and his voice was heard. "I will admit, Miranda, you were always my favorite."

She could not hide the bitterness from her tone as she spoke words without thought. "You had a fabulous way of showing it."

"My life has been nothing but a series of mistakes." At that point, Dell let go of his hand and sat back in her chair. "But the only one I regret is my absence in my daughters' lives."

She crossed her arms under her breasts, the bitterness growing, but her tone was soft. "'Tis too late for regrets."

"Aye," he gave a small nod, "but not too late to share them."

"You may venture to the heavens in peace, Papa; I do not harbor resentment toward you." The lady forced the sincerity into her tone, hoping it would please him to hear it.

The corners of his mouth turned up in a grin. "You are as terrible a liar as your mother."

Miranda shifted on her feet, feeling uncomfortable. She was overcome with the need to flee. "What do you require of me, Papa?"

He closed his eyes for many moments. His strength was dwindling rapidly. Miranda felt a stab of guilt. Her father was dying; it was not the time for bitterness and resentment. It was time to tell him what he wanted to hear. But he had already called her out for lying. He would see through any fabrication she made. She was caught up in a whirlwind of emotion, and it was mentally and physically sapping her strength.

She moved forward and dared to sit on the edge of the mattress.

He gazed up at her, his eyes steeped in sadness. "Watch over your mother and your sister." His cool hand reached for hers. She allowed him to hold it, feeling her walls break down. "With your strength, you can hold our family together. Do not let it fall apart as I have."

From the corner of her eye, she saw her mother rise and walk away. Then the distinct sound of sobbing drifted through the air.

Amherst's voice grew raspy with weakness and sentiment. "I have been a poor husband and an absent father. But I do not ask for forgiveness. I merely ask that you do not allow your bitterness to cloud your judgment in life."

"My son has known only my love, Papa. I speak the words every day." Miranda expected tears to take hold of her, but, miraculously, a strange calm settled upon her. She was able to think clearly, able to speak honestly without sounding bitter or angry.

"It pleases me to hear that." He attempted to smile, but his life was slipping so quickly that he failed.

Ever so slowly, his amber eyes closed. The rise and fall of his chest was dangerously shallow.

Miranda raised his hand and pressed a kiss to his knuckles. He responded with the barest hint of pressure when he squeezed her hand.

She sat there for several minutes, knowing he stood on the precipice of death. His breathing slowly stalled, and the hold on her hand grew limp.

Dell returned to the bedside and stared down at her husband while muted tears rolled down her cheeks.

The sun was at its highest point in the sky when he passed into the afterlife on that beautiful summer day.

Time seemed to suspend as Miranda studied her father's figure. He was gone. There were no more words to say, no more bridges to repair. They had not fixed a lifelong relationship of withheld love and affection. But they had reached a fragile truce. Miranda let go of her bitterness and any lingering resentment.

"Goodbye, Papa."

She could see her mother's shoulders shaking with grief, so she stood, circled the bed, and held open her arms. Dell did not hesitate to take the offer. She walked into her daughter's comforting embrace and wept.

Broken sobs filled the stone chamber. Miranda did not make any attempt to soothe her distraught parent; she simply allowed her to spill her sorrow.

Finally, Dell stepped back and wiped the tears from her eyes.

"He is at peace now," Miranda reasoned, but the response in her mother's eyes was that of war.

"Nay, he is in hell now," Dell spit out. With that, she ran from the room.

"Mama!" she called after her back, aghast at her behavior while her husband lay dead in their bed.

But Dell did not stop; she did not return.

Uneasy about her mother's outburst, her eyes shifted to the man she had never really known. They had made their peace with each other. But clearly husband and wife had not done the same. Her tears had been real, but her fury had also been real. Perhaps Dell could not forgive his faithlessness, even in death? Perhaps there had been more standing between them than his adultery? Perhaps Miranda would never know.

It was useless to ponder the possibilities. She had news to impart and arrangements to make.

The Great Hall was vacant. And the noise from the bailey announced that the men were in the midst of drills.

Tiny feet carried her out into the sunlight. At her right, the men were paired off, swords clanging against each other in practice of their skills. At her left, Reissa and Rowena lounged upon a blanket on the grass. Reissa was reading, and Rowena appeared to be resting, stretched out with her eyes closed. Both were oblivious to the racket of war on the opposite side of the bailey.

Reissa looked up. When she saw the determined look on Miranda's face as she approached, Reissa gently nudged Rowena.

Amber eyes opened, then shifted to her sister. Gracefully, she pushed herself to her feet. As always, Miranda's face was set in lines of stone, but Rowena was able to read the feeling in her eyes.

"He's gone?" she whispered.

A head of unbound raven locks nodded in response. Then she opened her arms expectantly, knowing the news would affect her sister more than she wanted it to.

Rowena's beautiful face broke down into tears as she moved into Miranda's arms. While consoling her forlorn sibling, the noise at her back began to decrease. Sword tips lowered to the ground as the men turned to take in the sight. The hush rolled through, like dominos falling. At long last, all was silent with the exception of Rowena's weeping.

Soft footfalls sounded, slowly, tentatively. Her head turned to find that several men had stepped away from the group. Viktor, Crogan, Alfred, and Brodie moved toward them. She could not meet Crogan's gaze, not when she was on such precarious ground emotionally. She looked to Viktor.

"My wife and I shall make the arrangements, my lady."

Her gaze turned to Reissa. She simply offered a forlorn smile and a nod to confirm her husband's decision. Reissa touched her forearm for a moment, offering silent support, then husband and wife walked away to prepare for a funeral.

Hooded eyes turned to Brodie for help. "My mama fled when he passed. Please find her; I am concerned."

"Of course," he assured in a confident tone. With that, he disappeared into the keep.

"My heart goes out to you both," Alfred spoke humbly, his eyes lingering on Rowena's tear-stained face.

Hearing his voice, her sister looked up, and her eyes sought him out. "Oh, Alfred," she choked. With that, she retreated from Miranda's arms and moved into the captain's.

His cheek fell to the crown of her head, and his eyes closed. The bailey was filled with men, yet no one would even think of calling them out for their embrace.

Miranda watched them for a moment, grateful her sister felt compelled to seek her comfort in his arms. She could only wish that she could do the same as she heard Crogan move forward.

"Please accept my condolences," he said softly.

"Thank you," she returned in a polite manner. Their gazes met and locked for a brief instant. Fearing she would lose her composure, Miranda turned and followed Brodie's path to the keep.

Chapter 36

Miranda watched the flames lick her father's makeshift casket with dry eyes. The partial numbing sensation that had claimed her after Edwin's abduction settled upon her with full force. In the hours following Amherst's passing, all of her feelings seemed to have washed away and dried up. She took everything in like a spectator who watched a scene that was unfamiliar to her.

They stood several hundred yards beyond the curtain walls. The casket was simply a massive pile of branches that had been cut down and lashed together. A navy velvet draping was placed upon the center to support Amherst's body, and then the whole thing was set ablaze.

Due to the situation with Edwin, Viktor and Reissa felt it was not appropriate to vacate the keep for an ocean burial. They felt it was necessary to remain on Lady Wilkes's property. And Miranda had wholeheartedly agreed. Their consideration for her was not overlooked. She could not thank them enough for everything they had done and continued to do for her.

Once the casket had been fashioned, the castle's occupants formed a large circle around it and silently watched as the flames took the place of a burial ceremony. Rowena stood at her left and discreetly wiped moisture from her face. Dell stood at her right, as dry-eyed as her eldest daughter.

Miranda looked at the reflection of the flames in her mother's amber eyes and wondered what she was feeling. Clearly, there was so much the woman had left unsaid since their sudden arrival at the manor. Despite her stunning announcement at dinner about Amherst's infidelities, she had kept up the pretense of a contented, if somewhat bitter, wife.

Feeling a gaze upon her, Dell glanced at her daughter, then, without warning, she turned and marched back to the keep.

The fire roared on as rain clouds floated across the sky. Seeing the impending weather, people began to disperse. Viktor and Reissa calmly walked from the scene. Alfred put an arm around Rowena's shoulder, and they walked away.

Miranda's gaze shifted to the sky. She watched the smoke rise up toward the clouds for so long that she learned she was alone when her eyes returned to her surroundings. At least that was her first impression. As she observed the first drops of rain fall onto the dying flames, she was accosted by the distinct impression of another presence at her back. It was a presence she realized she would know anywhere.

"You have not gone," she spoke in a monotone.

"Ye know I would not leave ye out here alone," his deep voice drew closer.

Her petite frame turned to meet Crogan's figure as he approached. Their eyes locked.

"What do you want from me, Crogan?" she tested point-blank.

A hand rose to tenderly wipe a drop of rain from her cheek. He was quiet for a moment, then his hand fell away. "I am uncertain," the Scotsman confessed honestly.

"Then allow me to remind you why you're here—"

He held up a palm to cut off her emotionless tirade. "I know why I am here."

Unable to stop herself, she put a palm on his chest, but her demeanor remained icy. "I need you to devise a brilliant plan to retrieve my son, then you must take yourself back to Scotland and marry your bride. 'Tis our only purpose at this point in time." She turned to walk away, but his voice forced her to halt.

"Previously ye claimed I looked upon ye with cold eyes. Now who looks upon whom with cold eyes, Miranda?"

Without turning, she mentioned, "My father has passed this day, Crogan; please impress your concerns upon me another time."

"Aye, your father has passed, but ye have not shed a tear." He stalked up behind her, clutched her shoulder and spun her around to face him.

"Tears will serve no purpose," the lady spoke as if from another person.

"Do ye hear your words, Miranda?" Strong hands clutched her upper arms, forcing her to meet a gaze that searched her own.

"Nay, I hear nothing but useless questions."

He gave her a slight shake. "In the night, I held a passionate lass in my arms. Now I hold an emotionless shell of the lass I have known." An auburn brow furrowed in confusion. "Where has she gone?"

"She has been beaten down with the abduction of her son, the illness of her sister, and the death of her father. She is lost. She is merely attempting to survive."

The muscles in his jaw clenched, then his eyes dropped to her lips. "She is not lost." His kiss was gentle, undeniably attempting to draw out a response. When he lifted his head, he pinned her with a questioning stare.

Moved by his touch, yet determined to show that she was unmoved, she gazed up at him with her mask firmly in place. "Find my son." With that, she pulled from his hold and headed to the keep without looking back.

Chapter 37

Miranda was physically present for the evening meal, but her thoughts were so distant that she might as well have been somewhere else. Amherst's life had been cut short by an illness, and that knowledge brought Edwin's absence into sharp focus. Their time on earth was not guaranteed. She wanted her son back.

The lady felt someone's gaze linger on her as she stared down at the food on her trencher. Her eyes lifted, expecting to lock gazes with Crogan, but she was surprised to find Dell studying her with a pensive expression. They shared a silent moment, then Dell's eyes fell to the table.

Her mother's look had gained her attention. And it was only then that she became aware of the subdued atmosphere at the table that evening. Voices were hushed, and the subject matter was safe.

The lady of the manor was quite relieved when minstrels and storytellers arrived to help lift the mood of mourning that was thick in the air. Another thoughtful product at the hands of her guests, the Colvilles.

"Miranda, I would like a moment," Dell declared when everyone rose to gather around the fireplace for a good story and some festive music.

She nodded. They descended the dais as a pair and crossed to the entrance, then passed into the bailey for a stroll. The fresh scent of cleanliness after the fall of rain tickled their sense of smell. And they walked out into a pleasantly warm evening.

Two pairs of gray eyes lifted to the sky, where they saw the moon peek through cloud cover overhead, giving off a modicum of light. Several torches in the bailey had been lit, so there was plenty of illumination to see the way as they followed the keep's perimeter.

Dell did not make any attempt to chit chat. She jumped in with both feet, beginning with a statement that shocked Miranda into reality: "I never loved your father."

A petite figure ground to a halt and gaped at her mother. "I could not have heard you correctly."

Dell shrugged and repeated her words, "I never loved your father, Miranda."

Her speechlessness continued.

"And he never loved me."

Finally, she found her voice. "I do not understand. Your lives have been a lie?"

"Nay." She began walking, forcing Miranda to fall in step. "I merely clung to a childish dream of happiness for far too long. Your father was not the husband I had hoped for when we married. The other women, the lack of respect, I was nothing but a sullen trophy on his arm."

As her mother spoke, Miranda picked up on a close parallel between their lives. And she did not hesitate to put a voice to her thoughts. "Mama, because of your absence in the course of my life, you do not realize how much we share in common."

A sniffle sounded. Her gaze shifted to see tears that glistened on her mother's face.

"In the beginning, I hoped and prayed he would change, and foolishly I allowed my hope to take priority over yours and Rowena's happiness," Dell confessed.

They walked for many moments. Then, "Why did you never leave him?"

"I did not possess the strength to strike out on my own. And I had nowhere to go." She sounded defeated.

Raven brows furrowed. "You could have come here, Mama."

"I burned that bridge long ago, my dear. I have lost you and your sister's trust."

"I know we have never been close, but I would not have turned you out. You are my family."

The sniffles erupted into heartfelt sobs. Without warning, Dell turned and pulled her daughter into her arms. For the third time that day, Miranda allowed someone to cry on her shoulder.

Her mother seemed so distraught about her choices, and she felt it was too late to make amends. But that simply was not true. She sired two daughters who would never throw her out onto the streets.

"I do not believe I ever spoke the words, and shame on me for that, but I do love you, Miranda. I always have."

She could not return the sentiment, simply because she did not know the woman who clung to her. They shared the same blood, but their lives had been so disjointed that they were virtual strangers.

"You are welcome to stay as long as you like," she offered in response.

"Thank you," the elder woman whispered with a crack in her voice.

They walked for many minutes as they quietly pondered what they had shared.

"Your father chose your husband."

Miranda felt her jaw clench. "And I have learned on this eve that he chose a man much like himself." Her gaze rose to the sky. "I do not know how I feel about that."

"I was not aware Gerald treated you in such a deplorable fashion," Dell's voice was steeped in guilt.

"'Tis all in the past now, Mama. But I cannot fault him for giving me the greatest gift in my life."

"My grandchild," Dell confirmed.

"Your grandchild is not visiting with friends, Mama; he has been abducted by a neighbor and is being held for the ransom of this property. Even now we are forced to await word of the next step in his devious design," Miranda ground out, hating Bishop with every syllable.

"Oh my," Dell breathed, clearly stricken by such news. "I have felt such tension in you following our arrival, and now I know why. I cannot imagine what you have been going through."

"I admit, 'tis a struggle. But I cling to hope. I will see him home again and pay any cost I must to do so."

Chapter 38

Mother and daughter continued their walk. They discussed many things, getting to know one another like never before. Miranda had no illusions that their relationship would mend into a friendship, but she welcomed the transition of stranger to acquaintance.

Once upon a time, she had considered the woman critical and cold, but she realized those traits had been misinterpreted. Her mother had merely been distracted and desperate to please a man who could not be pleased. Certainly, Dell was hopelessly flawed, but Miranda knew she was also far from perfect.

She surprised herself with an open willingness to forgive and start anew. And the elder woman seemed more than willing to attempt stepping into a mother's role, at last.

Deciding it was time to return to her guests, Miranda and Dell entered the keep. The once hushed and somber atmosphere had turned lively and energetic. Minstrels played in one of the empty corners, and a large group of guests had formed a dance floor of active bodies. An animated storyteller stood before the fireplace in the midst of a comedic tale that had people holding their aching sides from excessive laughter. Countless barrels of ale had already been consumed, and countless more would be drained before dawn arrived.

Miranda felt mixed emotions as she observed the revelry. She acknowledged guilt when she gazed upon a keep steeped with joy while her son remained in the hands of her corrupt neighbor, but at the same time, she would not expect any of them to remain cloaked in a shroud of misery while they were forced to wait for Bishop to make contact. They were simply making the best of a bad situation, and she must commend them for it.

With that thought in mind, she wandered over and joined the audience crowded around the evening's storyteller. She folded her tiny frame on a bench next to her sister and attempted to focus on the old man's tale.

But her mind refused to concentrate. Rather than listen to the story, her eyes strayed to the enthralled crowd. First, her gaze settled on Miles. He sat on a woven rug near Brodie's feet with his legs folded like a pretzel.

His state on the day they met had been worrisome. He had been unkempt, on the verge of starvation, and stricken by abandonment. In such a short time, the boy had made a miraculous recovery. Not only was he clean, but his blue eyes shone with humor as he watched the entertainment. He remained stick-thin, but he had not been in residence long enough yet to add pounds to his little figure.

It seemed as though Brodie had taken him under his wing without the least bit of hesitation. Miranda could not help but silently commend the man for stepping into that role of mentor for an orphan child. They did not share the same blood; there was no obligation for him to do so.

And clearly the boy had grown attached to his surrogate father figure. Miles followed the Scotsman everywhere, like a second shadow. He looked to him often for approval and commendations, and Brodie did not withhold his praise.

In response to one of the storyteller's jests, Miles burst into childish laughter, catching Miranda's rapt attention. The sound reminded her of Edwin's laugh. It drove a knife into her heart. For a moment, she felt tears threaten, but she quickly swallowed over the emotion and felt a bittersweet smile touch the corners of her mouth.

Miranda forced her gaze to travel. It settled on Viktor and Reissa. The pair sat on an oak bench nearby, side by side, without a breath of air between them. Lady Colville also giggled as a result of the show. Her husband glanced at her for a moment, obviously taken with her laughter. Affection was written clearly in his black eyes. He brushed an errant strand of hair from her cheek, then returned his attention to the old man who stood on one foot with a leg wrapped around the other and his arms entwined together to represent the massive vine in his tall tale.

The vine transformed into a horse. On hands and knees, he whinnied.

As they continued to watch, Reissa hooked her arm around Viktor's, and she rested her head on his shoulder.

Miranda hated her envy as she watched their close rapport. She had been robbed of that feeling with a crude husband, and she would never be able to indulge in that feeling with Crogan. Her heart felt heavy, yet hollow.

The lady told herself not to, but her eyes refused to heed the warning. They followed where she felt Adair's presence to be. He was seated at a distant trestle table, in conversation with one of his knights. While they spoke, he sipped from a tankard of ale, then laughed at something the younger fellow said.

Miranda's stomach tightened. Generally, she witnessed the man in a state of anger or passion. To see him thusly, so casual, was heartwarming. In a navy-blue tunic with his deep auburn hair unfettered and windblown and a day's worth of stubble on his chin, he was a handsome sight. So handsome, it was painful.

She was struck by a strong need to go to him, but logic was quick to follow. She remained seated on the bench but continued to covertly observe him. Her eyes dropped to his hands. A blush heated her pale cheeks. She could not help but be reminded that those hands had touched her intimately the previous evening. Those palms had passed over her skin, creating sensations her previous husband had never introduced her to. Those skilled fingers had dug into her hips, helping to guide their friction.

Her gaze rose to the smile upon his mouth. She had kissed those lips of her own free will, ignoring the truth that she did not possess the right.

As if he felt someone watching him, his head began to turn in her direction. Certain he sought her out, she quickly shifted her eyes away before their gazes locked.

As she pretended to be enthralled with the storyteller, she could feel those eyes upon her, and she could not help but wonder what Crogan was thinking. He had made it clear he had no desire to desire her. But he had also made it clear he had no intention of fighting his desire any longer.

Apparently, she had wounded his male pride when she confessed that their night in each other's arms was a mistake, but he had swiftly recovered into fury. Then her father passed, and Crogan had been willing to be there for her. He had offered the solace of his presence out there beyond the curtain walls. And she had denied him, even though it took every ounce of her willpower to do so.

Now it seemed as though he was content to maintain his distance. Miranda knew that was the right thing to do, but at the same time, she wanted to run into his arms and let him hold her, let him offer the comfort she so desperately needed.

A sound of applause rang in her ears, and she noticed the old man bow in gratitude. Many people rose with the intent to seek further entertainment elsewhere.

"I believe I shall retire now," Rowena decided.

Miranda looked at the weary girl at her side. Her sister tried to hide a yawn.

"Aye, 'twould be best," the elder woman agreed with an affectionate smile.

Rowena gave her a quick embrace. "Sleep well, Miranda."

"And you as well."

With that, the girl rose from the wooden bench and glided across the keep.

Reissa filled the empty seat beside her, and they both watched as the youth disappeared into the stairwell. "Rowena has recovered well."

"Aye, due to you."

"Due to both of us," she corrected with a matronly expression.

Miranda regarded the vacant bench Viktor and Reissa had occupied during the show. "Your husband has abandoned you?" she teased as she strived for a moment of normalcy in her chaotic world.

A strawberry blond head nodded, and she displayed a lovely grin. "Aye, he seeks male sport. Why do men feel a pathological need to compete with one another day in and day out?"

"'Tis in their blood, I fear."

Reissa laughed softly. "We jest, but 'tis likely true."

Miranda felt herself laugh in return. It felt so good to laugh.

Reissa's slim hand pointed to an empty corner where several of the men began setting up targets for an archery contest. Her laughter deepened. "Proof of our pondering, there they are. The choice of sport on this eve, archery."

Miranda's laughter grew, tickled by the sight after they had been picking on the men for that same reason. She placed a hand on her abdomen as it began to hurt from the joy of it.

Their giggling caused several heads to turn in their direction, including the men they were laughing at.

Both of them sobered instantly. But it only lasted a moment. They could not contain themselves. Reissa gave in, and Miranda quickly followed, bursting into hearty laughter that had eyes rolling with the belief that they must be well into their cups.

Alfred passed by them with his bow and arrow in hand. He glanced in their direction, taking in the scene. A stern expression formed on his face. "Do I need to separate you two?" Then he broke into a comedic grin.

The ladies took in the sight of the weapons in his hands and his add to their jest, and they were overcome by another round of humor. Reissa slapped the bench at her side, unable to contain herself, and Miranda wiped at the moisture in her eyes, awed that she had been moved to tears in her humored state.

Finally, they settled down and both took a deep breath.

"Oh my, I cannot express how much I needed that, Reissa," Miranda mentioned as she wiped the last of the water from her eyes.

"Always pleased to lend a hand." She grinned.

They watched in contented silence for many minutes as the men took turns competing to hit the center of the circular target.

Alfred pulled back his arrow, then let it go, seemingly without taking the time to aim, yet he nearly hit the center. He stepped back, and several of his companions patted him on the back for a job well done.

Brodie stepped up and mirrored the same stance. His action was leisurely; clearly, he was attempting to win. The arrow cut through the air in a streak and also nearly struck the bullseye. He shook his head; apparently he had expected better of himself.

Viktor moved into position. It also appeared that he did not take a moment to find the bullseye. But his feathered weapon found the center and embedded itself there without fail.

Several people in the audience whooped for joy, including Reissa. After giving him a round of applause, she leaned toward Miranda and stated, "I taught him that."

Her eyes swung to her companion, suspicious. "You jest?"

Reissa laughed. "Aye, I do."

Miranda giggled, but the sound broke off as she saw Crogan move forward. He took the position like every other man had, but for some reason, she found herself holding her breath. She could not help but notice the muscle in his arm bunch as he pulled back on the butt of the arrow.

His concentration was not to be distracted by the noise in the hall. Without warning, he released the weapon and lowered the bow. The arrow nearly split Viktor's with its proximity.

Another round of cheering sounded in the massive expanse of the keep. Miranda let go of her breath, startled to feel pride in his skill. She smiled.

The knight they had deemed as their referee moved forward to determine the winner. He looked closely at the arrows, then turned around and announced, "'Tis a draw. Lord Adair and Lord Colville are equal victors!"

Applause ensued as the men graciously bowed for their audience. Then the crowd of men dispersed. Some sought more ale, while others flocked to the music of the minstrels and began to dance.

Viktor began in their direction, approaching his wife. Miranda's gaze remained on Crogan. He stood there, staring at the target, obviously lost in thought. As he did so, Miles stepped up and gently tugged on the hem of his navy tunic, gaining the man's attention.

Curious eyes looked down at the child. Although she could not hear the boy's request, it was clear what he had asked as he pointed to the target, excitement lighting his expression.

Vaguely she heard Reissa say goodnight, then rise and depart. Husband and wife were gone. She was too engrossed in the scene to take notice. The lady stared as the man taught the boy the art of the bow and arrow. He patiently showed him how to hold the arched piece of wood, obviously encouraging with his smiles and the softening of his features.

Miranda was stupefied. Miles was only a couple years older than her son. It was not a difficult leap to imagine that Crogan was teaching Edwin, as a father would teach his son. The scene was endearing and heartbreaking on so many levels. She became alarmed as she felt her throat begin to constrict.

Widow Wilkes

Seated alone, there was no one to make excuses to. She simply rose from the bench and crossed to the stairwell. As she climbed the stone staircase, she pushed all thoughts from her mind, allowing her to maintain a modicum of composure.

Chapter 39

Miranda had every intention of ringing for Winny to aid her evening routine. Yet she seated herself at her vanity and began to pick the pins from her hair without the help of the maid. She felt cold inside as she pulled the silver-handled brush through unruly curls.

Finally, she could not deny the thoughts that demanded entrance. Eyes stared without seeing her reflection in the mirror.

She loved Crogan, and her father had passed away, but when all was said and done, none of it made any difference without Edwin. A piece of herself was missing, and she would not be whole again until his return. That hollow place inside her heart seemed to expand until finally, she fell into it.

A tear formed, blurred her vision, then streaked down her cheek. Another followed. Her hair had been combed through, but she acted mechanically. While the woman cried her sorrows in silent tears, she continued to brush through raven locks.

The sound of the door creaked on it hinges and snagged her attention. She put the brush down. Miranda already knew who stood there, staring at her from the open doorway of her bedchamber. She stared up at the figure in the mirror, unwilling to wipe the moisture from her face.

Crogan.

Miranda had lost her hope. Her father's death had simply been the last support of foundation to crumble. But Crogan's unexpected arrival caused a spark of hope in the depths of her misery. "You have not given up on me," she decided, choking on her anguish.

He shut the door and moved into the room. As he approached, Miranda shifted away from the vanity but remained seated. He dropped to bended knee before her, and his eyes stared into her grief-stricken features. "I am drawn to ye against my will, lass. I cannot give up on ye, not by will, or by choice."

She wanted to smile, but it only caused tears to form in greater quantities. She swallowed over a sob and peered at his handsome features. "'Twould seem I suffer a like affliction."

He gave her a tender smile, and, for a moment, it was as if time stood still. They had formed a fragile truce. She took down the wall she held up against him, no longer caring about right and wrong. Miranda allowed the dam to break loose, and doing so caused sobs to rise within.

"I miss Edwin. I miss him so much."

"I know," he whispered. Crogan rose and lifted her into his arms. She clung to him, burying her face in his neck as he carried her over to the bed. He sat there and simply held her, allowing her to pour out her sorrows on his shoulder.

Miranda's limbs were trembling with emotion as tears drained from the well she had pushed deep down inside. She wanted to scream; she wanted to shout; she wanted to do whatever was possible to get rid of the knot of frustration in her stomach, but all she could do was cry. Her strength had temporarily fled, and desperately she clung to Crogan, welcoming his presence.

She could feel his hands on her back, her hair, soothing her tumultuous emotions. The warmth of his body seeped into her petite figure, melting the tension into oblivion. As the minutes ticked by, her cries decreased into sniffles.

When her tears had completely dried up, she continued to pillow her head on his shoulder, unwilling to break contact. They sat like that for so long that Miranda's eyelids began to droop with fatigue.

Miranda woke from her dozing state when Crogan began to ease himself away and gently shift her figure onto the mattress. She hooked her arms around his neck.

"Stay," she whispered.

Their gazes locked.

"Stay with me, Crogan," the lady pleaded.

His eyes glanced down at the bed.

"What is it?"

His jaw clenched, and indignation shone brightly in his eyes. "I cannot."

Her mouth opened, but she could not form words, too hurt and disappointed by his abrupt rejection to speak.

"I cannot lay with ye in a bed ye shared with your husband."

Startled by his admission, she demanded, "Do I detect jealousy?"

"Give it any name ye wish, but I cannot stay, Miranda. I am tempted to set the structure aflame when I think of ye an' another man in it." With that, he acted out of context and placed a quick kiss on her cheek, then rose from the bed and sauntered from her chamber without a backward glance.

Miranda stared at the door in utter disbelief at the about face that had just taken place. She had never considered his feelings in relation to herself and Gerald. But now she was most certainly aware how he felt about her marriage.

The longer she sat there and considered his words, the angrier she became. And she would not let her thoughts remain silenced.

Once again, she stormed into her guest's chamber unannounced. This time Crogan stood there, as if he had expected her to follow him.

She marched up to him and clutched his tunic in her fists, her eyes flashing. "How dare you condemn me for a marriage that visited upon me nothing but misery. How dare you!"

Iron arms banded around her back. He gazed down into her face, his voice saturated with guilt. "I do not condemn ye, Miranda. But I cannot shake those thoughts from my mind."

She glared at him. "I cannot shake thoughts of you and Alice from my mind."

"I feel nothing for her," he confessed.

"Gerald is my past. Alice is your future." Miranda spelled it out for them both.

He gave a growl deep in his throat. "But I have ye now." With that, he fused their mouths together.

Crogan's kiss was filled with so much hunger that Miranda's body exploded with life. Passion consumed her to such a degree that she wanted him in that instant. The ardent lady could not wait a moment for the pleasure she sought in his arms.

Her hands dropped to the leather belt at his waist. She tugged at it, broke it free of its restrictions, and tossed it aside.

It seemed Crogan was also in the same impatient state. The hands that had moved to the buttons of her gown could not free them fast enough. So he clutched the neckline and ripped it down to her waist.

The noise of her gown being torn caused Miranda to break their kiss. She glanced down at the ruined garment. For a split second she was surprised, but then a throaty laugh erupted into the room. It was no loss. She owned more gowns than she could possibly wear in a lifetime.

Crogan yanked her into his arms and carried her to the bed. Their need continued to flourish in an animalistic form. They tore at each other's clothes until, at last, they were naked in one another's arms.

Finally, Crogan was inside of her and carried her to heights that pounded her into oblivion. She could not help but cry out as she hit that peak and felt an exhilarating freefall that ended much too soon.

From Crogan's position above her, he continued to hold himself up. It was obvious he had no intent to let the whole of his weight collapse on her. His head dropped to her shoulder as he attempted to catch his labored breath.

Miranda could feel the perspiration on his brow mingle with the glow of moisture on her skin.

Unable to contain herself, she let out another deep laugh, a bit startled by the electric charge that had just passed between them. It had swept them beyond themselves, beyond their control. She may have been slightly battered after that experience, but it was pleasantly so.

The Scotsman lifted his head and smiled down at her, his expression radiating awe.

Miranda opened her mouth to speak, but suddenly he kissed her again, cutting off her thoughts. He rolled onto his back and pulled her on top of him without breaking the contact of their mouths.

The warmth of his palms gently caressed her back, then slid down to cup her derriere. He deepened the kiss, tasting her, drawing her into his world of sensuality.

Overwhelmed by the range of emotion he had inspired within her that evening, she pulled back, needing a moment to catch her breath. He had drawn out a raw, violent need that she never could have imagined she possessed.

Then he treated her to tenderness that made her feel treasured, almost loved. And that was a sensation she was not used to receiving from a man. She needed to take a step back and force her feet to the ground, because she had allowed him to sweep her away.

Unwilling to withdraw in spite of her apprehensions, she lay her cheek on his chest, content to stay there.

Crogan's hand moved to beneath his head. He stared up at the canopy, his free hand thoughtlessly drawing circles on her naked shoulder. "I feel ravaged." He chuckled softly.

Suddenly concerned, Miranda lifted her head to gaze down into his face. "Have I hurt you?"

He stared at her and shook his head, a twinkle in his eye. "Nae, lass, that was amazing." His head rose enough to press his lips to hers, then dropped back onto his palm. But his gaze remained. "Your passion mesmerizes me."

In spite of all they had shared, his compliment brought out a shy side. What he made her feel was so new to her that she was not confident in herself. Clearly, she had not been enough to arouse Gerald's passions in the same way. Definitely not in a way that mirrored Crogan's desire for her.

Miranda's gaze dropped to his chest. She didn't want him to see the thoughts in her eyes. Her defenses were down, and she couldn't summon her wall of strength. The night of Gerald's birthday assaulted her introspection.

"What is it, lass?" His gaze searched hers.

She smiled, but the smile did not reach her eyes. "Forgive me, I was taken back to some unpleasant memories."

A low growl sounded in Crogan's throat, drawing her gaze. The twinkle had disappeared, and in its place were piercing questions. "Your husband?"

Her eyes dropped a second time.

Crogan clutched her shoulders. He guided her to shift to her haunches while he sat up, then his palms moved to cup her face, forcing her to look at him. Those sea-green eyes were so dark with feeling, they appeared black in the soft candlelight. "What did he do to ye, Miranda?"

The sadness in her eyes was there only a moment as she looked at him. Somehow, she managed to disguise it with indifference. "Please, let us not discuss Gerald."

His gaze softened. "His memory hurts ye."

"It is all in the past," she assured.

Crogan's head shook, his sea-green depths darkening once again. "It is here, now."

Her gaze lifted to the canopy, not seeing anything but her thoughts. Her sigh was ragged. "Gerald—" She couldn't find the right words. It felt as if Crogan was trying to peer into her soul. It scared her. She didn't want to bare it to him.

Glossing over the truth seemed to be the best route. "As a husband, he never gave me any reason to be pleased with him."

His eyes narrowed. "Emotionally or physically?"

She shrugged. "Both." When he continued to gaze at her in questioning silence, she added, "He never gave anything."

"He took," Crogan declared in another low growl. For a moment, he closed his eyes. At last, he looked to her, but his eyes still appeared black. "He raped ye?"

Miranda pushed his hands away, desperately needing some room to breathe. But even as she did so, her head shook from side to side in denial. "I never fought him," she confessed humbly.

Crogan grunted and leapt off the bed. He instantly began to pace, murder in his eyes. His hands rose, fingers combing through his hair, noticeably infuriated.

The stunned lady continued to sit back on her haunches as she watched his display. Clearly, he cared not that he was unclothed as he continued to pace. It seemed as though he had forgotten she was still in the room. His behavior was startling in its intensity. However, the knowledge that he felt so deeply on her behalf warmed her heart.

She crawled off the bed and crossed to stand in front of him, halting his motion. "Crogan."

He looked to her. His eye flashed. "I would run him through if I could," he uttered.

Slightly trembling hands lifted, and her palms pressed to his torso. Her head rose up to his massive height. "Come back to bed."

It was as if she had thrown a wet blanket on the flames of his fury. His palms returned to her cheeks, and for many long moments, he simply gazed into her eyes. "Ye deserved better."

She gave him a forlorn smile. "That may be so, but I have the gift of my son, so there must not be any regrets."

He sighed unsteadily, then his hands moved, and his arms curled around her. He swept the lady from her feet and carried her back to his bed. Ever so gently, he lay her on the mattress and covered her body with his own.

His eyes looked down upon her. "Ye are so beautiful."

A slender hand smoothed auburn locks from his brow, her eyes also moving over his face. She opened her mouth to speak, but then he kissed her, cutting off her words.

His mouth was extremely gentle, at first. The moment she returned his kiss, he deepened it, tasting her, re-igniting the spark within them both. Her fingers wove into his hair, then banded into fists as his tongue entered the recesses of her mouth and danced with her own.

His knees straddled her legs, and his hands moved around her back, lifting her ever so slightly. Then his lips shifted, and he kissed her jaw, her neck, her breast, her navel.

A work-roughened palm slid around to the back of her knee and lifted, guiding her left leg over the back of his shoulder. He pressed her right knee over, against the mattress, giving him access to her.

Wondering at his intent, Miranda looked down just in time to see and feel that beautiful man kiss her in a way she had never been kissed before.

She cried out at the pleasure of feeling his mouth against her. Her head fell to the mattress, and her eyes squeezed shut in disbelief. Her hold on his silky locks tightened further as his tongue pressed against her, bringing her up, up, up until she spiraled into an abyss of ecstasy.

Miranda was dazed as she gasped for air. She was only vaguely aware when Crogan moved to lay by her side and pulled the coverlet up and over them. He drew her back against him and threw an arm over her waist.

Ever so slowly, her breath began to come down, and finally she realized he held her close. The warmth of his breath was on her ear as he pillowed his head on his bent arm. The length of his arm was enough that she was also able to rest her head on his elbow.

With her thoughts finally intact, although, only slightly, she spoke, "Crogan?" She knew he had not found his own release, and she wondered at his intent. He was close enough that she was able to feel that he was still ready and able to take her if he chose to.

"Shh, sleep, lass," he ordered gently.

Miranda lay there, dumbfounded. He had given, and he had taken nothing in return. The realization of his generosity had her fighting back tears.

Chapter 40

Miranda teetered on the line between slumber and wakefulness when she heard Crogan's voice interrupt the silence. She opened her eyes and shifted to peer at him through the darkness. He remained in the same position as he had been when he transitioned into the world of unconsciousness.

The widow was not accustomed to sharing a bed, so she had slowly turned away, giving him the space she felt he needed to be comfortable.

As she gazed at him and allowed her eyes to adjust to the lack of light, she realized he was still asleep. He mumbled, his words unintelligible, but it was written in the lines on his face that he was distraught. Small beads of perspiration glistened on his furrowed brow.

Miranda acknowledged a modicum of concern. He was having a night terror; there was no doubt about it. She sat there, indecisive. Should she wake him or allow it to run its course?

Before she could come to terms with any type of decision, he abruptly sat up, his eyes opened wide, and his breath came in deep, labored gasps.

"Crogan?" she queried, then reached out to touch his forearm.

His head spun. He seemed startled to find her beside him. Like lightning, he yanked her across his lap and wrapped his arms around her. His brow fell to her naked shoulder.

When her hands hooked around his neck, she was caught off guard; he was shaking as a result of his unconscious horror. She thought of Crogan Adair as strong and indestructible. To see him in a vulnerable and stricken state was more than disarming; it cut at the heart of her being.

This man had offered her support when she needed it the most; now she wanted to return the favor. Her arms tightened, pulling him close.

She knew little of Crogan's past, but there could only be one tragedy great enough to replay itself in his mind against his will.

"You continue to be haunted by Dana's death?" Miranda put forth the question in a whisper. She ignored how the idea of his love for another woman wrapped around her heart and squeezed so hard that it physically pained her.

"I am haunted by that morn," his deep voice reverberated throughout her body while they held each other close. "But 'tis not her death I see."

Miranda's brow creased, perplexed. "I fail to understand."

"'Tis yours," he revealed in a breath.

A tempestuous shiver rolled down her spine. In response, Crogan's arms grew more secure.

"Mine?" she asked, uncertain how such news made her feel. He had dreamt of Dana's fatal fall down the staircase, but it was not

Dana he saw in that dream, it was Miranda. She took a deep breath in an attempt to calm her elevated pulse.

"Aye," he confirmed. "An' 'tis not the first time."

"'Tis not real, Crogan. The proof is in your arms."

The warm breath of his heavy sigh caressed her back. "I apologize if I alarmed ye." He dropped a light kiss onto her shoulder, then leaned back against the pillows, guiding her cheek to rest on his chest once again.

Before long, she heard his even breathing through the dark of the night. But Miranda lay awake for hours, unable to sleep. Unable to calm her churning thoughts.

Chapter 41

"Mama…"

She could hear it. She could hear him call for her.

"Mama!" his sweet voice echoed throughout the space of Bishop's dungeon.

Miranda raced down the corridor, desperately seeking her son. But one corridor looked like the next.

"Mama, I need you!"

Tears blurred her eyes as she turned the corner and faced yet another passageway. She continued to run down the long stone halls, but her efforts were futile. She was hopelessly lost, and Edwin continued to cry out for her.

"Edwin!" she shouted, her voice hoarse with frustration and desperation. The tip of her slipper banged against a raised stone in the floor. She stumbled, fell, and scraped her hands. "Edwin," she choked on a sob.

"Please, Mama!"

Despite the sting that radiated in her palms, she pushed herself to her feet and continued on, refusing to give up. "Hold on, Edwin, Mama is coming for you!"

Miranda's eyes snapped open. The dream had been so real that she could still feel the effects. Nevertheless, she was startled to realize she was in a strange state of calm. Her mind was clearer than it had ever been. And it was in that state of calm that she had a startling epiphany.

The plan went against every instinct she possessed as a mother, as a human being, but a voice from somewhere deep inside of her convinced her that it was right. Miranda knew in that instant what she needed to do. Her lips thinned into a grim line of determination.

The night had not yet lifted, and Crogan slept on, oblivious to her wakened condition. Ever so slowly, she eased away and prayed she did not rouse him from slumber. If he learned of her plan, he would lower the gates of denial down upon her without hesitating to consider it.

She could not allow that to pass. Miranda bit her lip as she moved an inch at a time. She needed to reach the edge of the mattress without creating a sound.

It seemed an eternity passed before her bare feet touched the cool stone floor. Miranda let out a silent breath, grateful she had accomplished that small feat. She glanced at Crogan through the darkness. His chest maintained its steady rise and fall.

Convinced she had not interrupted his sleep, she tip-toed to the bedchamber door and paused long enough to grab her torn gown from the floor. She held the material against her unclothed body, gritted her teeth as a slim hand clutched the brass handle, and pulled the door free of the latch. It swung open, the hinges creaking only slightly. Unwilling to waste the time to close it, it remained open in her wake.

She fled down the passage. The darkness of the corridor and the gown clutched to her chest were her only forms of concealment as she sprinted to her personal chambers.

The unclothed figure rushed in and pushed her antechamber door closed at her back. She tossed the ruined gown aside and padded to the bedchamber. She crossed directly to her wardrobe. Her eyes scanned through the garments. Miranda chose a clean cotte and a deep violet gown with split skirts.

Within minutes, she had managed to clothe herself without extra aid and weave her curls into a flawless plait. Her mind worked methodically as she grabbed a few choice items from her chamber, then sat down at her vanity to pen a short message.

She left the parchment on the pillows of her untouched bed, grabbed the small valise that contained her necessary items, vacated her chamber, and continued on to leave the manor behind.

***

Crogan's eyes creaked open. He blinked several times to push his slumber away. Through the cracks in the shutters, he was able to see that the sun was approaching the horizon. His head turned on the pillow, looking for Miranda.

The space beside him was empty. He scowled. A large muscular frame sat up and scanned the expanse of his chamber. He hoped to see her dressing, or seated near the fireplace, but he did not. The lady was nowhere to be found.

He gritted his teeth together. She had done it again; she had abandoned him in the night. Only this time, she managed to flee without waking him.

Following their truce the previous evening, he had expected to wake with her in his arms.

He would be married with the arrival of the new year. They both knew what they were doing was a bad idea. Perhaps staying at his side was too much to expect of her. It was too much to expect of anyone. But, damn it, he hated to see her withdraw from him. He hated how it made him feel.

From his perspective, he had not wed yet. Although he did admit of twinge of guilt for his actions because he had already bedded his future bride.

From Miranda's perspective, it was wrong for them to be together. She had reminded him of that over and over again.

Nevertheless, he could not deny his anger as he rose from the bed and stepped into his discarded braies. Miranda wanted him as much as he wanted her. She had not made any attempt to hide it. She had spoken the words, and she had been a willing participant in their physical activities.

As he stormed down the corridor, his fury flourished. He could not abide it. There were several months yet before he wed.

Crogan threw open the antechamber door. When he saw that she was not in the larger outer chamber, he stalked into the next room, assuming she had returned to her bed after she left him. His

284

brow furrowed once again when he saw that the large canopy structure remained untouched. The presence of a sheet of parchment caught his eye.

Feeling the tension rise in his stomach, he walked over to pick it up. He scanned Miranda's neat scrawl:

Crogan,

I will not wait a moment longer. I have gone to collect my son.

Miranda

Crogan felt his stomach drop to his feet as he muttered a biting oath. The parchment floated from his grasp, and he turned to charge from the room.

As he flew down the corridor toward his cousin's room, he opened up his lungs. "Brodie!"

The Scotsman reached the south tower and pushed open the door with a resounding whack. "Brodie, rise!" he bellowed as he moved into the room, his gaze narrowed upon the still figure in the bed. Callused hands shook his shoulder none too gently. "Brodie!"

Finally, emerald eyes blinked open. "Crogan?"

"Rouse yourself. We need to gather the armies. Miranda's gone after her son," he breathed, feeling sick as he put a voice to the words.

"Alone?" his cousin demanded in disbelief.

"Aye." He did not wait for the news to settle any further. He broke into a full run, this time heading for the Colvilles' chamber.

Viktor must have heard Crogan's raised voice, because he was already stepping out into the corridor while Crogan hurried toward the door.

"What has passed?" His deep voice was laden with sleep, but his eyes were alert. Reissa appeared and stepped up to his side. Her strawberry locks were disheveled, and her bedclothes rumpled, but she listened avidly to the conversation taking place.

"Miranda slipped away in the night. She seeks her son without aid."

"Oh, dear Lord," Reissa whispered and looked at her husband. "Bishop will have the Wilkes heir and the lands without her presence here. 'Tis likely she will be discarded without thought."

"I will not allow that," Crogan gritted, clenching his fists at his side.

Viktor held up a palm to ward off any interruptions. "We cannot assume Bishop's intent. Murder may not be in his veins. We have seen nothing but his greed."

Reissa frowned up at him. "He sent Edwin's blood back to torture her."

"We do not have proof 'twas Edwin's blood," he offered logically.

"The man has spilled blood," she emphasized. "Perhaps 'twas not Edwin's, but he has set a blade to flesh."

"We do not have time to ponder the bastard's intent," Crogan nearly shouted, unwilling to hear more. "We will gather the armies an' depart within the hour."

***

Viktor simply nodded in agreement with the Scotsman's plan. With that, he watched as Crogan marched off to wake Alfred.

Viktor and Reissa returned to their chamber. As they collected their garments from a trunk at the foot of the bed, Viktor scowled darkly. "Has the woman gone mad?"

"She is a mother, Viktor, same as I. I do not know how she has remained patient so long," Reissa remarked softly, lifting a wine-colored gown from the trunk. She set it aside, pushed the bed robe from her shoulders, and began to untie the laces of her cotte.

"The choice was not hers," he mentioned as he thoughtlessly watched his wife disrobe. A black tunic and matching braies were clutched firmly in his hands.

"Aye. 'Tis precisely why she has executed a drastic action. She is taking back her life." The petite bare figure reached for clean undergarments.

"She has behaved foolishly." His disapproval was evident as he began to attend to his own state of dress while his eyes remained on his wife. As he took in the sight of her unclothed figure, he felt a modicum of resentment that he could not indulge in a lazy morning in bed with her. And that only increased his anger.

"If Bishop does not murder her on sight, then I must admit she has executed a brilliant plan. She is well aware that she has the support of a siege to collect her and her son. While we fight to breach their walls, she will be allowed to protect her son from within," Reissa offered.

"Aye, and who will protect her from Bishop?" he wondered, unwilling to admit that he was concerned about their hostess. She was a strong woman, and he admired that. Miranda and Reissa were more alike than either of the women realized.

Reissa stepped into the gown, threaded her arms through the sleeves, then settled an empathetic gaze on him. "She is a parent, as you are. You would react in a like fashion if Fulton was threatened."

He pulled the tunic over his head, displacing his black locks, and looked at his wife. "Aye," he admitted. "I do not fault her decision, but I do not like it."

"We will collect both and bring them back safely," Reissa announced with a determined glint in her eye.

Viktor frowned. "We?"

"Aye, I *am* going with you."

"The hell you are!" he roared.

"Viktor, she's my friend," Reissa returned, her features expressing her wounded state.

"I care not, you will remain in the manor. I will not allow you in harm's way." He strapped on his sword belt, and his head rose to find that his wife had presented her back, silently requesting that he button her gown.

"You refuse me?" she tested softly.

Deftly, his fingers worked to secure the material at her back. "Rowena will be alarmed by her sister's decision. I will need you to remain and console the girl," he reasoned in a quieter tone.

Her head bowed, obviously taking on the full weight of the situation. "What if Bishop succeeds? What if the siege fails, and he dispatches his army? You could be hurt, or worse."

He turned her to face him and pulled her into his arms. "Crogan and I will not allow such a conclusion."

Chapter 42

As Spectrum climbed the rise on Bishop's lands, his castle slowly entered her vision. The structure was large and foreboding, with high curtain walls and tall stone towers. By now the guard in the portcullis tower would have spotted her approach and sent a man to inform the lord of the manor. It was too late for any regrets, too late to change her mind.

Miranda felt as though there was a stone in the pit of her stomach. She knew her actions were impulsive, perhaps foolishly so, but as she looked upon her neighbor's dwelling, she thought of her son. He was in there. She could almost feel his little body safe within her arms. And that alone spurred her on.

She knew she risked her lands and her life by arriving alone, but they were risks she was willing to take to retrieve her child. She also knew it was impossible to theorize what Bishop's response to her presence would be, but it mattered not. All that mattered was Edwin.

With the reins in her hands, she pulled Spectrum to a halt and simply sat there. For what, she was not certain. Her heart raced, and she could feel her limbs trembling in apprehension, but she would not turn and run. She would face any obstacle she must to see her only child.

The sun was high in the sky and the humidity unforgiving. Perspiration caused her gown to cling to her overheated body, and droplets rolled down the valley between her breasts, but Miranda was unaware of her condition. She was distracted by dread and an unshakable determination.

Unable to help herself, her mind touched on Crogan. Miranda hated leaving the way she had, but it had been necessary. If she had confided her plan, she had no doubt he would have stopped her.

He never would have allowed her to walk into the lion's den alone. What had he thought when he woke to find her gone? Had he sought her out, or sent curses into the heavens?

She did not assume Crogan would find the note she had left behind, but she made it out to his attention because it was his duty to retrieve her son. It was his duty to ensure that Edwin was returned to the Wilkes manor safe and sound.

If Crogan had not ventured to her chamber when he woke to find her gone, then the chambermaid would have found it during her morning routine. At that point in time, the whole of the castle would be aware of her actions.

She shuddered to think of Viktor's response. The man was likely damning her to hell. Rowena would be worried beyond imagination, and she could not guess at her mother's reaction.

They would gather the armies and come after her and Edwin. She was certain of it. Not a soul in her home would allow mother and son to remain in Bishop's clutches for long. The idea of Crogan setting out to retrieve them was not as consoling as she had hoped.

Abruptly, she was stricken by the possibility that he may suffer at the hands of Bishop or his men-at-arms if they failed to surpass the walls. If Bishop refused to give Edwin up at her request, there would be a battle.

Miranda knew Crogan had fought in many battles. And she had been a first-hand witness to his skill during drills; nevertheless, her strength faltered. If he were wounded or killed as a result of her plan, she would never forgive herself.

The sound of grinding metal carried over the land, which announced that the portcullis was being raised. Her eyes settled on the massive gate and saw the proof for herself. Beyond the portcullis, four equestrian riders waited to pass under, clearly intending to greet her. At such a distance, she could not decipher the faces.

Miranda did not delude herself into believing she would receive a pleasant greeting. She expected a troublesome confrontation, but she had every intention of giving in to whatever demands they extended. In fact, as they spurred their mounts into motion, she decided it would be best to dismount, to give the impression that she was willing to submit without a fight.

Her gaze avidly watched their approach. She dared not look away. As they drew nearer, ever so slowly she was able to focus on the details. The shine of their leather boots, the cut of their tunics, finally, the features of their faces.

The lady recognized Bishop first. His unbound raven locks and cobalt-blue eyes were striking in spite of the distance. She was slightly surprised to see him amongst his men. She had not expected him to leave the manor to attend to the matter personally. He wore a smug smile that made her fingers itch to slap it from his face.

Two of the other men were loyal members of his entourage; they had always accompanied his visits to the Wilkes castle. And the fourth man she did not recognize at all. But it did not matter, Bishop was the only man she cared to speak to.

Patiently, she waited for them to rein their horses to a halt. And at long last Bishop stared down at her from the height of his seated position.

"My Lady Wilkes, I have not yet sent for you. Your visit is most unexpected," he purred arrogantly, his eyes glittering.

Miranda crossed her arms under her breasts, feeling the need to shield herself. "I want my son," she stated simply, directly.

"I want your lands," he returned with an arrogant smile. He dismounted and approached.

Miranda forced herself not to retreat. She raised her chin and met his steady gaze without wavering.

"But for now, I want you in my dungeon." He reached for her with impressive speed. Strong arms banded around her petite figure, but she did not struggle.

Curious eyes stared down into her face. "You do not resist?"

"Nay, Bishop. I will not fight you," she confessed quietly. Being held in his arms made her skin crawl with revulsion, but she would not allow her feelings for him to show.

His gaze narrowed suspiciously. "You submit without a fight?"

She nodded. "I just want to see my son."

His smile was positively sinister. A chill swept down her spine. Without warning, he lifted her into his arms and seated her atop his horse. He pulled himself into the saddle behind her and snapped the reins, signaling his mount to leap into action. As they rode toward the castle, she saw his cohorts round up Spectrum and follow in the same direction.

When they passed under the portcullis, the lady was overwhelmed by a stifling feeling. The trepidation that she would not escape those walls before the end of her life beat against the inside of her head, screaming at her to run. She had to force such thoughts from her mind.

She focused on the sound of the hoof beats beneath them, the warm breeze caressing her face. Her eyes lifted to the blue sky overhead. A distant bird flapped its wings, effortlessly carrying itself through the air. The sun was bright; the air was damp.

As she came to the realization that it was a beautiful day, the portcullis lowered at her back, slowly, slowly. After what seemed an eternity, the reverberating sound of the gate closing echoed in her ears and shook her slight figure.

Miranda's gaze scanned the high curtain walls surrounding them. She had willingly entered into a prison. It was strange to know that when she looked at the similar walls of her home, she felt nothing but security. Freedom meant everything, but she was willing to give it up for the welfare of her child.

Bishop dismounted and turned back. He lifted his arms to offer to help her down. Even though she cringed inside, she put her hands on his shoulders and jumped to the ground.

A hand clutched her arm in a biting grip, and he yanked her toward the keep. His stride was so quick that she was forced to run to keep up with him. He guided her through a massive hall crammed with tables full of men, currently feasting on the midday meal.

They were all adorned in Bishop's colors, wordlessly stating that the lady looked upon his army. She felt more and more stares turn in their direction as he weaved toward the rear of the keep, his hold unrelenting. They approached a stairwell leading below. It was dark and dank and offered a musty smell.

He pushed her ahead of him, forcing her to traverse the narrow corridor while he followed closely at her back. She strained her eyes to see through the shadows. Unable to dispatch the weakness and trembling in her limbs, she stumbled on the staircase.

She could have fallen to her death there in the shadows of the stairwell, but an arm circled her waist, catching her weight. He held her until she steadied her stance, then released her.

For a moment she simply stood there, confused by his response. "So, you are not wholly evil, after all, Bishop," she decided out loud.

"I have always been fond of you, my lady. But I find that the greater attraction is your land."

"You do not intend to kill me, then?" Miranda wondered. She held her breath.

He did not hesitate. "Nay. Murder is not part of my plan."

"What is your plan?" It was bold, she knew, but she could not stop herself.

He leaned forward and whispered in her ear, "If I told you, then I *would* have to kill you."

Not amused by his jest, she continued down the staircase without prompt. When they reached the basement level, Miranda peered down a long corridor, not unlike the one in her dream. It continued beyond the light of a solitary torch held in a sconce on the wall. However, this corridor was lined with impenetrable metal doors. Immediately, the thought struck, wondering which door would reveal her imprisoned son.

Aware that her voice would carry down the length of the stone passageway, she opened her mouth and cried, "Edwin!"

A hearty laugh sounded at her back. Miranda spun on her heel to confront Bishop. She clenched her hands into fists and took a step toward him.

"You may scream as you wish, my lady. He will not hear you, and not a soul will come to your aid." He snickered.

"Where is my son?" Miranda's frustration finally superseded her fear. She reacted impulsively rather than logically. A hand curled into his tunic, and her eyes flashed with fury.

"He resides elsewhere," the man admitted. With that, he clutched her wrist and yanked it from his tunic.

"You will take me to him," she ordered as if he were her servant to do her bidding.

Rather than give a response to her command, he continued on down the corridor, with her wrist held in a brutal grip, dragging her with him.

Near the torch, he halted and opened a door on the left. The squeak of the hinges grated on her ears. She was not given the opportunity to gaze into the black space. He pulled her forward, placed a palm on her back, and heaved her into the room.

As she stumbled and fell onto the earth floor, the clang of the door as it swung shut echoed in her ears.

"Bishop!" she cried. Miranda pushed herself to her feet and turned around, but as she did so, she saw there was nothing to see. She had been swallowed up in blackness. There was not a trace of light in the cell.

She took a deep, steadying breath. She had expected precisely this; however, in her plan, she had expected to be held in the same cell as her son. The cruel bastard. Her knowledge of Edwin was no greater than it had been in the security of her own home.

Widow Wilkes

A shrill cry echoed throughout the small chamber.

Chapter 43

Miranda sighed. It was impossible to determine how long she had been held captive in Bishop's dungeon. For lack of options, she had searched the whole of the little room. It was completely empty, with the exception of a chamber pot. There were no windows and no furniture; however, she did stumble upon a row of shackles embedded in the far wall, across from the door. Each set was held in place by chains, enough to secure five adults in the space she estimated was fifteen by fifteen feet in size.

She sat with her back braced against the stone wall, knees pulled up to her chest, cheek resting on her knees. Her plan had been a complete failure. Not only was she not able to protect her son; she didn't even know if he was safe.

It was possible Bishop had shipped Edwin off to another one of his properties. The man had said that murder was not a part of his plan, but that could have been a lie. What if he had Edwin dispatched? The idea was too disturbing to entertain.

The lady wanted to cry, but her eyes remained dry. Once again, she could do nothing but wait for Bishop's next move. It was an incredibly frustrating situation, but, miraculously, her patience held out.

Eventually, she began to doze, and her limbs grew lax, causing her to jerk awake when she teetered and nearly fell over. Finally, giving in to her fatigue, she lay down on the cool earth and allowed sleep to carry her away.

The noise of creaking hinges intruded upon her slumber.

She blinked open her eyes. A minute amount of light poured in from the corridor, but what allowed her to see that Bishop stood there was the candle in his hand. In the other, he held a tankard.

Miranda sat up and rubbed the sleep away as he moved into the room. He knelt before her and placed the brass candle holder on the floor near her feet. Then he offered the tankard to her.

She looked at it, trying to decide if he meant to poison her.

"'Tis water, my lady. Drink," he prodded gently.

Tentatively, she took the tankard from him. She stared down into the clear liquid. She was parched, and for some reason, she believed he did not yet mean to kill her. Finally, she held the tankard to her lips and drank a sip. When she was able to taste the truth that it was just water, she tipped her head back and swallowed the remainder of its contents.

Bishop took the tankard from her and placed it near the candle. Without warning he grabbed her wrist.

"Bishop?" she asked fearfully.

He pulled her into a standing position and pushed her back toward the wall. When the cool stone bit into her flesh, she watched, helplessly, as he pressed a slender wrist into one of the shackles and secured it.

"You have imprisoned me in your dungeon. Why must you imprison me within the chamber?" Miranda requested, observing as he clamped the other wrist into the round metal cuff near her shoulder.

He stepped back and gazed at her. "You will learn the answer to that in time."

With that, he spun on his heel and exited the room. The sharp clang of the door shutting in his wake caused her to snap her eyes shut, her hope quashed. He may have shackled her to the wall, but he had also left the burning candle behind. She was grateful for that small gift. At least she was not cloaked in blackness any longer.

She stared at her prison. Perhaps the blackness had been better after all. She was surrounded by stone and emptiness. The illumination only reminded her that she had clearly made a terrible mistake.

A lonely tear formed and slid down her cheek.

***

Crogan was certain the element of surprise was not in their favor. Once Bishop had Miranda in his clutches, he would anticipate an attack. So, the armies marched toward their neighbor's castle, prepared to approach and siege without hesitation. Hundreds of men were accompanied by war horses. But hundreds more were foot soldiers, which, unfortunately, slowed their travel time considerably. They would not reach their destination until well after nightfall.

Crogan was unaware when Miranda had slipped from his bed, so he could not estimate how much of a head start she had.

Whatever the case, one minute with Bishop was too long, as far as he was concerned.

Alfred rode at his left, and Viktor and Brodie were at his right. All four men had said little since leaving the Wilkes castle behind. At that point, what could they say? All of them were worried for mother and son, but Crogan felt real fear for the first time since finding Dana's broken body in his stairwell. And he was loath to admit it, even to himself, but his fear for Miranda was magnified tenfold in comparison to what he felt when he heard Dana's cry as she slipped to her death.

He could not guess at Bishop's capabilities, and that was terrifying. Miranda might have been at the mercy of a madman, or a man without morals. He may not have any qualms about hurting her.

He glanced down at his hands as they held his mount's reins. They were clenched into fists so tight that his knuckles were white.

Crogan drew the back of a palm across his brow, wiping away perspiration. The sun was high in the sky overhead, and the day was stifling. Their slow journey weighed upon his frayed nerves. He just wanted to get there and find Miranda and Edwin.

He simply wanted to hold her in his arms and know she was safe, but it would be beneficial for them to attack after the sun sank below the horizon. Without direct rays of sunlight and the suffocating heat, his men would be invigorated, and he needed them to be in top form when they fought to surpass Bishop's curtain walls.

Alfred cleared his throat. "I wouldst speak with Henry. I will return." With that, he broke away from their party and journeyed back toward the mass of armored knights trailing behind them.

Crogan scanned the crowd of experienced warriors. Every last one of them was adept with a sword. The knowledge should have been a comfort to the Scotsman, but it did nothing to calm his racing heart.

His eyes returned to the lush hills stretching out for miles in front of them. "We are moving too slowly," he voiced his frustration aloud.

Several moments of ponderous silence followed.

"Miranda will endure, Adair," Viktor assured, addressing the heart of the matter. "Mentally, she is stronger than our two minds combined."

Crogan's lips thinned. "I will not argue that token. But, physically, she is weaker."

"The woman has a quick wit. She will survive."

"I agree with Viktor. She is an extraordinary woman. Ye need not concern yourself with unwarranted fear, Crogan," Brodie added.

The Scotsman nodded. His cousin and the Englishman were rather perceptive; he should trust in their opinions.

The three leaders continued on, pensive.

Finally, Viktor spoke, but his voice was tentative. "Do you wish to discuss it?"

"To what do ye refer, Colville?"

Black eyes turned to look directly at him. "The lady."

"Ye see all there is to see, Colville." He could not deny that the Englishman was well aware of everything that occurred around him.

"I see a man who has progressed beyond the role of protector."

"An' ye see a man who is betrothed," Crogan unhappily pointed out.

"You have overstepped your bounds," Colville stated, clearly feeling the need to step into the role of guardian for Lady Wilkes.

Crogan was caught off guard by Viktor's need to play sentry over Miranda, but he shouldn't have been. Her father had passed. She was unmarried, and vulnerable to the charm of the Scotsman, well, himself, in this case. And he was honor-bound to wed another. Viktor was too perceptive by far, and it was likely he had stepped into the role of her protector without thinking twice.

Crogan felt an immediate need to defend himself and take the offense on her behalf, but at the same time, he knew the man was right. He never should have allowed himself to harbor feelings for her. But that choice had been out of his hands. He tried to deny her, but it had been impossible to do so.

"Aye, I have," he confessed in a monotone.

"You will depart when we have returned the lady and her son to the manor?" It was presented as a question, but his tone was commanding.

A heavy sigh hung in the air. Crogan resented him for it, but Viktor was right once again. He could not remain in the manor once he had fulfilled the king's task. He needed to return to his own life; he could no longer be a part of Miranda's.

The words were but a whisper: "Aye, I will."

Chapter 44

Miranda's legs ached from standing. She had tried stretching them and leaned against the wall to offer a different position, but her confinement was taking its toll on her slender limbs. And her arms had been on fire from holding them up for far too long. Unwillingly, she was forced to let them drop, causing her wrists to bear the weight.

The shackles were loose, but not loose enough. Metal bit into the fleshy part of her palms, and her wrists were badly bruised from her movement.

Refusing to acknowledge her physical pain and give in to her helplessness, she began to hum. When her humming grew weak, she opened up her mouth and sang, giving herself up to it. She sang Edwin's lullaby. For a moment, she returned to the woods on her property; she returned to that evening when she had lost herself. Crogan had found her. And they had shared their first kiss.

Would she ever see Crogan again? Would she ever see her son again? Would she survive to see the sunlight overhead, hear the birds in the trees, feel the wind upon her face? The questions renewed the melody in her soul.

Her soft voice echoed throughout the room, bouncing off the stone walls of her prison. Her eyes closed, resting, though she knew she could not sleep.

Somewhere inside of her, an inner clock ticked away, creating an instinctual feeling that night had fallen. Perhaps it had fallen long ago. She still could not determine how long she had been held at Bishop's mercy. But for some reason, she decided the moon must be hanging in the sky.

Was it raining, or were the stars twinkling brightly for all to see?

Without warning, the heavy metal door creaked on its hinges. Her breath caught, cutting off the song.

She stared at the door as it swung open. A figure appeared in the candlelight, and her heart burst with joy.

Victory!

Alfred walked into the room. His face was expressionless as dark eyes settled on her. Miranda breathed a great sigh of relief. The armies had surpassed the walls; they had taken control of the castle's defenses. They had triumphed. At last, she would have the freedom to search for her son.

"Alfred, thank you Lord—" Once again, her voice halted, distracted as Bishop followed her captain into the dungeon.

Her brow furrowed, utterly confused by this unexpected turn of events. Then she realized the meaning. They had not won the battle; they had fallen prey to Bishop's force of men-at-arms. They had lost the battle, and the victor had taken prisoners.

Had Crogan been hurt?! Killed?! Her mind screamed the possibilities.

She stared, with her heart hammering in her chest, waiting for Bishop to force Alfred into the shackles beside her on the wall.

But Alfred drew to a halt, and Bishop stood at his side. The pair gazed at her.

It was then that she put a halt to her thoughts and surveyed the men standing before her. Bishop had not shackled her captain to the wall. He moved about of his own volition; there was no weapon threatening at his back.

Once again, her brow creased into crisp, confused lines.

"I do not understand," she whispered, feeling her heart break. It seemed as though a knife twisted in her gut.

"I am truly sorry, Miranda," Alfred spoke quietly, confirming her worst fears.

"Alfred," the lady choked on her disbelief. "What have you done?"

Bishop began to grin. But her eyes remained on the tall dark man who had been the leader of her army for many, many years.

There was a soft light of regret in his eyes.

True comprehension slapped her in the face, and a grunt of horror slipped past her lips.

"Alfred?" she demanded as tears began to blur her vision. There were no thoughts of holding them back. The lady allowed the moisture to stream down her cheeks, unchecked, too stunned by his betrayal to care. "You have joined forces with this criminal?"

"I have simply looked after my own interests, Miranda."

Her mouth fell open for a moment. "Your own interests?" Her voice was raspy with emotion. "Your interests include playing a part in my son's abduction?"

"Allow me to explain the man's interests." A new voice sounded in the corridor, causing Miranda's gaze to shift.

That voice.

She knew that voice…

A tall, lean figure stepped into the room. The man approached, and Miranda blinked, certain her eyes deceived her.

It was not possible.

Alfred's betrayal had caused her mind to topple, to create some form of dementia. Black spots fluttered in her vision, forcing her to blink more rapidly. For many moments, Miranda thought she might swoon.

A sinister laugh she remembered all too well gave her the strength to fight the faint that had nearly overwhelmed her. She clawed for her strength, held her legs steady, and raised her eyes to the man who had made her a widow three years ago.

"Gerald."

"Greetings, Wife," he drawled, stepping closer, blocking out her view of Alfred and Bishop. "I am loath to admit it, but you are looking rather well."

Her thoughts were still too perplexed by his abrupt return from the dead to acknowledge his flimsy compliment. Speech failed her as she took in the sight.

He had aged only slightly. The man still presented a striking figure. Teal eyes burned with brilliant color, and his shock of white-blond curls were neatly combed back. As he had always catered to his vanity, his jaw was clean-shaven, his black tunic tailored immaculately. The lines around his eyes and mouth were more pronounced, but they only proved to make him more distinguished, certainly not old. Absently, she did the math. On that day, he was four and thirty years of age.

After the blow of Alfred's betrayal and the disbelief of seeing her husband alive and well after three long years, it was miraculous that she was able to find a firm voice. "And you look to still be alive."

"Have not lost that quick wit, I see," he mocked dryly.

At last, Miranda realized why Bishop had put her in the shackles. He knew that learning her husband was still alive would inspire a violent response. And he had not been wrong. She wanted to lurch forward with claws bared and beat Gerald to a bloody pulp. She wanted to put him back into that watery grave she believed he had sunk into ages ago.

His eyes narrowed upon her. "I do not recall ever witnessing your tempestuous nature transform into violence, Miranda. You wish to hurt me?" He moved forward but remained inches from her reach, openly taunting her.

Miranda refused to bite. She simply stood there, raising her chin in defiance.

"Your husband is alive, Miranda; you should be overjoyed to see me," he ordered, pressing his palms to the stone wall beside her shoulders. He leaned close; she could feel his breath on her face.

With the wall at her back, she could not retreat, even though she desperately longed to. The unnerved lady gazed up into eyes she had thought she would only ever see in her nightmares.

"Welcome my return properly," he ordered, bringing his mouth to within inches of hers.

Miranda heaved in a breath, then reacted to instinct rather than logic. She pursed her lips together and spit in his face.

He stumbled back, clearly disgusted by her action. Callused fingers wiped the spittle from his cheek. Gerald looked at her, his gaze smoldering. She saw his arm rise and squeezed her eyes shut.

The blow was devastating. The force turned her head. For an instant, her eyes watered, and her cheekbone felt as though it had been split open. The resounding throb worked through her skull swiftly, then ebbed away into an ache.

When she had regained herself, she managed to drag her head back to stare at him. He simply stood there glaring, simmering in his fury.

"I do not welcome your return," she confessed boldly. Not once in all the years they had been married had he ever raised his hand to her in such a brutal fashion. He had claimed his rights to her body, but he had never struck her.

Much had changed. But much had stayed the same.

He scowled. "Clearly."

Miranda's gaze continued to move over him, unable to understand the circumstances. She wanted answers.

"I attended your funeral, Gerald."

The scowl swiftly transformed into a self-righteous grin. He retreated several steps and took up a stance beside Bishop. "Aye, that you did." With that, he turned to the man at his right. "You may go."

Miranda observed, startled that Gerald had so easily dismissed Bishop. The short statement announced the truth that her husband was the man in charge. When her neighbor merely gazed back for a moment, then exited without a word, she saw the truth of her assumption.

Gerald was the mastermind behind the plot to abduct her son. *His son.* Bishop was merely a pawn in whatever game he was playing. And she suspected Alfred was as well.

Her eyes shifted to the captain. Their gazes locked. His face was set in taut lines, obviously uncomfortable with the situation but willing to go along with it despite his feelings to the contrary. Why?

She opened her mouth to voice the question aloud, but Gerald spoke up, "Let us go, Alfred." His eyes remained on his wife. "We have business to tend to."

A shiver shook her spine. What business was he referring to?

With that, the pair quit the room.

Once again, she was left alone.

Plagued with more questions than ever.

***

Crogan looked on from his distant place outside Bishop's castle. Night was upon them, but the massive stone structure was aglow with burning torches. The sky overhead was clear; the moon shone brightly, lighting their way across endless green fields.

Aware of their impending arrival, the battlements were loaded with men-at-arms, watching, waiting, preparing for the enemy to siege.

His gaze turned to his right. Viktor sat on his mount, appearing confident, determined. Then they turned to his left. Brodie also appeared ready to act on a moment's notice. He noticed Henry had moved up abreast of his cousin.

"Henry," Crogan addressed, "where is your captain?"

"My lord?" With the helmet guard raised, he was able to see the knight's confused expression.

"Alfred did not speak with ye earlier?" he wondered, a feeling of unease fluttering in the pit of his gut.

"Nay, I have not seen him."

Crogan's jaw clenched. His gaze shifted to Viktor. Were they both thinking the same thing?

"A traitor?" Colville tested.

"But why?"

"That I cannot answer," the younger man replied.

"Perhaps there is a logical explanation for his disappearance," Crogan offered, not wanting to believe that Alfred may have played a part in Edwin's abduction.

"Perhaps there is not," Brodie added. "A man inside. 'Twould explain the ease of her son's disappearance."

"Aye," Viktor agreed.

"'Twould also explain Miranda's odd feeling of being watched," Brodie mentioned.

Crogan's eyes narrowed upon his cousin, silently demanding answers.

"I have not spoken of it previously, but one evening, the lass rushed into the hall. When she saw me en route to Winny's private quarters, she believed I had been observing her in her chamber."

"Ye were dallying with the lady's maid?" Crogan inquired.

"Aye," Brodie admitted. "I dismissed the charge, believing the lass was merely fatigued. But if Alfred is involved, he could have been watching her. It may not have been a figment of her imagination a'tall."

Crogan growled deep in his throat. "I will kill him myself."

"Let us not rush to pass judgment," Viktor moderated. "If Bishop installed a man in the castle to abduct the boy, it could have been another one of his men. We cannot be certain 'twas Alfred."

Crogan nodded. Viktor was right. They were simply speculating at that point, and to do so would not aid their cause in retrieving Miranda and Edwin. An intense battle loomed before them. But his men were ready and waiting. All they needed was one word from their leader to act.

Their plan was already in place. A large group of men would feverishly work to undermine a section of the north wall. It was there that they would seek entrance to the bailey. Of course, Bishop's men would retaliate with cauldrons of boiling hot water and other various weapons to ward off their efforts. But Crogan would have men posted on the hill far beyond the curtain walls, prepared with bows and arrows to pick off any soldiers bent on quashing the undermining. It was dangerous, and it was likely that many men would be lost, but such were the spoils of war.

Crogan anticipated hand-to-hand combat once they claimed their entrance to the bailey. But that was simply another obstacle he intended to overcome. His men were skilled, as was Miranda's army. They would arise victorious; he could not conceive of it any other way.

All in all, it could take hours to surpass the curtain walls, possibly days, so he would not waste another moment in thought.

He pulled his sword from its scabbard and raised it in the air, sending a signal to all. "Attack!"

Chapter 45

For the second time that evening, the heavy door of her prison creaked open. Miranda raised her head. Alfred entered, carrying another candle. For a moment, she was grateful. The one Bishop had left hours ago had nearly burned down to nothing. But as she observed him kneel to replace the old with the new, she was reminded that her trust in him had been cruelly betrayed. He was no longer the man she could confide in, no longer the man she would turn to for counsel.

He stood to his full height, and their gazes locked.

Once again, she felt tears rising to choke her. "Why, Alfred? I must know."

The regret returned to the depths of his black eyes. He glanced at the cylinder of wax in his hands. He had blown it out, but she knew it must be hot on his skin.

"I am in love with Rowena."

His words only caused more confusion. "How does your love for my sister relate to my son's abduction?"

Finally, he lifted his head and stared directly at her. "Your death is a part of Gerald's plan."

Miranda felt as though he had struck her. Her knees grew weak; her breath stalled. The world seemed to tilt.

Alfred quickly stepped forward, clearly intending to catch her swoon. But his movement renewed her strength. She blinked the terror away and drilled him with a glare.

"Go on," she ordered angrily.

"Your death will drive a grief-stricken Rowena into my arms, where she belongs," he explained his twisted reasoning.

Miranda took a deep breath as his confession registered in her thoughts. "I was such a fool to trust in you." At last, she understood what he had meant by declaring that he intended to look after his own interests. Those interests included her sister.

"You would have never condoned a marriage," he charged.

A tear streaked down her cheek. "You are wrong, Alfred."

He threw the candle aside in a fit of rage. "You lie!"

"I was merely waiting for you to ask for her hand. It would have been her choice to make, but I would have given you both my heartfelt blessing to wed." What she spoke was true. She had consented to his love for her sister all along, but she had not made her thoughts known.

"Your death is upon the horizon. You are simply speaking that which I long to hear." He pointed a finger at her. "Well, I will not hear more!" With that, the traitor turned toward the door.

"Alfred, please," she implored, appealing to his human nature.

He stalled, clearly affected by the sorrow he heard in her tone.

"I trusted in you. Believed in you. We do not share blood, but you are my family. 'Tis time to make a second choice. Please, Alfred, my life is in your hands."

His head shook, denying her words, then he stormed from the room, slamming the door so hard, she could feel it in the stone wall at her back.

For an instant, it appeared as though she was getting through to him. Was it possible he was angry with himself, and not with her? In the end, she decided it was simply a hopeful imagination searching for Alfred's redemption.

Miranda allowed her sobs to break. She gave in to the need to cleanse herself of her fear. Alfred revealed Gerald's plot to murder her. Would he take it upon himself to kill her? Or would he delegate the task to another? Whenever that man came to dispatch her, she needed to be strong.

What would become of her son, her sister, her mother? It was not herself she despaired for—it was them.

Crogan, she cried silently, *hear me. I need you.*

***

Two hours passed, but in Miranda's mind, it seemed like two days. Her prison opened, and men filed in, filling up the space of the little chamber. As she stared at the faces, she realized every last one was familiar to her. Several members of the army had deserted following Gerald's death, and all of them stood before her now.

Her husband wandered in, his stride casual. He stopped before her, his expression cold.

"You seek my death at last?" she asked.

An eyebrow raised curiously. "Alfred has revealed my ultimate goal?"

She simply stared back, neither confirming nor denying his question. Hate flowed through her veins.

He shrugged. "It matters not. You are my wife, and as such, I feel I owe you an explanation of my choices."

Did he expect her to be grateful to him? She just continued to stare, her stone mask firmly in place.

"Ask what you wish, Miranda. I will answer all." He paused, and a malicious glint entered his eyes. "Then I will dispatch you."

Truly frightened by his admission, she swallowed over a lump of fear in her throat. Unwilling to give in without a fight, yet ultimately hindered by the shackles, she realized she needed to keep him talking for as long as possible.

She repeated the statement she had voiced earlier. "I attended your funeral, Gerald. How do you stand here, alive and well?"

He held a finger up, and his brows rose. "You attended *a funeral*, Miranda, not *my funeral*."

"Excuse me?"

"'Twould be best to start at the beginning." He began to pace in front of her. "I despised our marriage." The man paused and glared at her. "I despised you, Miranda."

With that, he continued his pacing. "I was not prepared to commit murder, but I did not desire to be married any longer. So, I enlisted the aid of my most trusted men." His lean frame halted, and his arms stretched out wide, referring to the room full of familiar faces. "These men."

He took a hiatus from his tale and looked at the men-at-arms. "You have aided the illustration of my point. Thank you all; you may go."

She observed with growing apprehension as the men filed from the room. For some reason, being left alone with her husband was more alarming than being watched by a handful of betrayers.

Finally, he turned back to her. A chill swept down her spine as his gaze settled on her face. "I formulated a plan to escape my life." The words were spoken so lightly that he could have been discussing the choice of the evening meal.

Miranda recalled the day they learned of Gerald's murder. "The messenger who brought word of your death, what of him?"

"Paid a mighty sum to deliver a lie," he returned with a grin on his handsome face.

She felt her fingers itch to slap it from him.

Images of the funeral returned with full force. Miranda, Edwin, Rowena, Alfred, and the whole of the army watched the hemp raft float into the open sea. Flames roared, biting at the structure carrying Gerald's body. No, it had not been his body after all. The man she watched sink into a watery grave had been masked in a velvet bag, as was typical for the Wilkes family burials.

She had simply assumed the body had been her husband's. She never questioned it, never thought to be suspicious of his death. The men who had deserted the army were the same men who had attended to Gerald's body for burial. Why had she not put those two facts together and questioned it? How could she have been so blind?

"We sent a man to a watery grave, Gerald. Who was he?"

He shrugged again. "A vagabond living on the streets of London. He was not to be missed."

Miranda let out a slow breath, stunned by his words. "You were not prepared to take on my murder, but you were willing to murder a complete stranger? I fail to understand your logic."

"A vagabond would not be missed; the titled wife of a wealthy man would be."

It was the lady's turn to scowl. "He could have had family, friends."

"'Tis done," his voice was clipped, dismissive.

She took a moment to send a prayer into the heavens for the stranger her husband had used in his fake death plot. Then her thoughts returned to the captain. "Alfred was not a part of your demonstration."

"Alfred was not initially included in my escape. He also believed I had been murdered by a highwayman. I approached him a year ago, determined to win him over by any means necessary. During our hours of conversation, it became clear that he harbors feelings for your sister. I knew that was the mark that would gain his support. He agreed, albeit reluctantly, but he agreed, nevertheless. The man is not comfortable with the knowledge of your imminent death, but his feelings for Rowena rule his judgment.

"I needed him. I needed an ally in the castle, someone who could provide the concealment of my entrance without others' knowledge of it."

Miranda's gaze narrowed as understanding dawned. "'Twas you? You abducted my son. You watched me from the shadows. You who combed through my quarters."

He nodded, a licentious smile lifting the corners of his mouth. "I also watched your stunning display by the pond. Rather out of character for you, Miranda, I must admit."

She gasped.

"I attribute it to the presence of that Scotsman you have allowed into my home." He moved closer, his handsome face set in lines of fury.

A hand rose to gently touch her mouth. "It is obvious to me he has known you intimately. Kissed these lips." Abruptly, he clutched her jaw and lifted her head, forcing her to meet his hard stare. "You are *mine,* Miranda. Another does not own the right to spread those pretty legs of yours."

He let go and took a step back, his eyes moving over her in a scathing fashion. "Now I may address you as the whore you are."

Her grin held no humor. "'Twas a pleasure to be his whore. 'Twas not a pleasure to be your wife."

Gerald stared at her. "Rather bold for a woman whose life grows shorter with each minute."

"I have nothing to lose."

A single blond brow arched. "Touché, my dear."

Miranda tilted her head as more questions arose within. "What part does Bishop play in your plot?"

"Bishop was merely the face. I was thought to be dead. I could not arrive and give cause for you to believe I intended to abduct my own son. Bishop was promised the holding in return for his aid."

"I do not believe for a moment that you intend to relinquish the holding to him," She stated.

"You may trust that he is not a concern."

Another shiver coursed down her spine. "You intend to dispatch him as well," she realized.

"The man is dead," he stated casually.

Miranda nearly choked on her gasp. Bishop was dead, merely another loose end that had needed to be tied off. It seemed to be a foregone conclusion that her actions would result in a siege. It would be simple to explain away Bishop's death as a result of battle.

Her husband was truly a concentration of evil. "Will you murder Alfred as well?"

"Nay, I need him to continue on as guardian of the manor. The king believes I am dead. Edwin will turn of age and take ownership of the holding, and I will continue on in silence, making my rulings behind the scenes. I desire a return to the life I abandoned, but my death has created unfortunate obstacles."

Another concern claimed her. "And what of my sister? She will not abide it."

He crossed his arms over his chest. "Admittedly, she is the wild card here. I cannot explain away her death as easily as Bishop's. I know she is in the safety of the Wilkes castle walls, currently out of my reach. She must be looked after. She cannot relate the truth that I have created the ruse of my death."

"You will imprison her?"

"If necessary, aye. 'Twill be done."

"You bastard," she whispered, unable to contain herself. Each reveal only added to her frustration, her fear, her fury. If she were free of her shackles, she knew without a doubt she would seek his death.

"Not wholly the bastard you believe me to be. You may go to your grave with the knowledge that I have not harmed our son in any fashion."

"The blood did not belong to him?"

"Nay." He pulled up the sleeve of his black tunic, revealing a healing wound. "'Twas mine. He has been well cared for."

She was able to breathe one sigh of relief. All her days of worry over his health had been for naught. Her son was fine. With that weight lifted from her shoulders, the weight of her impending death became more real. And she was running out of questions. He had explained his plot. So, she quickly searched her mind for others, needing to buy herself more time.

"Do you love him, Gerald?"

His brow furrowed in confusion. "He is my son."

"You never showed him the attention he required from a father."

"A boy does not need to be coddled, Miranda. He must be strong. He must grow into a man."

"You have not answered my question."

He grunted angrily. "I see your ploy to delay your death, Miranda. I have explained all, and time grows short. The siege has already begun."

"Crogan?"

He nodded curtly.

She felt a bud of hope. He had come for her.

He reached for a piece of rope that had been tied around his waist. Miranda had been too distracted by his story to take notice. He also wore his sword belt, with his sword tucked away in the scabbard.

Her hope transformed into panic.

The lean figure moved forward. For a moment, he simply gazed at her. It seemed as though he was feeding off the fear she could no longer hide.

A hand rose to touch her. His fingertip traced over the bruise on her cheek. "Before this day, I have never raised a hand to you in anger."

"And now you intend to murder me," she said quietly, her voice slightly unsteady. "Why must you see my death?"

His expression grew icy. "I do not have any use for a wife."

Her thoughts were running wild. She was desperate. "I could take Edwin; we could leave; you would never have to see us again."

"I will not allow you to take my son."

"Halt, Gerald," she heard Alfred's voice as he moved into the cell without warning.

Gerald turned, puzzled.

"I cannot allow you to take the lady's life."

Instantly, Miranda's eyes shone brightly with forgiveness. He was not able to go through with it after all. Her earlier words had slipped into his heart and found the good man she knew resided within.

"You jest." Her husband breathed, unprepared for defection.

"I do not." A hand moved to rest on the hilt of his sword, causing action to speak louder than words.

Gerald tossed the rope aside and withdrew his sword from its scabbard. "Are you prepared to defend her life with your own, Coombs?"

Alfred's eyes glanced in her direction. He clearly read her unease in the expression on her face. His gaze shifted, and he squared his shoulders. "I am."

Miranda opened her mouth to stop him, but then an image of Edwin passed before her eyes. She could not only think of herself; she had a child to consider. Nevertheless, she spoke up, knowing her conscience would not abide it if she simply stood by and watched while he selflessly risked his life for hers.

"Alfred, you do not have to do this. I forgive your betrayal; I must attend to my own battles."

"Listen to the wench," Gerald ordered.

He responded without meeting her gaze. "I have brought this upon myself, my lady. I must set the circumstances right." With that, he pulled his weapon and held it up, signaling that he was ready to follow up his decision with action.

"Very well," Wilkes sighed. Abruptly, he lurched forward and thrust his sword toward Alfred, but the experienced captain easily side-stepped and retaliated in kind. Gerald managed to avoid the cut of the blade.

Miranda had witnessed numerous drills—she was no stranger to the art of war—but to see these men facing off with the blatant intent to inflict real harm weakened her resolve to stay strong. She wanted to scream for Alfred to watch out, but she dared not voice her concerns, afraid that speaking up would prove to be a deadly distraction.

So, she viewed them, mute, sucking in her breath every time Gerald nearly opened Alfred's flesh.

In an open bailey, both would have moved gracefully—their footwork had always been impeccable—but in the dungeon, the confined space hindered their efforts. Sword tips glanced off the stone walls, creating a show of sparks, accompanied by an awful grating noise that caused Miranda to cringe inwardly. And they were mindful of the walls looming at their backs. One would quickly dash to the right or the left in order to gain distance from the solid structure of the room.

As the minutes stretched, she heard their exerted breath between the clang of their swords as they attacked and defended. Neither man had gained a substantial offense. Their skills were perfectly matched.

Gerald must have continued his routine of swordplay during his long absence, because he did not falter and did not tire. And he was slightly smaller in terms of muscle mass, which she felt gave Alfred a distinct advantage over his opponent. But she was not witness to a sliver of advantage on either side as they continued to cross one another.

Finally, when she believed their battle would last forever, Alfred took a misstep, bringing him too close to the wall. He lifted his sword to block one of Gerald's thrusts, but the obstruction caused his timing to fail.

Miranda gasped as Gerald's blade sank deeply into his flesh. Her husband gave a triumphant grin and yanked his sword from the gaping wound in Alfred's belly.

The captain's black eyes turned down at the blood oozing from the wound, aghast. His sword fell uselessly to the dirt. He dropped to his knees, ineffectually clutching his stomach.

Tears welled in Miranda's eyes in an instant. "Nay," she whispered, unable to believe that her husband rose victorious.

Alfred looked at her, his gaze imploring. "I have failed you."

"In my eyes, you have found redemption," was all she could say as she sobbed openly.

The light of life flickered in the depths of those black windows to the soul, and then unconsciousness claimed him. He slumped forward, creating a horrifying thump. His body simply lay there, face down, blood slowly seeping onto the dirt floor.

"Oh, nay!" Miranda cried, unable to deny the sorrow and regret that overwhelmed her.

"Bloody fool," Gerald growled as he glowered down at the captain. He spared only a moment, then his gaze eerily rose and settled on her.

Miranda knew her time had run out. Terror washed over her. Gerald dropped his sword. Without searching the floor with his eyes, he knelt down and picked up the rope he had discarded when Alfred interrupted his sinister intentions.

He stepped forward.

She watched as a hand moved to one shackle and released it. Her eyes swung back to his face. He was going to give her a fighting chance. But she could not be grateful for it. He was taller and stronger. She did not have any hope to match him in a struggle for her life.

The second wrist was released. She was free. But he stood before her. Waiting, watching for her to make a move.

"One day you will burn in hell, Gerald."

"Not on this day."

With that, she made a dash to the left, praying her speed would not match his. But he was able to catch the swinging plait of her hair, and he gave it a hard yank. She was lurched painfully backward, thrown off balance and falling on the compacted dirt. Her lungs gave a rush of air from the impact. In a flash, he was upon his knees, moving to straddle her waist.

She looked up into his determined eyes, and as he wound the rope around his hands for better leverage to use against her, she let out an ear-piercing scream.

He leaned forward and pressed his fists to the ground on either side of her neck. The rope was stretched across her throat, cutting off the scream and her ability to breathe.

More tears formed in her eyes and rolled back into the hair above her ears. Her legs kicked uselessly as she bucked against his relentless weight. Her hands lifted up to his face, and she raked her nails down his cheeks, drawing deep ribbons of blood.

He cursed violently, but he refused to relinquish his hold on the rope. The bastard simply locked his arms straight, so his face was beyond her reach.

Her desperate efforts to breathe in air and offer the relief she needed were unobtainable. The lack of oxygen was beginning to take its toll. Lights danced in her vision. She was growing too weak to fight. And even though she refused to give up, she felt that death was near.

Chapter 46

Crogan drove his sword into the kinks of another stranger's armor, killing him instantly. They had surpassed Bishop's walls with little loss of human life, at least little loss of the men in his and Miranda's armies. Now they were battling the men-at-arms in the bailey. Ever so slowly, he was making progress toward the entrance to the keep. He was drawing closer to Miranda.

He ignored the truth that he had taken yet another man's life; he ignored the blood that sprayed from the wound onto his armor. He had one goal, and that was to find Miranda. Nothing would be allowed to stand in his way, and he would strike down any man who dared to do so.

Brodie and Viktor were in the vicinity, their swords blazing with the blood of fallen knights. They were as vigilant as Crogan, striving to reach the manor interior, concerned for mother and son.

The trio cut down the enemy's army without remorse. There was no room for it when defending one's own life and when determined to save others in congress.

The hours wore on, and, ever so slowly, Bishop's army grew weak, and their numbers dwindled. It was midday, and the sun was shining brightly upon them. The light of day revealed that the bailey was littered with bodies and stained crimson with blood. But Bishop's army was relentless; they fought to the death. Surrender was clearly not an option for them.

Crogan glanced around him. Everywhere he saw men continuing to fight. They had not secured a victory yet. Men continued to come at him, but his strength held up. He cut them down, one after another.

Finally, Crogan saw an opening to dash into the keep, and he did not hesitate to take it. His massive frame pushed through the heavy double doors. His gaze scanned the spacious hall, desperately searching for the sight of gray eyes and raven curls.

A grunt sounded behind him. He turned in time to see Viktor thrusting his sword into the armor of a man who had intended to attack at Crogan's back.

The knight slid off the bloody sword and fell in a heap at Viktor's feet. They did not spare the dead man a glance. Crogan sent his companion a curt nod of thanks, and they rushed into the hall.

Both men slowed as the sight of Bishop's corpse appeared, sprawled out on one of the trestle tables. His throat had been slit. Sticky, blackened liquid pooled around his neck and head, announcing that he had been dead for quite some time.

Crogan removed his helmet and tossed it aside. They exchanged a perplexed glance.

"Miranda?" Viktor wondered, referring to Bishop's state.

"'Tis possible. But if not her doing, then who?"

Two of Bishop's men-at-arms charged into the keep, intent on dispatching the intruders.

Viktor followed their approach with his eyes and braced himself for the onslaught of battle. "Go, Adair. Find them." When his companion hesitated, unwilling to leave a man behind, the Englishman shouted, "Now!"

He knew Viktor was right. He moved toward the rear of the keep, certain there must be a stairway to the basement somewhere. After giving it careful consideration during their journey to Bishop's holding the previous morning, Crogan had decided it would be logical to check the dungeon first. That was where prisoners were held, and that was likely where Edwin and Miranda would be. Bishop would treat them as hostages, used simply to barter for his greed.

After seeing Bishop's lifeless form, he was uncertain of the situation, but rather than wander around in confusion, he stuck to his original plan.

A scream sounded in the distance, then abruptly cut off. It was a primal, terrified shriek that penetrated his defenses.

At once Crogan knew it to be Miranda. The pitch could only be hers. And the feeling of dread in his stomach was no mistake.

With jerky movements, his head turned, seeking the origin of the scream. He spotted the darkened shadow of a stairwell near the kitchen entrance and immediately broke into a dash for the lower level.

A single torch lit the passageway, but it was easy to see that only one door stood open. As he flew down the space, he began to fear what he might find.

If she had been hurt… He could not finish the thought. He would not allow himself to think it.

Crogan turned the corner and met with a sight that stopped his heart.

***

Miranda felt blackness closing in. She was slipping away from herself and into a realm of unknown.

Then Crogan's voice sounded in her imagination. It seemed so far away. It could not be real.

She vaguely felt the rope lift away from her throat as Gerald jumped up to confront their unexpected guest. Instinctually, air flooded into her lungs, and she gasped, heaving, fighting for more.

"Miranda!" Crogan's voice sounded again, followed by the familiar noise of swords clanging together.

She blinked against the blackness while sucking in breath after breath. Thoughtlessly, she rolled over onto her stomach and clutched at the earthen floor.

Light began to filter through, allowing her to see the flickering of the candle not a foot from her head. She stared at the flame as her breath labored. For a moment, she lay there, regaining herself, regaining the life that had nearly been extinguished. Her throat burned and throbbed, and it felt as though she had swallowed knives.

Once she gained a semblance of control, her head turned. It had not been her imagination after all. Hope washed over her as Crogan's face registered in her mind. But it was quickly dashed as she observed the scene.

Crogan and Gerald were locked in battle.

Alfred's body still lay on the floor, a brutal reminder that her husband dispatched the last man who had made an attempt to save her life. Because of the small space, they were forced to step over him time and time again, as if he were some discarded refuse that was merely in their way.

A hand moved to cup her throat, attempting to soothe the agony there. "Miranda, are ye hurt?" Crogan demanded without taking his eyes from his opponent.

It was nothing that she would not recover from in time. "Nay," it came out as a croak.

She saw Gerald sneer as he sidestepped, deflecting Adair's weapon. "My wife is my concern, not yours."

"Wife?"

"I am Lord Gerald Wilkes, the lady's husband." In that situation, he clearly relished speaking the words.

"Gerald Wilkes is dead."

"He speaks true," Miranda confirmed in a whisper. It was difficult to speak.

She saw Crogan's brow furrow, mystified by this newfound information. But he did not relent.

"As such, Miranda is mine to do with as I please. I will dispatch you, then I will dispatch her," he purred confidently.

"She will not be harmed, by ye, or anyone else," the Scotsman growled.

With that, Gerald charged forward, forcing Crogan into retreat. Unprepared for the sudden onslaught, he missed Alfred's body at his back. He tripped and fell hard on his backside.

Gerald laughed.

Miranda's heart leapt into her throat, constricted in horror. While her husband laughed, the Scotsman appeared to see an opening and did not hesitate to take it. His movements proceeded in a flash as he grunted and thrust his sword into Gerald's abdomen. The dreadful sound of metal grating against flesh and bone entered the silence.

Gerald gasped and looked down. There was a sword penetrating the man's body.

Crogan held it there. He didn't move.

The lady observed as that smug bastard's expression fell into defeat. With defeat came fury. Gerald hissed, then forced himself to back away from the blade in his stomach.

At last, he was free of it, and he halted, staring as blood soaked his tunic.

Miranda pushed herself to her feet.

Gerald's gaze moved to the bloody sword in Crogan's hand. The corner of his mouth curled, and hate leapt in his eyes. His mouth opened, and he let out an enraged shout. He rushed forward, undoubtedly intent on driving his own blade into Crogan's neck, but Crogan was ready for it. He plunged his sword into Gerald's heart. With that, he released the hilt, and as Gerald staggered backward, he jumped to his feet.

Miranda watched as her husband abruptly sat down hard. His hand moved to the hilt, as if he meant to pull it from his chest, but his strength must have failed him. His arms fell away, and he slumped over onto his side, his eyes open but unseeing, his breath stalled.

The lady moved over to stand beside Gerald's dead body. Unable to help herself, she fell to her knees, and her shoulders slumped, staring into lifeless eyes. Her own husband had meant to kill her, and he nearly had. All those years and he had been alive while everyone believed him to be deceased, but that had been devised merely as an escape from her. What had she done to deserve such hatred?

Miranda felt Crogan standing at her back, waiting silently.

Now she was truly a widow.

Abruptly, Viktor rushed into the room and took in the scene.

"Help me with this," Crogan ordered, referring to his hauberk.

The Englishman easily lifted the heavy metal structure over his head.

Once he was freed of it, Crogan spun on his heel, dropped to his knees beside Miranda, and pulled her into his arms.

At last, feeling the security of his embrace, she breathed an unsteady sigh of relief. She held on to him, her limbs trembling, eyes blurred with tears.

She wanted to speak her gratitude aloud, but following her brush with death, it was difficult to talk over the pain in her throat. So, she held him in thankful silence.

Finally, he pulled back and took stock of her appearance. His eyes paused on her bruised cheek, then settled on the angry red rope burns cutting across her neck.

"Are ye well?" Callused fingers moved to touch the skin of her neck, but then it appeared as though he thought better of it.

"I will mend," she whispered. "I want my son."

"I will locate him, my lady," Viktor announced. With that, he quit the room.

Miranda stared at the open doorway. Freedom was hers.

Anticipating her silent intent, Crogan aided her rise.

The couple walked out into the empty passageway, moving away from the bodies lying on the dungeon floor. She turned to face the man who had saved her life.

Her brow dropped to Crogan's chest, and she allowed quiet tears of relief to fall. It was over; it was finally all over.

Chapter 47

When Viktor descended the staircase holding her son, Miranda felt her heart burst. Edwin was pale and terrified, but other than that, he was healthy. Gerald had not lied; her boy had not been harmed.

In spite of an aching body, she rushed forward.

His little teal eyes settled on her, and the joy that shone brightly within them filled her heart with happiness.

"Mama!" he cried.

Viktor set him on his feet, and he flew into Miranda's open arms. She curled him into a tight embrace, at last able to feel him close and safe. A laugh sounded in her injured throat as she dropped kisses onto his brow. Moisture pricked her eyes.

"You are safe, Edwin. Mama is here."

He clung to her, tears streaming down his wan cheeks.

"I found him locked in the east tower," Viktor declared as both men observed the reunion between mother and son.

Her eyes settled on the Englishman. "Thank you." Then they shifted to Crogan. "Thank you both."

Then her eyes shut, and she gave her son another firm squeeze. "Thank you, Lord."

***

While mother and son continued to embrace, Brodie joined their party, and Viktor turned to his elder male companion. "We are victorious. The holding is yours."

Crogan glanced at Miranda, uncertain if he wanted the property neighboring that woman. He had made a promise to leave once Edwin had been returned. And he was due to be married in short order. He knew the right thing to do was to deny the property and cut all ties, but he spoke contrary to his thoughts. "I want those fallen in battle removed before Edwin is taken above."

"Alfred," Miranda whispered as she gazed at them over her son's shoulder.

The trio gave her their full attention.

"He must be given a Christian burial," she rasped and winced.

"The man is a traitor," Viktor asserted.

"His death is not a result of Gerald's evil disposition; his death was given to save my life," she whispered.

There was a pensive pause in response.

"Your words are strained, Miranda; rest your voice," Crogan ordered protectively. His gaze shifted to Brodie and Viktor.

He did not have to speak a word. Viktor nodded, understanding. "We will have the men remove the fallen at once." With that, Brodie and Viktor slipped past mother and son and climbed to the main level.

Crogan stepped forward and offered a hand. "Let us move away from the cell while its contents are addressed."

Miranda took his hand and held Edwin's little one in her own, then they all wandered down the passageway past the lady's prison cell. When they struck the end, Crogan seated himself, using the wall to support his back. Miranda and Edwin took up a place at his side.

The lady's son was upon her lap, and she pressed his head to her chest. "Rest, darling." The boy obeyed instantly. With his mother's arms around him, he was assured of security. His eyes closed, and, in moments, he dozed.

"Ye must be exhausted," Crogan whispered so he would not disturb her son.

She nodded, and her temple fell to his shoulder. "As you must be."

"I should throttle ye for slinking away in the night," he growled softly. "Bishop could have murdered ye."

She grinned up at him. "I am well. My son is well. 'Tis a satisfactory end, is it not? With the exception of Alfred's untimely death."

His head moved closer. His eyes blazed intensely. "Ye *were* nearly killed."

Miranda merely shrugged. "I shall mend."

He frowned down at her but said nothing more, unwilling to aggravate her after all she had been through.

Before long, the lady's eyes drifted shut, and her even breathing met his ears.

While they slept, Crogan's gaze lingered upon them. The sight was amazing. Mother and son had been reunited. Edwin was perfect; there was not a mark on him.

He wished he could say the same for her. As his eyes moved over them, he noticed something he had not prior. Her wrists were scraped and bruised, which meant she had not only been imprisoned in that room, but she had also been held in those shackles on the wall. When Miranda related the events that had occurred while she was held hostage, he was certain she would not divulge that detail.

Crogan sighed regretfully. The task he was assigned had been accomplished, but at what cost? Both of them were certain to be mentally scarred by the events. And then there was the relationship that had developed between Miranda and himself during Edwin's absence. The couple cared for one another, but it could not continue. Their lives would part. He would marry, and he was prompted to wonder what the future held for her.

Would she find another to care for? Would she ever remarry? The feelings those thoughts invoked were not welcome, so he pushed them aside and considered the mundane details of the journey back to Scotland.

At long last, Crogan's eyes began to droop, and he gave in to the need to rest.

The sound of approaching footsteps caused his eyes to snap open. He looked up to see Brodie standing over them.

"The evidence of battle has been cleared, cousin."

"We all need rest. We will stay the evening an' depart at dawn."

Brodie nodded. "Aye, Viktor believed ye would feel so. A room has been prepared for the lass an' her son."

His eyes turned to Edwin. "Please take the lad."

Ever so gently, Brodie extracted Edwin from Miranda's arms. Both were too deep in slumber to be roused by the movement. With the boy held effortlessly in robust arms, Crogan lifted Miranda and held her close.

They were carried up to one of the guest rooms and deposited in the same bed. Two pairs of eyes watched as Miranda instinctually pulled her son close and settled into comfortable unconsciousness.

Her heavy sigh emitted palpable relief.

Brodie turned to leave them in peace, but Crogan felt as though his feet were rooted to the floor. They were safe. The threat to their well-being had been extinguished. Yet he could not force himself to exit the room. His protective nature would not relent.

Although he knew it was the lingering effects of seeing Miranda in peril, he felt as though a shadow continued to hang above them all. Gerald was dead. Bishop was dead. Edwin was healthy and within his mother's loving embrace. So why did he remain, watching over them? Why was there a nagging feeling in the back of his mind that perhaps it was not over?

In that instant, he knew. His task had been accomplished, but his feelings for Miranda would remain. When he left her behind and journeyed toward his future, the ties would not be completely severed. He would not be able to forget her. Perhaps she would fade in time, but he feared that the months following his departure would be more difficult than he initially anticipated.

In several days' time, they would part forever. But she was in his life now. And he was unwilling to divide their company for the short while she remained in it. Rather than leave the room, he eased himself into the bed beside her, draped an arm over her waist, and drifted off into slumber.

***

The whole of their party departed shortly after dawn the following morning. Edwin rode in the saddle, along with his mother, a secure arm curled around his tummy. Crogan, Brodie and Viktor were dutifully by their side during the length of the journey.

The silence stretched for many minutes, but finally the boy spoke. He turned his head to gaze at his mother out of the corner of his eye. "Where's Papa?"

Startled by his question, her eyes jerked over to Crogan. Miranda had expected the boy to question his father's whereabouts, but the abrupt request had caught her off guard.

She curled an arm tightly around her son and dipped her head to rest against his pate. Her throat held a mild ache from the previous evening's scuffle, but she ignored it. "Papa has gone up to heaven. He is in the Lord's hands. He is safe." She had to force her voice to be steady, because she nearly choked on the lie. There was no doubt in her mind that Gerald had gone straight to hell for his misdeeds.

"But Papa came back," he argued, believing Gerald had returned from the dead.

"Nay, sweetheart," she whispered compassionately, "'twas a mistake. We believed a terrible accident had sent your father up to the heavens, but we were mistaken. He was simply absent from our lives. But I am sorry, Edwin, Papa has truly gone to heaven. I have seen his departure."

The boy was thoughtful for a moment. Miranda stared at his profile as his brow furrowed. Then he looked at her. "Should I be sad, Mama?"

Her eyes widened, his question most unexpected. She cleared her throat. "You will feel how you feel, Edwin; 'tis not wrong."

He frowned. "Papa never smiled."

Miranda sat up straight in the saddle, haunted by the past. The only smiles he had bestowed upon her were leers, meant to be hurtful and humiliating. She opened her mouth to respond, but what could she say? His words were true.

She struggled to find a proper reply.

Without warning, Crogan broke into their conversation with a change of subject, and Miranda was so grateful for that. She had no doubt it was intentional.

"There are many guests waiting at home to welcome your return, Edwin. Your grandmamma, a nice lad named Miles, and Lady Colville." He grinned brightly.

The boy turned a delighted smile in Adair's direction. "Guests for me?!"

Crogan chuckled. "A whole castle full."

The boy and the man continued to chat for the remainder of the journey. Miranda listened with mixed feelings. She was impressed by Crogan's ability to befriend her son so easily, and at the same time, she felt sorrow burgeoning in her heart. She knew he would leave them and go on to marry another. He would find a place in Edwin's heart, just as he had found a place in her own, and then he would be gone.

Several times she found herself biting back tears.

Chapter 48

Miranda stood at Edwin's bedside, watching the steady rise and fall of his little chest. He was home, tucked safely in his own bed. The side of herself that had been in a frenzy of worry for so long was finally at peace.

She took in a deep breath and let it out slowly. From the moment he had been returned to her, she could not leave his side. They shared a night of slumber in the guest room at Bishop's castle. When they awoke alone, she aided the boy's morning toilet. Then they shared a mount for their return home.

Once they finally arrived at the manor, and he was passed from person to person, receiving heartfelt hugs of welcome, including from his grandmamma, whom he was able to meet for the first time, she selfishly dragged him around with her while she tended to necessary castle chores. And she even sat him directly on her lap for the evening meal.

At last, nearly falling asleep while on his feet, she led him up to his chamber and pulled the covers up to his chin. He was oblivious to her presence in moments. His soft, even breathing sounded like music to her ears.

The moon was high in the sky, but she was not yet ready to leave him. She sat down in a chair near the blackened fireplace and continued to watch him sleep. There were no guarantees that he would make it through the night without having a bad dream. And if he was susceptible to them after his ordeal, she intended to be at his side in a moment's notice, there to soothe him. There to chase his fears away.

***

Miranda woke before dawn, with a stiff neck and tired eyes.

As she roused herself from the chair she spent the night in, Edwin turned over and opened his eyes to find her there.

He sent her a beaming grin. "Good morn, Mama."

Miranda's morning began with a beautiful grin from her son, but more than an hour later, she stood present at yet another burial. While Dell and Reissa gladly watched over the children within the manor walls, Miranda watched the flames lift Alfred's ashes into the cerulean sky. As a sign of respect, they had transported his body back to the Wilkes manor for burial.

Gerald remained in a shallow grave along with his fallen cohorts beyond the curtain walls at the Bishop holding. Reluctantly, Miranda had identified every traitor. Every man who had stood in that dungeon next to Lord Wilkes had been victims of the siege. Perhaps some unseen forces of vengeance had sought them out.

The widow had no regrets for her husband's death, particularly after three years of believing it had already been so. But Alfred's passing left her torn. She had witnessed the captain's deceit firsthand, but even as she experienced the warmth of his burial flames, she could not believe a man she had trusted above all others had plotted against her. His heart had been in the right place. He had wanted nothing other than to love Rowena, but his mind betrayed him, and he had forsaken the morals bred within him.

Rowena stood at her side, tears shining upon her beautiful face. Miranda could not tell her the truth. She knew her sister would feel responsible if the thoughts behind Alfred's actions were known.

By that time, the only thing Miranda had revealed about his death was the truth that he had saved her from her husband. He was nothing but a hero in Rowena's eyes, and she would not take that away from either of them. She would allow his pristine reputation to continue into the ages. And at that point, only Miranda knew the reason why he had temporarily defected. Viktor, Crogan, and Brodie knew he had done so, but she had no intent to reveal the "why" to them, or to anyone else, ever.

Her thoughts touched on his behavior in recent months. His personality remained the same, as did his actions. There had been no sign to indicate he had been betraying her in all that time. Miranda's head bowed, and she felt moisture sting her eyes. How could he have lived with the charade of duplicity so long? How could he have looked her in the eye while knowing he had taken up with her conniving husband?

Her disappointment in him weighed heavily on her shoulders. What if Edwin had been hurt? Alfred played a large part in that plot. He was partially the cause for her panic and stress over her son's disappearance. And he had stood at her side and watched it all without wavering.

She allowed him the concession of stepping onto the right path in the last minutes. She forgave him for his betrayal, but she would not feel guilty for his loss. She would not look upon the situation with regret. She would not see the hole in their lives that his absence revealed. It was to be treated like a book that had been finished. The last page had been turned, and now it was time to return it to the shelf and move on to the next. His secret would be guarded well. And life would go on without him.

Miranda blinked back the tears that threatened, then looked to the burial fire. As she stared into the flames, she could feel Crogan's gaze upon her from his place at her side. She shifted to her left and locked on his questioning stare. She loved him. There was no question there. But at the same time, circumstances dictated that she must deny her love for him. So, she masked her feelings, swallowed over the burn in her throat, spun on her heel, and marched back to the keep. She wanted to see her son's smiling face.

The remainder of the afternoon, the ladies of the manor spent with Miles and Edwin, playing games and enjoying the sunshine out of doors. For those few hours, Miranda denied any thoughts of Crogan. She simply enjoyed the company of her family and guests.

But then the dinner hour arrived, and everyone took their seats at the table. She could not help but gaze at him when he was not looking in her direction and feel the heaviness in her heart. Then she saw him glance in Viktor's direction, and he visibly breathed a silent sigh.

His gaze unexpectedly turned on her, and his voice opened up. "Edwin has been returned safely to his home. My service has been fulfilled. We shall depart at dawn."

For a moment, she merely stared at him while the words took effect. Even as it registered in her mind that he would be gone in less than twelve hours, she was working to conceal the truth that she felt an unbearable weight settling on her chest.

With all eyes on her, she swallowed hard. "On behalf of my son, please accept my most heartfelt gratitude for your aid during our unfortunate situation. I wish you good luck, and Godspeed." She lifted her chalice of wine to toast him, causing everyone to follow suit and offer a hearty "hear, hear."

Then everyone drank, and the conversation that continued centered around Crogan and Brodie's departure. And as Miranda listened to the preparations that needed to be made for the morrow, she felt the emotion rising, stinging her eyes. And this time she could not stop them.

So, rather than show an open display of emotion, she murmured to the crowd, "Please excuse me," and hurried from the Great Hall without a backward glance.

The sentiment that had forced her from the hall faded as she climbed the staircase. It receded into a tight ball of tension deep in the pit of her stomach. She wandered into her bedchamber and crossed to the window. Outside, the moon was full, giving off a beautiful white glow. Miranda crossed her arms under her breasts and gazed up at it, a pensive expression on her lovely face.

She had been content with her life before Crogan arrived on her darkened doorstep. She would find a way to go back to that contentment. She felt helpless, frustrated, and lost. Edwin was home; she should feel nothing other than relief and joy, but her heart was breaking. In spite of the warmth of the evening, a shiver rolled down her spine.

Her gaze dropped to the horizon. Clouds hovered there, slowly rolling toward the keep. Soon they would cover the moon, and its beautiful light would blink out, leaving the world around her in shadows.

Her sigh of relief was cloaked in misery. Thoughtlessly, she lifted her hands to the buttons at her nape.

"Allow me."

A startled gasp erupted. She spun around to find Crogan standing at her back.

"I did not hear your entrance," Miranda spoke breathlessly.

"Ye appeared rather distracted by your thoughts." His gaze moved over her face, then locked on the depths of her gray eyes. "Has the funeral upset ye so? Or dare I hope that your flight is a result of my departure?"

Miranda could not lie to him. "I have made my peace with Alfred."

His head tilted. "So your flight *is* a result of my departure."

She shifted uncomfortably on her feet, and her eyes dropped to his chest. "I have acquired undeniable feelings for you, Crogan."

The tip of his index finger pressed to the underside of her chin, forcing her head to rise, his eyes searching. "Will ye miss me, Miranda?"

Rather than answer his question, she evaded it with one of her own. "Why are you here, Crogan?"

His hand fell to rest on the buckle of his belted waist. "I have made a decision."

Miranda's heart began to thud in her chest, uncertain what he intended.

"When I have gone, an' ye lay in that bed at night, I do not want ye to think of your husband. I want ye to think of me." With that, he unfastened his belt and dropped it on the floor. Then his hands clutched his tunic and pulled it over his head. It fell onto the belt. There was no mistaking his meaning.

Miranda stood there for a moment, enjoying the sight as he finished undressing. He would be gone from her life forever, so she would not even consider denying him, or herself, this last evening.

Her body began to burn as she looked upon the magnificent display of his unclothed figure. Her breath labored. Trembling hands moved to the buttons at her back, but Crogan stepped forward and swept her into his arms.

He carried her over to the bed and gently laid her petite figure upon the coverlet. Miranda raised her head to fuse their mouths together, but he pulled back and smiled down at her, removing the pins from her hair.

"'Twill be a night never to forget, lass." With that, he slowly disrobed her. Once she lay naked beneath him, he treated her to a sweet exploration of her body with his tender kisses. He started with the tips of her fingers, then moved over her shoulders, down across her torso, and concluded with an intimate kiss that brought her to the heights of ecstasy.

Miranda was still floating upon the wings of pleasure when he entered her and carried her away. She was lost, writhing beneath him, prey to the convulsions throbbing in her core.

Finally, Crogan joined her in the world he had raised her up to. As he found his climax, she stumbled into a third round of waves that had her lifting her hips to meet him. Her arms wrapped tightly around his neck as she experienced the pleasure that reached deep inside and touched every nerve ending in her body.

At last, she returned to reality and gulped for breath, brow aglow with perspiration.

Crogan rolled over onto his back, his chest heaving, temples damp.

They lay there for many minutes in silence.

When Miranda was able to speak with a steady inflection, she turned to look at Crogan.

His head rolled to the side, and he gazed at her. A licentious grin tugged at the corners of his mouth. "Will that be sufficient?"

At first she giggled, but then the smile faded. Miranda glanced at the mosquito netting overhead, then rolled away and sat up, placing her feet on the platform. The widow stared into a lonely future and realized she would not want to suffer it without a body by her side.

She may not find another to love, not while her love for Crogan lived, but she could find someone to ease the solitude of a dark night. "You have taught me what I may find within the arms of a decent man, Crogan. You will be gone, and I may not want to lie in this bed alone."

Without warning, an arm snaked around her waist and yanked her back under the prison of his pressing weight. "Ye will not," he growled, eyes burning with anger as he gazed upon her.

She glared up at him, furious that he would dare to order her about when he had no right to do so. "I am a widow, not an innocent. I have the right to choose for myself."

His expression transformed into one of frustration. "Ye would seek another in my absence?"

"You will be married with the new year, Crogan. Our union must end at dawn," she asserted, hating hearing those words spoken out loud.

He shook his head, clearly coming to a realization that he was not willing to accept. "'Tis not necessary for our union to end, Miranda."

Her brow furrowed, disgusted by the implication there. "I am to be used as mistress?"

His head shook again. "'Used' is not an appropriate word."

"Nay, the correct word is 'whore.'"

He scowled. "A mistress is a far cry from being a whore."

"Is it not?"

He stared down at her. She pushed on his chest, and he moved, allowing her to rise. Nude, she sat on the edge of the mattress with her back to him.

"A mistress is used for the pleasure of her body, and she is given extravagant gifts as a result. How is that not the definition of a whore?" the lady wondered.

A response was not forthcoming.

"I believe I have made my point," Miranda added. Thoughtlessly, slim fingers rose and delved into her raven locks, separating it into three long sections. Her hands worked, plaiting the shiny black tresses with ease.

Crogan was at her back, his eyes on her. "Ye refuse to be my mistress, yet ye will seek the arms of another?"

Miranda finished the plait, then bowed her head and sighed, feeling defeated. "I truly regret speaking that thought aloud."

She heard the bed shift and glanced over her shoulder. Crogan had moved into the same position on the opposite side, so they sat with their backs to each other.

"As do I," he growled quietly.

The silence stretched between them, thick as fog.

Finally, Miranda decided. "I cannot live that life, Crogan."

"'Twould be a good life, Miranda," he assured, but his tone lacked conviction.

"Then tell me. Tell me how 'twill be between us." She gazed at him over her shoulder, and he did the same. Their eyes locked.

Crogan's mouth opened, but the moments stretched as she saw thoughts swirling in those sea-green depths. He broke eye contact and turned back.

With that, he rose. His motions were jerky and angry as he pulled on his clothes. Miranda observed, feeling the need to mend the rift she had just created, but words failed her.

When he finished dressing, he moved to look down at her from his massive height. "Ye deserve better," he barked angrily and stormed from the chamber.

The lady bowed her head. A feeling of defeat washed over her, overwhelming her. And the emotion that had coiled itself into a ball of tension prior to Crogan's visit returned with a vengeance. She was unaware that the tears had begun until she felt warm liquid rolling down her cheek.

Chapter 49

Miranda tossed and turned fitfully that night. She rose feeling exhausted and drained. And she dreaded going below. Crogan would be walking out of her life in minutes. She knew there was no preparation for such a farewell. And he was cross with her, which only added to the difficulty of their situation.

Bleary-eyed from crying herself to sleep, she dragged her feet as she descended to the Great Hall. When she looked up from the bottom step, she saw that the hall was empty. Her heart stopped. Was she too late? Had they departed early? Had Crogan left without a word?

She ran to the front entrance and pushed on the heavy double doors.

A sigh of relief escaped her. Crogan's army was milling about in the bailey, awaiting word that they were moving out.

Her eyes scanned the crowd. She spotted her family and guests near the portcullis, speaking with Crogan and Brodie, clearly expressing their goodbyes. Miles stood at Brodie's side, prepared to depart with the elder man. Following the burial the previous day, Brodie had approached with a request. He wanted to take on Miles as a ward. He would be given a good home and raised as a knight. Miranda could not deny the request. She would be sad to see Miles go, but the boy would want for nothing, including a generous and caring father figure.

As if feeling her approach, Crogan's eyes shifted. They turned on her, cold and unyielding. Miranda's gait slowed, beaten down by his unwelcome greeting.

She halted and looked at Brodie. "'Twas a great pleasure to meet you, Brodie. You are always welcome in my home."

He kissed her hand affectionately. "Please visit us in Scotland soon, lass."

Miranda simply smiled, aware that she would never be able to visit the country, not while Crogan resided there. Her gaze shifted to Miles. She pulled the boy into a close embrace, then retreated and grinned down at him. "Take care of my good friend, will you?" she mentioned, referring to Brodie.

He gave her a sweet grin and nodded happily.

Regrettably, she turned to Crogan. As she spoke, she could feel numerous pairs of eyes upon them, spectating. "Once again, I must extend my sincerest gratitude for your help in collecting my son." She curtsied politely, gave him a perfunctory nod, then took a step back.

Outside, she appeared civil and gracious, but her insides were quivering. "Farewell, Crogan." There was the tiniest catch in her voice, but she was unaware, because she was too distracted by his steely gaze.

Unexpectedly, he stepped forward and pulled her into his arms. His mouth claimed hers, warm, hard, and branding.

Several gasps erupted from the crowd.

He released her before she could form a thought, leaving her slightly dazed and extremely surprised by his daring move.

"Farewell, Miranda," his voice was a low monotone.

He rode from her life with the tingle of his kiss upon her lips.

Chapter 50

Crogan walked through the door of his luxurious castle in Scotland, looked around the massive hall adorned with velvet tapestries, gold candelabras, and ornate chandeliers, then looked at the empty space at his side. It felt wrong that Miranda was not standing there beside him.

He scowled, silently chastising himself for the thought. She had denied him, refused his offer to be his mistress, which meant she would not play any part in his life at all, and that enraged him to no end.

He wanted her, and she wanted him. Nothing should have stood between them. He deemed it as simple as that. But she felt differently, and he resented her for it. No, perhaps that was not quite true. He resented himself and his impulsive decision to allow the King to choose his wife. Now that he was tied to Alice for life, he felt as though he was living in a prison of his own making.

There was no denying that his desire for Miranda raged on, but she was gone, and there was nothing that would change that.

Aware that he had arrived, Alice rushed up and threw herself into his arms. "At last, ye have returned," she purred, pressing her buxom body close as she held him tight.

Crogan pushed her back the length of his arms and pinned her with a volatile glare. "Leave me be, Alice." With that, he walked away, leaving her to stare after him, obviously insulted by his instant dismissal.

She began to move forward, clearly intent on chasing after him, but a hand reached out and clutched her arm. Chestnut eyes looked up into Brodie's stern expression. "Do not."

"But—"

He shook his head negatively. "Nae, Alice. Leave him be. 'Twould serve ye best to retire." The hour was late, but the kitchen had prepared a meal to fill their bellies prior to seeking much-needed slumber after a swift journey.

"But—"

A callused palm lifted. "Go, Alice!" he growled in a low voice.

"Vile man," she snapped, then clutched her skirts and stomped off to her chamber.

Brodie crossed to the head table, pulled his seat, and sat down hard. His emerald gaze swung over to his cousin.

Crogan was eating in silence. Feeling a heavy stare, his head rose, and their gazes locked. He sat back in his chair, his eyes narrowing. "What is on your mind, cousin?"

"Ye dug yourself a big hole, Crogan."

He squinted in anger. "I am aware."

"Alice is—" Brodie frowned, obviously searching for the right epithet.

Reluctantly, Crogan ended the phrase for him, "—my future wife."

"Aye, she is that," Brodie agreed, clearly disgusted by the notion.

"Nothing has changed."

"All has changed." He pounded the table for emphasis, causing several knights' eyes to shift in their direction. "Miranda was not a figment of your imagination—"

Crogan quickly spoke up, "I will not hear her name in my presence. Not ever."

Brodie's brow creased darkly. "Ye refuse to discuss it?"

"Aye, I refuse to discuss it." With that, he rose from his chair and sauntered from the hall.

Once he was in the solitude of his chamber, Crogan tossed his tunic and belt aside, then sat down and dispensed with his boots. Clad in a navy pair of braies, he lay down on his massive oak bed and stared through the darkness, willing sleep to come.

He had pushed them all too far too fast, and he was exhausted as a result. But in spite of his fatigue, his mind continued to buzz with thoughts he could not banish. Thoughts of his distant and immediate past plagued him, and even worse: thoughts of a bleak future.

An hour passed. And two more. Finally, he gave up on the idea of slumber and moved to sit on the edge of the mattress. Once that was accomplished, he rubbed his eyes and stood up. Without intent, he found himself wandering down to the hall on the main level. A majority of the castle had retired long ago, including the servants, so Crogan took it upon himself to pour a tankard of ale. He crossed to the dining table and filled his seat.

Not one of six chandeliers remained burning, but tiny shafts of moonlight filtered through the high windows in the structure, creating minimal light. The instant he sat down, his sharp senses picked up on another presence in the room. His eyes locked on a shadowed figure seated several feet down the table. Despite a lack of light and the late hour, he was able to see that Alice happened to be the second body in the hall.

He gave a silent groan as their gazes locked in the darkness. "Alice."

"Unable to sleep, Crogan?" she wondered with sour sweetness.

"Very perceptive." He swallowed his sarcasm along with a hearty gulp of ale.

For many moments, the betrothed couple simply stared through the darkness, the tension palpable.

At last, Alice opened her mouth. "I hate that ye look at me and wish I were her. I hate it."

He drank from the tankard, set it down, and gave her his full attention. But he did not speak up to deny it. The Scotsman simply stared, his eyes hard, defenses supported by an innate anger.

"An' I will never be her." She snorted derisively and stared down at the wine in her chalice. "Good Lord, I never thought I would envy another. 'Tis an unpleasant feeling. Most unpleasant."

Absently, she swirled the contents of the silver goblet. "Will I spend my wedding night in solitude?"

Crogan threaded his fingers together and rested his hands on a flat abdomen, his pose casual and relaxed. "I will not lie, Alice. My desire for ye has run its course."

Her eyes locked on him, burning with malice. "Then I shall find comfort in the arms of another."

He knew she said it to inflame his jealousy, but it did not arouse the least bit of response. "Very well."

"Ye will not be shamed while your wife carries on with other men?" she demanded.

"Ye will be discreet, or I will have ye banished for adultery." His tone was monotonous, bored.

The lady's spine grew rigid. "Damn ye, Crogan. Ye will not treat me as discarded refuse!"

The man's stone expression did not change. "I will treat ye as I see fit."

She abruptly broke into tears, but moisture failed to appear on her cheeks. Clearly, she was making an attempt to extract some compassion, but Crogan easily saw through her ruse. He rolled his eyes, disgusted.

"Your drama is unwanted, Alice. Leave me."

She glared up at him, her fit of sobbing completely wiped away and replaced with childish anger.

"I will not abide such displays."

"Damn ye," Alice scolded. "Our marriage will be nothing but a prison."

"Our marriage is written in stone," Crogan growled unhappily. "Ye cannot sever the contract. I will drag ye down the aisle if I must."

"'Tis ye who does not possess the desire to make that journey down the aisle."

"Nevertheless, I will honor the King's contract." He sat forward, eyes locked on her, his features set in ruthless lines. "And so will ye."

"I will wed a man who is cursed under the spell of another. 'Tis every woman's dream," she spat, then stalked from the room.

Chapter 51

Miranda watched her son chase after leaves floating upon an autumn wind out in the bailey. In spite of the beauty of the day and Edwin's joy, she stood nearby with a fixed smile upon her face. Outside, she appeared content and happy, but inside…

The woman's heart was overflowing with love for her son, her sister, and her mother, but there was a hollow feeling within that followed her like a shadow, constant and dark.

Crogan, Brodie, and Miles had gone from her life. Then Viktor and Reissa announced their exit. After all of her guests had departed, she peered around the manor one evening during supper and breathed a heavy sigh. The manor was virtually empty without them.

Miranda would only admit it to herself, but she was lonely. She always had Rowena to confide in, but she missed talking with Reissa, missed the ring of her laughter echoing off the stone walls. The woman brought a carefree spirit into her home that was most welcome. And she even missed Viktor's intimidating presence. He was a solid wall of security that she took for granted while he was in residence, and now that he was gone, she felt the absence of that support.

Then there was Crogan. And he was at the heart of her loneliness. He had succeeded in dousing thoughts of Gerald from her conscience. When she lay alone in bed at night, she could almost feel his arms around her. Hear the deep timbre of his voice in her ear. See him sleeping contentedly next to her.

She had cried into her pillow on more than one occasion, and she revisited their last conversation in her bedchamber nearly every night. She had denied his offer. While he had been in residence, it was a simple matter to cling to her moral and ethical pride.

She would not consider lowering herself into the position of a high-class whore. But now that Crogan had abandoned her to a life without him, she continually second-guessed her decision. Miranda was so desperate to see him again that her thoughts shifted into unknown territory. She found herself wondering what would be so bad about taking on the role of his lover while he was married to Lady Farraday?

While she stared into the darkness of the night and yearned for him to be lying next to her, she gave in to the temptation of re-considering his offer. But then she would fall into a restless sleep, wake in the morn, and come to her senses. She simply could not go to him. The idea was out of the question.

Miranda cared not about her reputation, but she had a son to consider. And a sister who had yet to jump into the marriage market. Soiling her own reputation would put a mark on Rowena's as well.

Miranda sighed and watched Edwin pounce on a leaf that crackled under his little foot. He giggled happily and looked to her for approval.

She gave him a beaming smile and a hearty clap that appeased him. With that leaf caught, he moved on to the next. A swift breeze surrounded them, causing the stray leaves that had found their way into the bailey to fly around without direction or purpose.

The air had grown cooler, and summer had eased into fall. Before long, snow would dance in the sky and settle on the ground. Before long, the New Year would arrive, and, with it, Crogan's wedding.

Miranda banished the thought. Dwelling on the idea would do nothing but tug on her emotions. They were raw, her wounds open, with no signs of healing. The best way to deal with her sensitivity to Crogan's loss was to ignore her feelings. She tried to concentrate on Edwin. But the man snuck into her mind more than she cared to admit. Mentally, she gave a mighty shove and pushed him away.

Her gaze shifted up. The sky was overcast, clouds hanging low above them. The air held a chill, announcing they may see the first snowfall before the day met its end. Edwin was bundled up tight, but his cheeks were rosy from the weather.

A particularly strong gust of wind hit her, and she felt as though it filtered through her tiny figure. A violent shiver shook her body. But she would not take her son inside yet. When winter arrived, they would be cooped up in the manor much of the time. So, she wanted to take advantage of the weather for as long as possible.

"You look cold. You should go on inside. I will watch him," Rowena spoke as she approached and halted at her side.

Miranda sent her sister an appreciative smile, but her head swiveled from side to side. "I would rather stay here."

"Well, I believe we are prepared for the change in season." The portcullis began to rise, and wagons heaping with supplies filtered into the bailey. "The manor has been cleaned from top to bottom and has been sealed up tight. The pantry will be stocked, and there is enough firewood to last us a year," Rowena announced with a sense of accomplishment.

During the last couple of months, the younger sister had taken on many of the castle's duties. Rowe had requested to do so with the excuse that it was time that she learn such things, but Miranda knew the root cause. Her sister was well aware that Miranda was nursing a broken heart, and the only way Rowe could offer any help in that area was to reduce her stress by bearing the load of the castle chores.

At first, teaching her sister all of the necessary tasks relating to the upkeep and supervision of the manor helped to keep her mind busy, but now that Rowe was working without any aid from her elder sibling, Miranda's days were free and clear to dwell upon much. She devoted her time to her son and visiting with her mother, but her loneliness in the dead of the night seemed to surround her, growing dense like the smoke of a fire. Lately, it seemed to be suffocating, nearly choking her.

"Fabulous, Rowe. You are doing a splendid job. Thank you for all of your help." The lady did not turn her head to look at Rowe. Her words were sincere, but deep down, she felt as though she was acting without feeling. She knew what was expected of her, and she behaved accordingly, but her heart was just not in it.

The idea to shut herself away, curl up into the fetal position, and feel sorry for herself was foremost in her mind. But she fought against it. She could not give in to her sadness. She would refuse it because she loved her son, and she needed to be in top form for him.

As Miranda continued to watch her son, she could feel Rowena's heavy stare. Finally, she looked at her sister expectantly.

The youth gave her a woeful smile. "We need to get you away from here, Miranda."

Her eyes narrowed. "I do not understand."

"Perhaps a visit to Scotland."

Miranda looked away. "'Tis over, Rowe. 'Twould serve you well to come to terms with that. I have."

Rowena gave a dramatic sigh, and her gaze shifted to the sky. "You do hide it well."

"Rowe," she chastised in a hoarse tone.

Her sister stepped into her line of sight, forcing the irritated lady to meet her gaze. "Miranda, break with convention. Go to him."

A hint of tears formed in her eyes. "I cannot." With that, she stalked away, dismissing the subject, dismissing her sister's attempt to change her mind.

Chapter 52

Alice giggled delightedly at a jest one of the knights made during supper that evening. She was in the middle of her third glass of wine, and she had no intention of stopping.

Unwillingly, greedy eyes shifted to her future husband, and the giggling abruptly halted. She sobered immediately.

She had followed him around for months, hoping, praying the man would snap from his dark reverie and see her standing before him. But all she saw was a distracted, quietly self-loathing man who refused to allow anyone inside.

Many nights had seen him sitting up at the table for hours, drinking ale until he passed out right there in his chair.

Many days he nursed a headache and barked at everyone who dared to speak with him.

When Alice first met him, she was drawn in by his overt masculinity, confidence, and strong sense of self. Now she looked upon a man who was nothing but a shell of himself, lost to the world around him.

His journey to England had changed everything.

Once upon a time, she had warmed his bed and stood at his side. But she had been cast aside without a second thought. Discarded without a care.

Alice gazed at him, feeling helpless and enraged. There was no chance for a healthy marriage with him while he continued to pine for another. No chance at all.

She would never find happiness in his arms. Never share a warm glance across the table. Never spend a lazy day in bed together.

As the lady realized all that had been robbed from her, a desperate helplessness began to wash over her, again and again.

She could not continue on as such. She could not watch Crogan mourn Miranda Wilkes forever. She could not sit idly by.

With her decision made, Alice did not hesitate to move. The buxom figure rose from her seat, stormed across the hall, and slammed out the front entrance without a glance back.

***

Miranda's eyes popped open in the deep hours of the night. Something had caused her to wake. She sat up and rubbed the sleep from her eyes, then blinked several times, waiting for her sight to adjust to the lack of light.

The moon was covered by clouds, so she could not rely on its white glow for illumination. She stared through the darkness as the hair on the back of her neck stood on end. The feeling of a second body in the room was palpable.

"Hello, Miranda."

The sound of a voice directly beside her bed caused her to jump in her skin. And her thudding heartbeat did not halt there. She recognized the voice immediately; a voice that did not belong there.

"Alice," she whispered, feeling uneasy. Why was she in England, in her home, in her chamber, in the wee hours of the night?

A match flared in the darkness.

The mosquito netting had been drawn aside before she woke. So, Miranda watched in muted silence as the intruder lit the candle on the table next to her bed. Then her eyes shifted, and her heart jumped into her throat.

Alice was holding a dirk. The candlelight reflected off the silver metal blade and glowed in the girl's dark eyes, creating a scene that Miranda knew had been permanently seared into the recesses of her mind.

She took in a deep, unsteady breath. "What brings you here, Alice?"

"A produce cart," the girl returned with a self-righteous grin. "It carried me directly into your bailey. What extraordinary luck."

Miranda thought of the supply carts she had watched enter earlier that day and gave a groan in the back of her throat. The bloody chit had intruded into the manor with very little effort, and she had not even had an insider help her do so.

The idea was daunting, but there was no time to dwell on the inadequacies of the castle guard. Clearly, Alice had arrived with purpose—an intent that did not bode well for her.

When the girl did not add an explanation for her cause, Miranda was forced to speak up. "Why are you here?"

Alice squinted, fury radiating from her. "It seems to be Providence that I arrive here on All Hollows Eve to dispatch a witch."

Miranda's throat went dry.

"Ye have stolen my right to happiness, Miranda Wilkes," she hissed, holding the blade in a threatening manner.

"I have stolen nothing from you," the widow defended casually, eyes locked on the dirk.

"Ye cast a spell on my future husband, a spell I cannot break through. The man would not touch me once ye entered into his life. He looks at me but does not see me. He sees nothing but ye. Ye are a witch; I am convinced of it."

From somewhere deep inside, Miranda acknowledged the fact that Alice had just confirmed words she had once thought to be a lie. Crogan had denied bedding Alice under her roof, but she had not believed him. Despite her situation, in that moment, she felt an ounce of satisfaction in knowing he spoke true. But then she returned her attention to the matter at hand.

"You are wrong, Alice. Crogan is haunted by another."

Alice shook her head vehemently from side to side. "Dana's name has not been banished from his home."

Miranda felt a stake to her heart. Not only was Crogan not in love with her, but Alice's confession also announced that the man clearly resented and despised her. In that moment, her will to live dwindled, but thoughts of Edwin instantly revived her. She could not give up on life. Edwin needed his mother.

Alice held the blade out, inches from Miranda's cheek. "Rise."

Ever so slowly, the youth allowed Miranda to move forward and step down onto the platform, but she remained vigilant, the dirk clutched tightly in her hand.

"What will you do, Alice?" she demanded, desperate to know her fate.

Her grin was terrifying. "I entertained the notion of burning ye at the stake; 'tis a befitting death for a witch, after all. But I was forced to reject that idea. 'Tis an announcement of murder, ye see. Nae, your death must be perceived as an accident." Gracefully, she backed down the platform and gestured for Miranda to do the same. "Let us go."

Miranda's pace lacked speed, grasping for time. She was uncertain how to extricate herself from the threat to her life. Alice's consideration of burning her at the stake was shocking and horrifying. It spoke of the lady's evil disposition. It was either that, or her desperation. Possibly it was a fusion of both. But that design for her fate had been discarded; she could be grateful for that. However, she had yet to reveal the scheme she had settled on, which could be equally disturbing.

Once the elder lady stared up at the girl from her inferior height, Alice continued, her voice low, noticeably reveling in the scene in which she dominated, "I have decided that Dana's death shall be your own."

Miranda gasped, thinking of the eve Crogan woke from a night terror. He had confessed that he saw Miranda's death upon the staircase, not Dana's.

The lady felt ill. Crogan had not been dreaming a morbid fantasy. He had a premonition of her demise.

Chapter 53

Crogan looked up from the ale in his tankard, an odd feeling settling upon him. Alice had been a constant irritant under foot for weeks, but as he considered the present, he realized he had not seen her for quite some time.

His eyes scanned the space of the hall, searching for the unmistakable sight of her buxom figure, but he came to the bizarre conclusion that she was absent.

It certainly was not like her to retire at such an early hour. They had just finished their supper. She generally remained in the hall, socializing with the knights while keeping a close eye on him.

He sat up straight in his chair. Something was wrong. It was nothing but a perception deep inside his being, but he knew it to be true. Like he knew the sun would rise with the morn.

And for some reason the sensation was accompanied by an image of Miranda.

Crogan frowned. Perhaps the ale had finally taken his sanity, along with his judgment.

He shook off the odd sensation and tipped his tankard back, draining the contents. It was early, so he had not yet succeeded in intoxicating his mind and body, but he had every intention of doing just that.

Unexpectedly, Brodie fell into a chair beside him. "Well, I cannot beat ye, Crogan, so I shall join ye." His cousin grinned, ostensibly referring to the man's withdrawn disposition and recent penchant for spirits.

His gaze turned to watch Brodie gulp from another tankard. As he stared, once again he was accosted by the feeling that something was amiss.

"Where is Alice?" Crogan demanded, unable to shake off the feeling a second time.

A head of brunette curls turned, taking in the view of a hall overflowing with knights and foot soldiers. His brow furrowed. "I have not seen her all day."

"'Tis odd, is it not?"

Brodie nodded. "Odd, aye. But then, the lass is odd."

A switch was triggered inside Crogan. He shook his head and stood. "Nae, Alice is not odd. She is envious and violent, and she has sought vengeance upon Miranda on one prior occasion. I do not like the feeling I have inside, Brodie. She's in danger."

"Ye believe Alice would visit violence upon the lass?"

"'Tis possible. If I am wrong, I have lost nothing, if I am correct—" He would not finish the statement. "I must go now." With that, he started across the hall, his gait steady and determined.

"Well, ye will not be going alone," Brodie declared, following his cousin.

***

Miranda peered down upon the shadowed staircase. Her breath labored in trepidation. Alice loomed at her rear, the sharp metal edge of the blade pressed against the fleshy space between her neck and shoulder.

"I do not want to die," she whispered into the darkness.

The blade lifted, causing Miranda to turn and face her enemy. For a moment, she thought her words had touched the youth. But she was horribly wrong. The dirk moved to delicately touch the tip of her chin.

"Ye cannot arouse my compassion, witch. I will have the marriage I desire. Crogan will mourn your death, as he has mourned Dana's, but he will heal. In time, he will seek the comforting arms of another. An' as his wife, my arms will be open to him."

Their eyes locked in the blackness of the top landing.

"I am truly sorry you believe I have cast a spell upon him, for I have not. The man merely aided in the return of my son. And now our association has met its end." Her voice was husky with unshed tears and apprehension.

Alice's eyes glistened with murderous intent. "Ye have met your end, Miranda." With that, her hand lifted, a palm pressed to her chest, and she gave a mighty shove.

The lady had been prepared for such action. At that point she knew there was no escape from her fate. Alice was taller and stronger than she. To lunge forward and battle her would simply result in a blade plunged into her heart, she was certain of it.

Regrettably, she accepted her tragic fate. But she would not accept it without a single act of retribution.

When she saw Alice's arm rise in the dark, a hand shot out to clutch the girl's wrist. "Aye, but I will not meet it alone," she breathed as she felt the momentum of the shove. Her tiny figure fell backward into the stairwell, and she pulled Alice right along with her.

In the Great Hall below, two massive figures burst through the front entrance and drew to an abrupt halt.

***

Two gut-wrenching screams entered into the night, followed by a short scuffle, and then, two grisly thuds.

Crogan and Brodie stared at each other, eyes wide with terror. Cousins raced to the stairwell and climbed to the first landing. A gruesome scene of Alice and Miranda's limp bodies lying in a heap ground them to a halt. Alice's neck was twisted at a macabre angle, her limbs splayed and bent. And Miranda's brow glistened with an exorbitant amount of blood.

"Oh, Lord," Brodie breathed, a hand raised to press against the wall for support.

"Miranda!" Crogan cried. He dropped to his knees on the landing and pulled her slack figure into his arms. "Miranda, nae." Muted tears dripped down his cheeks as his brow fell to rest against her chest. His soul-searing nightmare had come true, but it in no way had prepared him for the reality of it.

He was reliving Dana's death all over again. But this time, it seemed to reach inside and squeeze and torment him until the pain was unbearable, all-consuming. Uncaring that his emotions were visible to anyone who happened upon the scene, he allowed tears to drip down and catch on the stubble of his unshaven cheeks.

What would he do without her? He had been asking himself that same question for weeks, but now the request possessed infinitely more meaning.

The future stretched out before him. Endless, stark, agonizing. How would he drag himself out of bed every morning? What purpose was left for him?

And Rowena and Edwin would be devastated. The girl without a sister, and the boy without a mother. Rowena would not have the woman she loved so unconditionally standing by her side when she wed. She would not be there to hold her hand when she gave birth to her first child.

Edwin was far too young to suffer the loss of not one parent, but two. At such a tender age, would he remember her when he grew into a man? Would her voice fade? Her smile vanish?

His arms tightened about her, unwilling to let her go. He sucked in a breath and held it there, welcoming the lack of oxygen and its lack of significance in that instant.

But as he held his breath, there was something there in the silence. A muffled noise that gained his avid attention.

Crogan pressed his ear to her breast and closed his eyes.

"'Tis there. I hear it. I feel it," he whispered wondrously. He looked at Brodie, his expression steeped with hope. "Her heart. 'Tis beating." Two pairs of eyes dropped to her chest, waiting, praying.

It was faint, but neither man imagined it.

Brodie pointed, his face alight with joy. "She's breathing!"

"She's alive!" Crogan shouted. Once again, he pulled her into his arms, but his feelings in that moment had made a complete transformation.

"Miranda?!" Rowena shrieked, rushing down the stairway to take in the scene.

***

Miranda heard the high-pitched squeal of her sister's voice as the blackness fell away. The noise caused the throbbing in her brow to pulse unbearably. A groan whispered past her lips, and a hand instinctually rose to press against the pulsing pain.

"Miranda?"

The remaining remnants of slumber vanished. She must have struck her head hard because she thought she heard Crogan's voice.

Her eyes blinked open, desperate to learn if it was her imagination playing tricks on her. At first, her view was a bit blurred, but finally she focused on the figure holding her in his arms.

"Crogan," she breathed in disbelief. "You are here."

384

"I thought ye were dead," he murmured breathlessly.

She noticed the glistening of moisture on his cheeks. She gave him a tender grin and delicately smoothed the tears from his face.

His gaze shifted to the blood on her brow. "Ye have a horrible bump on your head. Does anything else hurt?"

For a moment, she focused on her arms and legs, but there was no injury to be found. "Nay."

"Alice?" Rowena questioned. Her sister's eyes shifted to the limp figure lying at her sister's back.

Crogan pinned the younger sister with a determined gaze. "Send for the physician immediately."

She merely nodded and moved past them to continue down the staircase, skirts clutched tightly in hand.

"The physician is unnecessary," Miranda voiced quietly, but the waver in her words announced a lack of strength.

"A head wound is not to be taken lightly," Brodie scolded.

"Aye, I will not argue," she returned, defeated. Her palm pressed to the throbbing in her skull. When it was lifted away and she saw the crimson liquid glistening there, she was ashamed to admit that she felt slightly woozy.

"Miranda?" Crogan tested.

"I will mend." She sighed, then her head turned to check on Alice out of the corner of her eye.

Three gazes fell upon the girl's broken body.

"Once again, I have escaped death, while those who sought to take my life fall prey to their own intent. I am not a witch, but perhaps I possess the blood of a cat."

"A witch?" Adair wondered with a furrowed brow.

"Your betrothed believed I was a witch who cast a spell upon you," Miranda confessed quietly.

A single brow rose. "I must confess, she was correct in her assumption, but we may discuss that another time. We need to get ye out of this damned stairwell." With that, he held her close and stood to his full height.

Thoughtlessly, her arms locked around his neck, and her temple was supported by his shoulder, blood soiling his tunic.

"I will see to Alice," Brodie announced. Crogan nodded, carried Miranda up to the top landing and moved down the hall to her chamber.

A single candle remained lit on the bedside table. The same candle Alice lit upon her arrival.

Ever so gently, he dispensed her tiny figure to the comfort of her feather mattress. She watched as he collected a clean cloth from the washstand and doused it in water, wrung it out, then moved to sit on the edge of the mattress. With a light touch, he began to wipe the blood from her brow. It had oozed into the hair at her temple and down to the delicate shell of her ear.

"Alice intended my death to appear as an accident. She intended to slink away unnoticed. How did you know, Crogan?"

Their eyes locked. He shook his head. "I did not. 'Twas simply a feeling. Alice was missing, and I feared ye were in danger."

The depths of her eyes glazed over with guilt. "I killed her."

Crogan stared, confused.

"She pushed me, and I pulled her down with me."

"Ye did not kill her, Miranda. Perhaps 'twas even her death that saved your life." He grabbed her hand and gave it a squeeze. "If ye had been the one lying there with a broken neck, I would have killed her, 'tis certain."

Her fingers lifted to touch his cheek. "I believed I would never see you again. I thought my mind deceived me when I saw you there."

"I am here, Miranda, in flesh and blood." He tossed the blood-soaked cloth on the bedside table.

"I wanted to go to you, so desperately." A shimmer of tears began to form in her eyes.

"I desired the same. I do not know how many times I looked at my door, hoping to see ye standing there," he spoke in a tortured whisper.

"When Alice relayed that you had my name banished, I was convinced you despised me. I was convinced you cared not." A tear trickled into her hair.

A head of auburn waves shook vehemently from side to side. He gave her hand another squeeze. "I care more for ye than I have ever cared for another, Miranda. While I held ye in my arms, when I believed ye to be lost to the heavens, I realized just how much I do care. It required your death to open my eyes to the truth that I have fallen hopelessly in love with ye."

Miranda grinned as tears continued to seep from her eyes. "You have?"

He smiled and pulled her into his arms. "I never want to be parted from ye again. Not for a moment." He dropped a tender kiss onto her lips.

Her fingers threaded through his hair, holding his head secure in her hands. Stormy eyes locked on sea-green orbs. "'Tis rather beneficial that you love me, Crogan, for I love you as well."

His smile grew luminous. "Ah, such sweet words to hear."

She giggled and lost her breath as he pulled her tightly to his chest. He fused their mouths together for a warm kiss, sealing their fates together without words.

Epilogue

Two days later, Miranda joined the rest of the manor to break her fast for the first time since Crogan and Brodie's arrival. She had been forced to remain abed for that amount of time, resting her head according to the doctor's orders. She had also been strictly ordered not to tax her strength, which had been the elder man's way of telling Crogan, "Hands off until she has healed sufficiently from her fall."

Crogan brought Edwin and visited with Miranda for many hours during the day, but he respectfully vacated to his own chamber in the evenings, allowing the lady to rest.

The gash on her brow had scabbed over and diminished in size. Miranda felt in top form, and she refused to lie abed another day.

Her appetite was ravenous, but she was distracted from sustenance by the weight of Crogan's stare. She looked up, and their eyes locked. She gave him a radiant smile.

He simply gazed at her for many moments, causing her to wonder what he was thinking, but in the next instant, he revealed the thoughts behind his eyes.

"Marry me."

A table full of heads swiveled in their direction, catching the public proposal.

Miranda's jaw dropped open, as shocked as the rest. His proposal had been so abrupt and unexpected that she reacted without thought. Her eyes dropped to the bread in her hand, then shifted back to him. "May I break my fast first?"

He chuckled happily. "Does that mean ye accept?"

She laughed, realizing her blunder. "Aye, I accept."

He jumped up and pulled her into his arms for a celebratory kiss, and as a result, their audience responded with whistles and whoops of joy.

"Congratulations!" Rowena shouted and clapped ecstatically.

Crogan looked at his bride-to-be. "First, the wedding night. Then ye may break your fast. Then, the wedding," he announced with a devilish grin, and with that, he lifted her into his arms and began toward the stairwell.

The crowd broke into hearty laughter.

"Crogan," she cried, her cheeks inflamed by his scandalous behavior, though she could not help but smile.

He was taking her exactly where she wanted to go. He was carrying her into their future.

Miranda grinned. It seemed she would be spending the day abed after all.

Other Titles by Shalene Marie:

Scandal

Colville Manor

Ocean of Fate

Echoes From the Past

Treasures

Justice

A Stranger's Vow

The Storm Breaks

The Spring

A Breath In The Rain

Secrets

Secret Sins (18+ Dark Historical Romance)

Amazon Link:

https://www.amazon.com/author/shalenemarie

Author Website Link:

https://www.shalenemarie.space/